THE HIGH PRIESTESS OF LUMERIA

DOMINIQUE WRIGHT

PRAISE FOR THE HIGH PRIESTESS OF LUMERIA

"This book is more than a story—it's a transmission of divine feminine wisdom. Solei's journey felt like a mirror of my own soul's purpose. If you've ever felt like you came here to awaken the world, The High Priestess of Lumeria is your portal of remembrance."

—Melinda Grubbs, *founder of Soul Care Intuitive*

"Dominique Wright's The High Priestess of Lumeria is a mesmerizing tale of divine awakening and ancient feminine power. Elegant prose and profound spiritual wisdom intertwine as Solei, a divine-born priestess, rises to protect her sacred land from darkness. An enchanting journey that beautifully reconnects readers with their spiritual core."

— Divine Zape, *Readers' Favorite*

"The High Priestess of Lumeria is a breathtaking odyssey of myth, mysticism, and soul remembrance. A radiant portal of divine storytelling, this visionary novel awakens ancient truths and stirs the heart of every seeker. More than a book—it is a gift to humanity."

— Genie Mergard C.HT, *founder of GenieMergard.com*

CONTENTS

"We do not awaken to become what the world accepts.
We awaken to become what the soul remembers— wild, radiant,
ancient, whole."

—Solei, Elu'Vara

B eloved one,

This is not just a story—it is a remembrance.

The High Priestess of Lumeria was not written from imagination, but from the soul. Solei is not a character I created—she is a part of me. She is who I once was, in another time, another form, when the Earth was young and the light still sang through the stones.

This book is a return. A prayer. A remembering of a lifetime I lived as Solei, when I walked as High Priestess upon sacred land, carrying codes of healing, unity, and divine feminine light. Her voice came through in whispers and waves, in dreams and visions, until it became impossible not to write.

I offer this story as a love letter to your own soul.
Because if these words found you, it is not by accident.
If you feel the ache of remembering in your bones...
If your heart knows things the world forgot to teach...

If you are drawn to the stars and the ancient feminine within you...

Then this book is for you.

Because this is not just my story. It is our story.

A sacred mirror for every woman who came to awaken the Earth through her light.

With reverence,
and with all my love,
Dominique Wright

DEDICATION

For the women who have been silenced, forgotten, or made to
fear their power—
This is for you.

For the priestesses, healers, mystics, and goddesses who remember a truth deeper than time—
This is your call home.

To the ancient ones who walked before me, and the starborn
daughters yet to rise—
May this story awaken what was never truly lost.
And to my soul family,
Thank you for walking beside me in this lifetime,

For believing in magic,
And for remembering the light in me that mirrors the light in
you.

TO MY FELLOW HEALERS

To the lightbringers, the energy weavers, the frequency keepers—

To the ones who feel deeply, love bravely, and walk through shadow with open hearts...

Thank you.

Your presence is a balm in this world.

Your work is prayer in motion.

Your love—when offered unconditionally—is a light that restores galaxies.

May you continue to rise in remembrance.

May you trust the wisdom in your hands, your hearts, your sacred knowing.

And may every healing you offer ripple across timelines, touching souls you may never meet—but always feel.

Keep shining. Keep loving. Keep walking with grace.

This world needs you more than ever.

I honor your path.

And I walk beside you.

With deepest gratitude and soul love,

Dominique

CHAPTER ONE

THE DESCENT OF LIGHT

S olei was not born in the way humans understand birth. She was dreamed into form—breathed into being from streams of light, consciousness, and love. Her essence was spun from the harmonic pulse of a star, her soul whispered into existence by the breath of creation itself.

To human eyes, her home appeared as a brilliant speck in the night sky—Sirius A. But in truth, it was not a place. It was a realm of light, memory, and sound. A sanctuary of pure resonance, where form and spirit were one.

Their energy flowed pure and boundless, effortless waves of light and thought. They did not tire, for they were sustained by the eternal current of Source. Their presence glowed—sometimes soft and silvery like moonlight, other times brilliant and blinding like the birth of stars. They were not beings of form, but of resonance—fluid and radiant, each of them a living frequency in the great harmony of existence.

And still, even in all that peace, Solei remembered the moment the call stirred within them. It did not come with words, but as a pulse in the fabric of their collective heart—an ancient knowing that rippled across the entire realm and changed everything.

The stars paused, as if holding their breath. The wind—a current of consciousness in that realm—fell into perfect stillness. And in that stillness, something ancient rose within Solei. It wasn't a thought, but a remembering. A slow and sacred opening, like the unfurling of a lotus made of light. She felt it in her core, where essence meets eternity. It stirred like a sacred bell being rung across galaxies—calling them home to purpose, to a promise made long ago.

It was Lu Mai.

She did not arrive with footsteps or shadow. She descended as presence itself—a consciousness that filled the skies and the spaces between stars. She shimmered in every ray of starlight, moved in every thought that passed between them. She was not felt as one being, but as the breath of Source—the Mother of Memory, the Weaver of Light.

Her essence enveloped the entire realm in a hush of golden stillness. The moment she entered, the crystalline winds shifted, forming spirals of living codes that pulsed around them in soft, luminous patterns. Her voice did not speak through sound—it rippled through their light, blooming as knowing in the center of their beings.

A golden hum echoed outward from her, and instantly they were gathered—five hundred thousand of them, standing in concentric spirals, floating in radiant formation around her light. No one moved. No one spoke. They simply listened with every layer of their being as her frequency began to rise.

Her light expanded like a sun within a sun, casting fractal rays across the sky. Then, gently, her voice resonated through the unified field—feminine, vast, and soul-born:

"My children... my starseeds... my healers of love and light... A great birthing stirs across the galaxy."

The air thickened with meaning. Their hearts opened wide. Lu Mai continued, each word weaving itself into the center of their light-bodies like sacred code.

"There is a new world forming. A living blue planet. She is Earth.

There, a new species will evolve—a species of potential, of longing, of chaos and beauty. But they will forget. They will suffer. And when they cry out, you will hear them. That is why I call you now.

They will not remember where they came from. Their souls will pass through the Veil of Forgetting, and with each life cycle, their connection to truth will dim.

They will be born into illusion, into pain, into separation—and yet the divine spark will always remain. Hidden. Waiting.

You will take on form, not once, but many times. Each of you will incarnate through countless cycles, each one unique, layered, and filled with its own lessons.

Some of you will be healers. Some, visionaries. Some, silent anchors of peace in places of great darkness. Your gifts will evolve, transform, and reawaken across lifetimes.

There will be joy. There will be heartbreak. You will fall in love, and you will feel loss so deep it cracks the soul open wide enough for the light to return.

And through it all, you will remember—not all at once, but through symbols, through dreams, through the ache in your chest that never quite goes away.

This mission is not to save humanity—but to walk beside them. To be present within their world, not as saviors, but as sacred witnesses and gentle reminders.

Your task is to embody the vibration of unconditional love, to emanate compassion in the face of division, and to become still points of light in places overcome by fear.

You will not preach. You will not convince. You will remember—and in remembering, you will reflect back to humanity what they already are, but have forgotten.

You will plant seeds of remembrance with your energy, your art, your touch, your silence.

You will heal not only through your gifts but through your presence.

Some of you will awaken in times of peace. Others will rise in the heart of chaos. But no matter where or when, your purpose will be the same: to hold a frequency so pure, so steady, that even in their deepest pain, others will feel it and begin to awaken.

When they doubt, you will see their light. When they fall, you will remind them of their wings.

You will not judge them for forgetting.

You will love them into remembering.

You will mirror to them what they have forgotten they are: divine."

This was not an easy path. But it was sacred. And she would walk beside them, lifetime after lifetime, in the whispers of the wind and the stillness of the stars.

A deep stillness followed. Not silence—but presence. The air shimmered with possibility, the field of their consciousness wide open, waiting.

Then Lu Mai's voice returned, gentle but resonant—like the sound of creation itself choosing to whisper instead of roar.

"You have a choice," she said. "This mission is sacred—and it is difficult. You will descend into form. You will take on flesh and memory and loss. You will forget who you are, again and again. But through every lifetime, the call to heal will stir within you. And if you listen, if you remember, your light will change worlds."

A quiet knowing passed between them. Some wept—rivers of light streaming down faces of energy. Others glowed more brightly, their inner flame rising in fierce clarity.

"You do not have to go," Lu Mai continued, her love unshaken. "You are already whole. But if you feel the call within you, if your essence burns to serve... step forward."

The moment Solei stepped forward, a radiant current surged through her—pure remembrance, fierce and sweet. Others began to follow, one by one, their light rising in response to the call. A soft rumble passed through the realm, not of fear—but of destiny moving.

Lu Mai's voice sang through the golden air. "So be it. You are the ones."

Above them, the skies began to part with a soundless crackle of brilliance. The firmament itself shimmered, as though the stars had peeled open a hidden seam in the cosmos. From this rift emerged a colossal spiral of light, spinning with breathtaking precision—each ring aglow with iridescent hues that shifted like liquid crystal.

It was more than light; it was memory made visible, a sacred current of soul-paths and purpose. The spiral rotated in slow majesty, revealing multidimensional gates layered within its core. Each gateway pulsed with ancient codes, flickering like stardust in motion. Prisms of violet flame and sapphire mist arched like bridges between dimensions, and waves of golden geometry spiraled outward like petals of an infinite lotus.

This was no ordinary portal—it was a divine threshold, crafted not from force, but from their collective willingness. It responded to intention. It pulsed with love. It shimmered with remembrance.

They gathered in sacred convergence once more, and their energies braided together—light wrapping around light. Their bodies remained for now, but their forms began to pulse differently. Denser. Slower. Readying.

Lu Mai came closer, her presence touching each of them.

"You will not remember me. Not at first. But I will be with you in wind and fire, in water and stars. You will find me in the ache of your longing and the love in your healing. You are never truly alone."

A wave of warmth passed through them like the breath of home. And then—together—they began to rise.

The spiral widened above them—its light pulsing in rhythm with their own. They moved as one, lifting into the current of the portal. The golden spiral enfolded them, and the tones of their realm began to stretch into silence. It was not a falling. It was a letting go.

They passed through layer after layer of frequency—each one painted in colors never seen by human eyes. There were rivers of translucent sapphire laced with electric gold, clouds of rose-lavender mist speckled with shimmering opal dust. Veils of emerald and violet shimmer cascaded around them like living silk. Some layers felt like warm breath; others like sound made visible. Crystalline webs of iridescent fire danced around them in fractal motion, shifting with sacred intelligence.

Vibrations slowed. Thought became sensation. Sensation became gravity. Light became matter.

Their luminous forms began to shift, their pure energy stretching into containment. Solei could feel her essence folding into something smaller, heavier. The unity between them remained, but it flickered—thinner now, veiled.

And still, they held to each other.

As they moved through the final layer, a roar of wind and fire burst around them. The veil of atmosphere burned against their light, like friction tearing through the fabric of who they had always been. The spiral shook with power, pulling them faster into gravity's embrace. Solei's light began to tremble at the edges, struggling to hold its shape as the pressure grew unbearable.

The winds screamed with a voice ancient and fierce, a thunderous howl that echoed through the cosmos and into the marrow of her soul. They plunged through clouds of glowing plasma, each wave pressing tighter against their essence, sculpting it into something finite. Lightning forked across the void in luminous arcs, and fire licked the edge of their spiral as they fell—not in panic, but in sacred surrender.

Emotion surged. There was awe. There was fear. There was the aching pull of all they were leaving behind. Solei could feel others near her—her kin—reaching inward, holding firm to the thread of unity they still shared. Though their bodies burned, their hearts remained linked.

She could feel the heat—intense and unrelenting, not just around her but within. She was terrified from the pressure, collapsing time and sound into a single vibrating moment. And she was mesmerized by the crackling distortion of entering physicality, as if being sung into a new dimension by a thousand forgotten voices.

Then—silence.

The ground received them like a drum receiving the strike of its first note—resonant, ancient, and alive. The land trembled, rippling outward in concentric waves of force and frequency. Where they struck, a crater bloomed like a sacred imprint, its pattern etched in spiraling geometry as if the Earth herself had been branded with the memory of stars.

The sky exploded in a burst of blinding white, a halo of radiance that lingered on the horizon like a second sunrise. The air cracked open with sound—deep and echoing, like the voice of creation responding to their arrival. A ring of brilliant energy shimmered out from the impact site, igniting the atmosphere in hues of violet, gold, and azure.

The basin glowed at the edges with residual starlight, still pulsing with the memory of their descent. The surrounding terrain was transformed—steam rose from crystalline stones unearthed by the blast, and pillars of light flickered where their bodies had landed. It was not destruction—it was activation.

From beyond the distant dunes, the ocean surged forward, a vast, living tide drawn by the magnetic resonance of their return. Waves rolled in like sacred drums, their rhythm echoing their own, crashing against the basin's edge with reverent power. Seafoam danced across the sand like luminous lace, and the shoreline shimmered with flecks of gold where saltwater met the starlit earth.

The impact had scattered them like luminous seeds across the sand and sea. For a moment, Solei could feel the memory of the stars trailing behind them, unraveling like silver threads.

Then came breath—shaky and foreign, yet filled with life. Air flooded her lungs, and she felt the strange miracle of density, of skin, of sound. She was wrapped in something solid, yet wondrous.

She was still Solei... but encased in mystery.

And then... she breathed

CHAPTER TWO

THE AWAKENED SHORES

The waves whispered as they pulled back toward the sea, leaving a gleaming shoreline dotted with the bodies of Solei's kin. They lay scattered in divine stillness, caught between worlds, cloaked in saltwater and sunlight. One by one, they began to stir.

As Solei blinked into the golden light, she became aware of the strange weight of form—not burdensome, but grounding. It was as though she had stepped into a symphony of sensation after eons of silence. Her limbs, once woven from light and song, now moved with unfamiliar gravity—a sensation both humbling and sacred, anchoring her spirit in this new world of form. She lay still, cradled between sea and sky, listening to the pulse of a living planet pressing against her skin.

The ocean whispered its welcome as it kissed her body, the water cool and soothing, like the breath of Gaia herself. The sand beneath her was soft and alive, molding to her shape like a second skin—as if the Earth had waited to cradle her in this exact form. Above her, the sun poured golden warmth into her chest, and she felt it—her first breath. It was like sipping starlight through lungs that had never known air.

Curiosity bloomed in her chest like a wildflower breaking through stone. She lifted her arms, watching them tremble slightly in the light. Her hands—long, graceful, tipped with fine nails—felt both foreign and mesmerizing. She turned them slowly, marveling at how they caught the sunlight, how the golden symbols etched into her greenish-blue skin shimmered like sacred runes. They pulsed in time with her heart, as if they remembered what she had not yet recalled.

She touched her face, her jaw, her brow—tentative at first, then with growing awe. Her fingers threaded through strands of thick, wavy hair, dark as the void, now heavy with seawater and glinting like obsidian silk. It trailed over her shoulders and down her back, anchoring her in this form. She could feel its weight and texture—every thread whispering: *You are here.*

Though the sensations were vivid, the memories behind them still danced at the edge of knowing—just out of reach.

With cautious reverence, she pushed herself upright. Her body unfolded like a new language spoken for the first time. Her legs, long and sinewy, trembled beneath her. When she finally stood—unsteady, yet open—the sand clung to her feet, and the sea curled around her ankles in swirling celebration. She curled and stretched her toes into the wet earth, marveling at how every grain, every splash of salt, was its own kind of miracle.

She stepped toward a pool of still water and knelt before it. Her reflection shimmered back—eyes wide and luminous green, rimmed in light and mystery. Her face was both unfamiliar and deeply, cosmically known, as if the very architecture of her features had been sculpted from memory itself—echoing lifetimes etched into the stars. As she stared into her own gaze, something within her stirred—not memory, but recognition.

She was beauty made manifest. She was soul clothed in creation. And as she breathed in the sweet air, she understood: she was born again to remember why she had come.

Her breath found rhythm again, and she turned to see others emerging—arms stretching, torsos rising from the sand like blooming flowers reaching toward the sun. Their eyes blinked open slowly, dazed but glistening with the sacred imprint of memory. They did not speak with their mouths—their thoughts moved like soft waves between them, and Solei could feel their emotions rising like tides: awe, reverence, confusion, curiosity.

She rose fully to her feet, her form still unfamiliar, but steadier now. Golden markings shimmered across her skin, glowing brighter as the sun climbed higher into the sky. The golden symbols that shimmered across her skin as if they has been etched by starlight itself-delicate yet powerful, ancient yet alive. Spiriling glyphs curved around her forearms like flowing water, whispering of timelines of memory. A crescent woven through a circle rested over her heart, symbolizing unity of the divine feminine and cosmic cycles. Down her spine, radiant lines branched like a tree of light- each mark an encoded memory from the stars, a map of her souls lineage. Upon her palm the most scared of all: a glowing- the infinity loop interwoven with a radiant eye- representing eternal embrace and sacred sight. It pulsed in harmony with her breath, marking her as Elu'Vara, the one who walks between worlds, carrying codes of awakening.

She looked out across the shore, watching the ocean's edge kiss the feet of her people, welcoming them like an old friend. They had entered a living sanctuary.

The sand beneath them was soft and pale, kissed with flecks of crystal that sparkled in the sun. A breeze carried the scent of salt, wild blooms, and something ancient—something that sang to their souls. The land stretched before them in waves of color and vibration: emerald leaves rustled high above, cascading vines hung from trees like celestial ribbons, and butterflies danced like floating prayers.

They gathered slowly, instinctively. No one gave direction—their hearts moved them. Hands reached for hands, fingers entwined as they stood in sacred circles. Solei could feel their energy syncing, grounding. The Earth received them not as strangers, but as returning kin.

She looked around at their faces—her family of light. Each form was distinct. Some tall and slender, others wide-shouldered and graceful, all glimmering with radiant symbols unique to their essence. Their skin, like hers, bore the shimmer of starlight in earthy hues of greenish blue. Their eyes—violet, amber, deep sapphire—each held galaxies of memory.

As she met each gaze, a name would rise within her. Not in words, but in tone, in light—a soul signature. These were not new companions. They had traveled lifetimes together.

Then she felt a presence beside her—Zambia.

Zambia stood tall with a quiet strength, her figure both regal and fluid, like moonlight given form. Her skin was a deeper shade of greenish blue, kissed with opalescent undertones that shimmered with every movement. Her long limbs moved with a dancer's grace, each motion purposeful, each breath in harmony with the rhythms of the Earth.

Etched across her skin were radiant golden symbols—sacred markings that glowed softly with every breath she took. Along her collarbone curved a spiraled sunburst, its rays extending like beams of memory. Across her left arm stretched a line of crescent shapes intertwined with delicate vine-like sigils that pulsed like ancient songs encoded in her light. On her back, partially hidden beneath strands of hair, Solei glimpsed a geometric pattern that mirrored the sacred geometry of the stars—a map of her soul's lineage. And she remembered it. She had seen that pattern before—etched into the temple walls of Sirius.

Her hair fell like onyx silk down her back, thick and flowing with subtle waves, adorned at the crown with delicate strands of golden vine that had wound themselves there as if by the will of the planet itself. Her eyes were wide with joy—deep violet, flecked with stardust, reflecting not just the present, but echoes of past lives and ancient wisdom.

But beneath her radiant beauty was the unmistakable presence of a warrior priestess. Her energy was sharp, focused—like lightning wrapped in velvet. She moved with the effortless power of one who had trained in countless lifetimes, her awareness ever-tuned to subtle shifts in energy. There was an intensity in her that felt like sacred fire held in stillness—a readiness to rise and protect. Her presence felt like the edge of a blade dipped in moonlight—elegant, but forged in purpose, honed by truth, and blessed by spirit.

They met gaze to gaze, and Solei felt their shared lineage, their promise. Zambia did not need to speak—Solei heard her clearly.

"We made it."

"Yes," Solei replied in thought, smiling. "And we remember."

A few paces beyond her, Pehani was kneeling in the sand, his fingers tracing the lines of his symbol across his arm—an intricate tri-moon sigil that shimmered with silver-gold light. His features were striking—strong jaw, high cheekbones, and kind eyes the color of twilight skies. His long, braided hair fell over one shoulder, adorned with tiny beads of polished stone that glinted in the sun. His physique was powerful yet agile, sculpted by lifetimes of protection and sacred discipline.

The energy that surrounded him was unmistakable—an aura of vigilant strength, tempered by wisdom. He radiated the essence of a guardian, a soul forged for protection and clarity. There was a quiet alertness in him, a readiness to act should danger ever threaten what he loved. He moved like a warrior at rest—always aware, always poised. Beneath his calm reverence was an unwavering resolve, and the Earth itself seemed to honor his presence.

When he looked up at Solei, his voice reached her like a song from the stars.

"It's all still here, Solei. I feel it all."

She nodded, moved. "So do I."

Lu Mai's presence brushed over them like a warm breeze, and her voice—pure, eternal—rippled through the collective, washing over their hearts with the resonance of a thousand suns:

"My children, this land will nurture your forms and deepen your purpose. Walk gently. Remember why you came."

She paused, and the air seemed to hold its breath. Her presence intensified, surrounding each of them in a cocoon of golden light.

"Are you ready?" she asked—not as a command, but as an offering. Her question echoed within each of them, calling them inward to the deepest parts of their soul memory.

"Are you ready to carry light through shadow? To anchor harmony in a world that has forgotten it? To feel love—and loss—and still rise in remembrance?"

The words ignited something in Solei. Not fear—but reverence. The gravity of their mission crystallized in that moment. She felt the soul of Earth respond, like a drumbeat pulsing beneath their feet.

Then came the answer—not in speech, but in unified stillness. A thousand heart-lights ignited in silent affirmation.

And Solei stepped forward first—not because she was un-afraid, but because she remembered. Because she had always known this was her path.

As one, they turned toward the rising sun, facing the vibrant expanse of forest and water. This was not simply a gesture—it was the invocation of an ancient Lumerian ritual known as *Sol'Shara*, the Ritual of Recalling. First spoken of by Lu Mai before their descent, it was the sacred act of reawakening their star-born essence through embodiment on Earth. It called forth the essence of who they were across the stars, grounding it into the flesh of this new form.

The air around them began to shimmer as if responding to their collective memory. The light grew warmer, richer, shifting from gold to rose to radiant white. Each ray moved like a living thread, weaving around their bodies in spirals, activating dormant codes in their cells. The sun itself seemed to pulse—not with heat, but with frequency.

They lifted their hands slowly, palms open, letting the sacred light flood into their cores. With each breath, their hearts beat louder—not in panic, but in recognition. The warmth kissed their skin like memory—reminding them not of what they were becoming, but what they had always been.

The wind danced between them, swirling with floral scents and subtle static. It braided through their hair, carried away tension, and replaced it with stillness. The sand beneath their feet hummed with awareness, as if Gaia herself rose to meet them. Energy spiraled upward from the ground, wrapping their ankles, thighs, spines, and hearts in a cocoon of deep remembering.

A collective hum began—first as a whisper, then as a resonance. No words, only tone. It moved through them like a sacred current, flowing from one soul to the next. Their golden markings began to glow in unison, flickering with soft pulses that echoed the hum. They became a field of light, a circuit of starlit memory.

In that moment, they remembered. Not all—but enough to begin.

They were no longer strangers to this world. They were its healers, its harmonizers, its sacred stewards. The Ritual of Recalling aligned their bodies, minds, and spirits with Earth's living heart.

This was not ceremony.

This was embodiment.

In the light, they were whole again.

Then slowly, the glow that bound them began to soften, like the fading warmth of twilight. They lowered their hands, but the energy still pulsed within their cores. The tones of the Ritual of Recalling remained like an echo in their blood.

As the last shimmer of unified resonance settled over the circle, they opened their eyes in reverent silence. There were tears on some faces—not from sorrow, but from awe. Others breathed deeply, their chests rising as if they were inhaling the very soul of the Earth. They turned inward, bowing gently, honoring themselves and each other for remembering.

Zambia touched her heart with both palms, then pressed her fingers to the earth. Pehani mirrored her, planting one knee to the ground, whispering a silent vow with his gaze fixed to the sea. The others followed.

Soft gusts of wind encircled their bodies one final time, as if Gaia herself had sealed the ritual with her breath. Overhead, a flock of luminous-winged birds crossed the sky in perfect formation, their calls piercing the moment with crystalline beauty.

Solei stepped forward first.

And the others followed.

They had awakened.

Not only into bodies—but into mission.

They were the Children of Sirius, light-born wayfarers seeded with memory and purpose—those chosen by Lu Mai to walk among humanity, not as saviors, but as reminders of the divine.

And they were home.

CHAPTER THREE

THE FOUNDATIONS OF LIGHT

From the moment their feet kissed the sacred sands, the Lumerians moved like breath—fluid, intentional, woven with remembrance. There was no hesitation, no uncertainty—only the deep soul-knowing that they were meant to build something not of stone and wood alone, but of light, love, and legacy. Though their bodies were new—fresh with the unfamiliar rhythm of form—their purpose burned bright within their hearts, ancient and radiant.

Tears shimmered in their eyes, not from grief, but from sacred awe. Every branch, every gust of wind, every patch of moss seemed to rise in welcome. The land held memory. The land knew them. And they, in turn, bowed to it with every step.

This was not a place they had found. This was a home they had returned to.

They had come not to survive, but to embody. Not to shelter, but to sanctify.

They moved hand in hand, soul beside soul, hearts open as the sky.

With glyphs glowing softly across their skin like celestial whispers, they began to construct their first dwellings. There were no blueprints. No orders. Only intuition, vision, and heart-sent messages. Branches bent willingly in their hands. Vines braided themselves into sacred spirals. Crystals hummed in harmonic response, lighting the way as their breath synced with the frequency of the land.

Solei moved among them with fluid grace, her High Priestess symbols casting arcs of gold through the trees as she directed with tenderness and clarity. She radiated the sacred knowing of one who carried the codes of remembrance in her bones. Her every gesture was both invocation and instruction. Pehani hauled stone with strength and devotion, his Thal'Vahir protector glyphs flaring with each movement. Every boulder he lifted became an offering. Zambia moved with fierce elegance, weaving the markings of the Sael'Vahara—the warrior priestess lineage—into the walls, her glyphs dancing with firelight and moonlight as they sealed the structures in protection and purpose.

For days, they labored. Sunrises melted into moonlight. Time became sacred rhythm. They built under the breath of starlight, through heat and mist, their hands blistered and blessed. Each step pressed into soil like a prayer. Each breath hummed with meaning.

Their bodies pulsed with exhaustion. Muscles trembled. Eyes burned. But their spirits soared.

Faces flushed with sacred effort, cheeks streaked with sweat and stardust. Eyes sparkled with the clarity of living fully awake. Some sang as they worked, their voices trembling with beauty. Others whispered blessings into the beams and woven roots, their glyphs dancing across bark and stone like spells.

The land responded. Vines thickened. Blossoms opened. Trees leaned toward the rising walls.

They shaped dwellings not from plans, but from presence. Not for survival—but for soul.

They were luminous.

And they were beautifully undone by love.

It wasn't until one golden afternoon, when the scent of blooming vines curled through the air and the sky gleamed like molten opal, that Kaelion collapsed, arms outstretched mid-weave, face-first into a freshly thatched roof.

His limbs sprawled like poetry across the structure. A beat passed.

"This vessel," he mumbled into the straw with a dramatic sigh, "has reached full capacity and is formally requesting divine intervention."

Laughter erupted.

Liora, breathless and red-cheeked, wiped her brow. "Why is it still light? I swear we've lived through three days already."

"No, beloved," Elina replied from a nearby archway, voice lilting like a lullaby. "That's still the same day."

Pehani looked up with slow, reverent wonder, his voice edged with the confusion of a soul meeting the limits of flesh. "Perhaps it is time we commune... with nourishment."

Zambia groaned and collapsed into the moss with theatrical flair. "I believe my legs have transcended the physical plane and left a farewell note."

They collapsed in laughter and tangled joy, sprawled across the forest floor in divine fatigue. In their shared surrender was something sacred—a collective understanding that even divine beings must learn the ways of human form.

It was then they realized: they hadn't yet eaten.

As the sun dipped low, hunger rose. Not pain—but a longing. A tug. A deep and unfamiliar emptiness.

Elina, a gifted plant healer whose spirit pulsed in rhythm with the flora around her, had wandered a little deeper into the grove. Her senses led her—not by sight alone, but by the energetic call she felt deep in the sacred center of her being, where intuition stirred like a golden ember beneath her ribs. She paused as a glimmering hue danced between the thickets, drawing her attention like a whispered name from the soil. There, nestled between broad, glowing leaves, hung a sun-fruit—a radiant orb of swirling amber, blushing rose, and soft luminescent gold. Its surface shimmered like a prism dipped in sunrise, with veins of opaline pink threading through its skin. It pulsed faintly like a heartbeat, as if infused with the breath of the planet itself. It called to her in vibration, its light syncing with the gentle hum of her palms.

She reached out slowly, reverently, her fingertips tingling with recognition, a soft glow blooming from her palms as her energy touched the fruit's radiant aura. It pulsed brighter in her presence, as if recognizing her as kin. The moment swelled with sacred intimacy—the kind felt at the threshold of becoming. Her breath caught, heart full and trembling as she cradled it gently in both hands, lifting it from the branch as one would lift a blessing gifted from the cosmos. The warmth of it spread through her arms, into her chest, lighting up her heart like a dawn unfolding inside her. This was not simply discovery. It was communion. It was remembrance. It was initiation.

Returning to the group with urgent steps, her hands cradling the glowing fruit like a living ember, Elina's breath came quickly—not from fear, but from the excitement of divine discovery. Her eyes shimmered with awe, yet her voice trembled with a kind of sacred urgency, as if what she held was not just nourishment, but a revelation. She raised the fruit aloft, its light flickering across every face. "We are supposed to... consume this?" she asked, voice caught somewhere between wonder and disbelief, as though this act alone could alter everything they knew about being in body.

"Inside the mouth, yes?" someone asked.

"Then what?"

Pehani took the first brave bite, pausing dramatically. "If I transcend this plane mid-chew... speak of me kindly in the starlit songs."

He chewed. Blinked. And moaned softly.

"Oh... that is divine."

The feast began.

They discovered the bliss of juice spilling like sunlight across their tongues, the surprise of texture, the awakening of flavor. They sneezed when blossoms tickled their noses, giggled at the mess of fruit juice trailing down their arms, and moaned in delight with each new sensation. Their laughter mingled with birdsong, rising in waves of childlike wonder. They drank from crystalline springs so pure they shimmered with the memory of starsong. They touched the water to their lips as if it were holy, then drank deeply, gasping in pleasure. They licked their fingers, sticky with nectar and pollen, and gave thanks with hearts wide open. Palms pressed to the ground, they sent their gratitude into the earth in silent prayer, their light seeding the soil with joy and reverence.

Their bodies, strange and beautiful, began to settle into rhythm.

They learned to surrender to sleep beneath the cathedral of stars, their bodies curled into the gentle arms of tree roots that cradled them like sacred wombs. The Earth hummed beneath them, lulling them into dreams woven with memory and stardust. Each dawn, as the first light pierced through the leaves in golden filaments, they rose in silence, breath soft and reverent. They pressed their palms to their hearts, eyes closed, and offered their light to the land—not out of duty, but devotion. The act was intimate, ancient, like lighting a candle inside the soul of the world. And each night, before rest returned to claim them, they gave thanks aloud and in thought—words of gratitude dancing like whispered poems across the canopy. It was a rhythm, a ritual, a remembering of what it meant to be in communion with all things.

They sang their gratitude into the soil, voices trembling with reverence, each note a thread of light weaving through the earth. They hummed into blossoms, their melodies like lullabies of devotion that made petals quiver and unfold. They whispered love into vines, fingertips glowing as they touched each leaf with tenderness. The vines responded, coiling gently as if hugging back. The land pulsed with joy beneath their feet, its energy shimmering in ripples of gold and green. Flowers opened wider, the trees exhaled fragrance, and the very air shimmered with the song of harmony returning. It was not just response. It was communion.

Flowers bloomed brighter. Fruit grew sweeter. Trees pulsed with harmony.

Now that they had learned how to nourish, how to replenish, how to care for their luminous new forms, they began to build again. But this time, with deeper knowing—with reverence not only for what they were creating, but for the bodies carrying the light of creation. Their movements were slower, more intentional. Each gesture a blessing. Each breath a prayer. They paused when needed, drank when thirsty, rested when guided. And in doing so, they discovered that embodiment itself was a sacred art.

They began to build again. But now, with deeper knowing.

They shaped spiraled homes of living wood and flowering vines, weaving branches that shimmered with bioluminescent tendrils into walls that breathed. Domed sanctuaries rose from the earth, crafted of luminous crystal that caught the sun by day and glowed from within at night. Trees arched in natural elegance, their trunks gently curved around the shelters as if offering their protection. The very ground pulsed with harmony beneath their feet, alive with the memory of every footstep. In each corner of every home, they placed a Lu'Shael protection stone—glowing softly with the encoded light of Lu Mai, pulsing with the frequency of guardianship, love, and radiant peace. These stones anchored the shelters not only to the earth, but to spirit, linking every dwelling to the greater energetic grid of Lumeria.

And the colony began to glow.

Healers blessed walls with chants that echoed like waves of soft thunder, their voices layered with ancient frequencies that wove invisible tapestries of light into every corner of the dwellings. Each syllable was a vibration, a thread of harmony sewn into the foundation. Their eyes glistened with tears as they felt the resonance of safety take root. Artists moved like dancers along the surfaces, adorning walls with radiant sigils that shimmered with memory—each stroke pulsing with story, with love, with the unseen dreams of the collective heart. Children giggled and skipped barefoot across smooth stones, singing light into their homes with crystalline laughter, their joy lifting the entire vibration of the village like a song rising to the stars.

Their voices created color, and color created protection. Elders, with weathered palms kissed by time and starlight, walked the thresholds with reverent grace. They placed their hands on the doorways, whispering blessings through trembling lips, sealing the entries with the strength of generations and the silent power of presence. Each touch was a ceremony. Each home, a temple.

No one was idle. No one rested until the last home stood.

And when they were done, they stood hand in hand beneath a sky brushed in twilight, the last rays of sun caressing their faces like the kiss of a blessing. A hush fell over the village, not from silence, but from reverence. Their eyes shimmered with tears—tears of exhaustion, of wonder, of deep sacred pride. Above them, the first stars blinked into being, mirroring the soft light still glowing across their skin. Their breath came slow, unified, like a lullaby woven through a thousand souls. For a moment, time bowed around them, and the land itself exhaled in harmony. It was not the end of a task, but the beginning of a life woven from light.

Their hearts opened like wildflowers at dawn, soft and unguarded, blooming wide in the glow of belonging. Emotion surged through them in waves—relief, awe, devotion—filling the space between them like a shared breath. It was as though the walls they had built now reflected the walls within that had fallen. They looked at one another and saw not just faces, but flickers of starlight, mirrors of soul-light, and the unmistakable presence of family long awaited and newly found.

Their bodies trembling with the sacred exhaustion of devotion—limbs heavy, muscles aching, and yet their spirits shimmered like dawn breaking through mist. Their fingertips tingled with the echo of everything they had touched into life, their hearts thudded like drums still playing the rhythm of the work they had done. It was the trembling not of weariness alone, but of wonder—of being fully poured out in love, and still overflowing.

They had not only built homes.

They had built belonging.

They had woven light into matter.

And in the sacred stillness that followed, they realized:

They were learning to live.

To grow.

To *be*.

Together, they were becoming.

And the land, cradled in their love, began to bloom.

CHAPTER FOUR

THE AWAKENING OF LUMERIA

I n the days after their shelters rose like sanctuaries from the soil, the Lumerians turned inward—not in isolation, but in discovery. They had built together, slept under the stars side by side, laughed as they learned to eat and drink, to rest and remember. But now came the deeper work: understanding themselves, understanding each other.

It began with subtle things. A glance held too long. A sigh that trembled with something unnamed. Confusion flickering in violet eyes. Emotions rose within them like waves—not foreign, but deeply felt in unfamiliar ways. They had lived as light. Now, they were learning to live as heart.

Kaelion, ever the grounded builder, had begun to work in silence. His form was tall and broad, with luminous greenish-blue skin—typical of the Lumerian people—touched by a soft opalescent sheen that shimmered in the light. He moved with the calm weight of stone shaped by centuries, his presence steady as ancient roots. Long, earth-toned hair, threaded with strands of vine and crystal beads, was tied at his back. His eyes—deep jade flecked with gold—held the quiet knowing of one who had sculpted form from frequency across lifetimes. Across his arms, chest, and down his spine, sacred builder glyphs glowed in intricate geometric spirals and angular forms—symbols of the Elar'Miran lineage, the sacred architects of harmony. These sigils pulsed with energy, aligning him to ley lines and resonant design. His structures remained perfect—curved with sacred geometry, balanced by magnetic lines—but his laughter, once easy, had faded.

One evening, as dusk spilled lavender and rose across the sky, Liora approached him. Her plant-healer aura shimmered faintly as she tucked a vine behind her ear. "You've been quiet."

Kaelion looked up, his hands still on a half-finished archway. "This body feels too much. Sometimes I'm building and suddenly there's... weight in my chest. Grief? But nothing's wrong."

Liora sat beside him, brushing her fingers over a nearby leaf. "Maybe it's memory moving through your heart. The Earth teaches differently than the stars."

He nodded slowly, blinking back wetness he hadn't understood. "I don't know how to talk about it."

"You just did."

Across the grove, Pehani and Zambia trained under the shade of the elder trees. Their movements were fluid but laced with a new, subtle tension. After a parry and a block, Zambia stepped back, breathing hard.

"You're holding back," she said, sweat glinting along her temple.

"I'm trying to be gentle."

She frowned. "Don't. Not with me."

He hesitated. "I'm... afraid to hurt you. This form—emotion—it moves through me like fire. If I let go... I might burn."

Zambia lowered her stance, meeting his gaze. "Then let's burn together. And learn how not to fear the flame."

Solei watched quietly from the edge of the grove. She had become the silent thread that wove the village into harmony—not with grand declarations, but with presence. A touch to a shoulder. A glance that softened conflict. A breath shared in silence.

That evening, as the light faded into shades of rose and indigo, she gathered a small circle—Kaelion, Pehani, Zambia, Liora, and Elina—beneath a flowering arch of moonbloom vines. They sat cross-legged on moss warmed by the sun, their eyes tired, hearts full.

"We are all learning to feel," Solei said, her voice a gentle river. "To carry light in bodies that tremble, to hold frequency in a form that forgets. This is the sacred edge of being human."

Kaelion looked up, his hands resting on his knees, his voice gravel-soft. "It's harder than I imagined."

Solei nodded. "Because it's real. And real is tender. You feel the ache because you are present."

Liora blinked back tears. "Sometimes I feel overwhelmed by love. I don't know where to put it all."

"You let it spill," Solei replied, smiling. "Into your work. Into each other. Into the soil."

Zambia's voice was quiet but steady. "And the fire we carry—when it flares too quickly?"

Solei turned to her. "You breathe with it. You hold it like a child. And if it grows too big, you bring it here—to be seen, not judged."

The group fell into silence, the kind that settles not from lack of words, but the fullness of understanding. Above them, blossoms opened slowly, releasing fragrance into the twilight air.

Solei looked around at each of them, her heart swelling. "We are not here to master human emotion. We are here to meet it, love it, and allow it to grow us. This is how we build not only homes, but each other."

She listened deeply.

She witnessed fully.

She reminded them without words that they were not broken. Only blooming.

Each soul carried brilliance. And slowly, their roles emerged.

The braiders—like Luneia—wove not just hair, but memory. Their fingers worked with herbs and strands of silk-vine, weaving protective glyphs into garments, beds, and ceremonial cords. They infused enchantments into everything they touched, their work grounding the people in remembrance and comfort.

The builders shaped space with intuition. Kaelion and his circle carved resonance chambers into stone that amplified healing tones. They listened to trees, asking permission before shaping, and formed spiraled homes that breathed in rhythm with their inhabitants.

The plant healers like Liora tended the living medicines. They spoke to roots and received answers in vibration. They grew gardens that responded to song. Leaves turned toward their voices. Fruit sweetened in their hands. Their gift nourished the body and soothed the soul.

The healers offered restoration. They traced light over skin, into organs, through emotional knots. Their hands were sacred instruments, tuned to frequencies of wholeness. With chants and herbs, water and light, they brought harmony to the spaces between breath.

The warriors trained to defend—not from violence, but from imbalance. They protected the energetic fields of the village, anchoring peace. Their movements were artful, synchronized with breath and heartbeat. They danced strength into the soil.

The midwives, luminous and gentle, held space for birth—not only of children, but of ideas, dreams, transformations. Their presence was warm moonlight, quiet yet immeasurably powerful. They taught others how to trust the wisdom of the body, the whispers of the womb, the rhythms of becoming.

And at the heart of it all was Solei.

One evening, the entire village gathered beneath the canopy of starlight. Vines wove themselves into lanterns that glowed with soft lavender and gold. A stillness settled, the kind that only comes before something sacred.

Solei stood barefoot in the center of the gathering, the earth beneath her feet pulsing gently with recognition. Her robe, woven from threads of stardust and blossom silk, fluttered like light caught in a breeze. Her glyphs shimmered like constellations awakened—radiant trails of golden light mapping her skin, pulsing with a sacred rhythm known only to those who carry the memory of worlds.

She was not just standing—she was anchoring.

Around her, the people encircled her in reverent stillness. Zambia stood tall, her fiery presence radiating from every line of her being, the glyphs of the warrior-priestess glowing along her arms like sacred sigils forged from courage. Pehani, grounded and luminous, emanated strength like a pillar of light, his protector markings pulsing with silent devotion. Liora and Elina glowed softly, their energies weaving together in the hues of plant-song and dream-memory, their eyes bright with compassion and reverence. Kaelion stood like a golden anchor beside the braiders and builders, his aura steady, his form exuding a warmth that felt like home.

All around them, the breath of the land held still—as if it too awaited the naming of what had finally become whole.

Then came the wind.

Soft at first. Then rising.

It swept through the canopy like a breath from the stars, alive with sacred force. The leaves rustled in unison, turning upward as if bowing in reverence to the presence descending. Flames flickered, then surged—not with heat, but with brilliance, casting waves of gold and violet across the gathered circle. Hair lifted, glyphs shimmered brighter, and the ground pulsed gently beneath their feet, as though the Earth herself was exhaling into their bones. A hush fell so deep it felt like time itself had knelt beside them.

Above them, the sky opened with breathtaking grace, parting like a curtain of silk woven from moonlight and stardust. Clouds shifted aside as if drawn by divine hands, revealing a vast tapestry of stars that pulsed with living memory. A luminous vortex spiraled into being—soft, iridescent, radiant—casting waves of color that painted the treetops in hues of violet, rose, and deep gold. The heavens did not simply open; they unveiled, revealing the breath of the cosmos itself preparing to speak.

And Lu Mai descended—not in form, but in a radiant cascade of starlight and divine essence. Her presence arrived on a spiral of gold and silver frequencies, threads of remembrance streaming from the heavens like liquid light. She was not seen, but felt—every soul stirred as her energy touched them, like being wrapped in the warmth of all the mothers they had ever known. Her voice rang out like a bell forged from the first breath of dawn, shimmering with reverence, beauty, and the weight of eternity.

"My beloveds," she said, "you have remembered your roles. You have built not only dwellings, but devotion. Not only form, but frequency."

Solei trembled, her hand pressed to her heart. Tears slid down her cheeks.

Lu Mai's light expanded, rippling outward like a luminous heartbeat sent from the core of the cosmos. Waves of soft gold and pearlescent blue radiated from her essence, bathing the circle in warmth and awe. The trees quivered. The soil glowed. The glyphs on every soul ignited in brilliant hues, responding as if called by their original name. The ripple moved through skin, through breath, through bone—awakening something ancient and eternal in every being present. It was not light alone. It was remembrance made manifest.

"This land shall be known as **Lumeria**—a sanctuary of light, remembrance, and rebirth."

The word vibrated through them all.

Lumeria.

The air shimmered like a living veil lifting between worlds. Glyphs lit on every face, each one glowing with the intimate brilliance of soul recognition—a cosmic signature illuminated. The Earth pulsed beneath their feet, waves of energy radiating outward as if the land itself was singing their name. Overhead, the stars blazed brighter, rearranging into unfamiliar constellations that felt deeply known—as if even the cosmos had shifted to honor this sacred becoming.

The name wasn't given.

It was awakened.

The people wept, some in silence, others with song. Their voices rose like rivers joining. Lumeria. Their home. Their prayer. Their vow.

And Solei, at the center of it all, closed her eyes, lifted her palms to the sky, and whispered, "Thank you."

In that breath, she felt her chest open wide—not just physically, but across lifetimes. Her heart trembled with awe, her ribs a cradle for a love too vast to name. She wasn't leading in this moment. She was *becoming*. Becoming the vessel, the prayer, the promise.

And around her, the people felt it too. Some dropped to their knees, overcome by the frequency of remembering. Others stood frozen in reverence, eyes turned upward, hands pressed to hearts. The trees swayed gently, as if singing in the language of leaves. The wind carried their stillness like a blessing.

They were no longer just a colony.

They were a people.

And they had remembered who they were.

And the land, now named, began to hum with the whisper of all it still held within its heart.

CHAPTER FIVE

A BREATH OF REMEMBERING

That evening, as the light melted over the ocean and the island glowed in its golden hour, Solei walked alone to the edge of the cliffs that faced the setting sun. The breeze lifted her dark blue-black hair as she stood barefoot on the smooth stone, gazing toward the horizon. Her heart felt full and silent all at once—a deep knowing stirring like gentle waves inside her.

She wasn't searching.

She was sensing.

Behind her, the sound of quiet footsteps approached—familiar, grounded, steady. She didn't turn. She didn't need to. Her soul had already recognized his presence long before her eyes could see.

Pehani stood beside her, his arrival silent, yet so deeply felt it shifted the very air around them. The descending sunlight draped his tall frame in amber light, illuminating the golden symbols across his chest and arms—each one a glowing testament to his sacred path as protector and guide. His skin, bronzed and radiant, shimmered with the final light of day, while his eyes held the calm of oceans and the depth of memory.

His presence was like the island itself—strong and unshakable, ancient and knowing. A quiet gentleness lived beneath his strength, a warmth that radiated from his very core. When he stood beside her, it wasn't as one arriving—but as one returning. It felt as though the elements had conspired to guide him there—the wind, the sea, the stones beneath their feet—all aligning to honor this sacred reunion.

For a long moment, they said nothing.

Then Solei turned to him, her voice low and unwavering.

"You feel like home."

Pehani didn't speak. He simply reached out and gently took her hand. The moment their fingers met, a warm current surged between them—like golden light pouring through their skin and into their hearts. The connection was immediate, electric, tender. It wasn't simply a touch; it was a homecoming. Their palms pressed together with a quiet ache, as if they were sealing something sacred, long-awaited, and already known.

Tears welled in Solei's eyes—not from sadness, but from the exquisite remembering that bloomed in her chest. A love so ancient and whole stirred within her, her soul trembling under the weight of it. Pehani's thumb brushed the side of her hand with a reverence that felt like a vow—unspoken, but eternal.

Their breath aligned. Their energy merged. In that one gesture, every part of Solei's heart opened like the petals of a sacred night flower, blooming only when the stars were brightest.

No words were needed. The silence between them pulsed with divine clarity.

They had found each other again.

In that moment, no ceremony was required. No vows to speak. No oaths to proclaim. The Earth beneath them recognized their union, and the wind carried it as blessing.

They stood together in the fading light—two souls remembering, two flames returning to one light.

Solei turned fully to him now, her emerald eyes shimmering with the reflection of the sun. The golden glow painted her skin like molten light, dancing across the sacred markings that adorned her body. In Pehani's gaze, she saw not only the present, but fragments of lifetimes they had once known—memories locked in shared silence, waiting to be awakened by the sacred bond now reignited.

He touched her cheek with reverence that went beyond the physical. It was soul meeting soul. The space between them shimmered like heat rising from sacred earth. Around them, the island responded. A gentle wind rustled nearby palms, and golden petals from an overhanging blossom tree floated between them like blessings from the unseen.

"In every breath I have taken here," Pehani finally spoke, voice deep and steady, **"I have been calling you back to me."**

Solei's breath caught—not from surprise, but from remembrance. Her heart, so strong and expansive, softened into the rhythm of his voice. She stepped closer. Their foreheads met—a sacred kiss of light and breath, of divine memory returning to form.

They spoke no further. Words were too small for such knowing.

Instead, they stood in stillness, letting their love root itself into the island like a blooming vine, weaving through the heart of Lumeria.

In that moment, the Earth pulsed beneath their feet.

It, too, remembered them together.

Above them, the first star pierced the sky—a whisper of destiny. Around them, warm winds curled in unseen spirals, stitching threads between their hearts and the heavens.

And so they stood—two souls, one bond, held by an island shimmering in the truth of their love.

In that stillness, they became more than partners.

They became a living prayer.

That night, beneath the velvet canopy of stars, Solei and Pehani returned hand in hand to a sacred grove deep within the island's heart. The path glowed with flowers that bloomed only in moonlight, casting golden hues across the mossy trail. The grove shimmered with enchantment—bioluminescent blossoms blinked like gentle stars among the ferns, and crystal stones embedded in the earth radiated violet and silver, creating a quiet breath of light.

Their shelter was open to the sky, woven from golden reeds and flowering vines. The scent of wild orchids and moon fruit hung sweet in the tropical air. Inside, the floor was soft with woven grasses and light-infused cloth. At the center, a pool glowed from within, reflecting the starlight and the sacred energy blooming in the air around them.

Solei turned to him fully, her body glowing in moonlight. The golden symbols on her skin pulsed with soft radiance. Pehani reached for her, not with urgency, but with devotion.

Their foreheads touched again. Eyes closed. Palms over each other's hearts.

A trembling began in Solei's chest—not from fear, but from a swell of love so immense it stretched her open. Her breath caught under the weight of such tender truth—vulnerability, reverence, the sacred sweetness of being truly seen.

Pehani's breath rose in sync with hers, shuddering slightly as old walls softened. In her presence, he was both strong and unguarded, his being laid bare to her light. He felt held, not just by her hands, but by lifetimes of soul recognition.

Tears rose between them—unbidden, unashamed. Joy. Sorrow. Longing. Fulfillment.
All lifetimes flowing into one.

Pehani cupped her face with both hands, his thumbs brushing away the tears she didn't try to hide. His voice came low, like a breath caught between dimensions.

"Even if I had to find you through a thousand lifetimes of silence," he whispered, his forehead pressed to hers, "I would choose you every time, in every world, until the stars forget how to shine."

Solei exhaled a breath that was half sob, half prayer. Her hands curled around his, grounding them in this now—this life, this love.

From that love, something ancient stirred.

Golden threads of light shimmered from their joined hands, rising like mist. Each thread pulsed with living memory, spiraling along their arms, their spines, into their hearts. The energy swirled in constellations across their skin, ancient glyphs illuminating with breath.

As the threads met at the center of their hearts, they spiraled outward, forming a cocoon of golden radiance—warmth, safety, and soul truth enveloping them completely.

As they lay together beneath the stars, their union became a current of remembrance. Energy flowed between them like a sacred river, warming their bodies, illuminating them from within. Each kiss awakened buried memories. Each sacred touch reignited a vow.

No words.

Only breath.

Only light.

Only love—pure, ancient, eternal.

The night held them gently.

The stars blinked their approval.

The earth hummed beneath them in tender resonance.

And in their divine union, the soul of Lumeria expanded.

At the height of their merging, the stars above shimmered brighter. Constellations shifted, drawing new formations across the heavens. A luminous wave of light burst from their hearts, spreading outward in ripples of gold and silver—through the jungle, the sky, and the sea.

The energy moved like breath—intelligent and alive—rising to the tallest palms, sinking into the deepest roots. The entire island vibrated with the echo of their sacred love. Every leaf trembled in reverence. Every wave bowed in rhythm. Birds fell silent. Blossoms tilted toward the glow.

From above, a single beam of starlight broke through the canopy, bathing them in celestial warmth. In that light, the golden threads dissolved into the night, becoming one with Lumeria's breath.

Solei opened her eyes.

Tears glistened on her cheeks.

Pehani's gaze held her like a sacred vow.

They were no longer just bonded.

They were consecrated—marked by divine love, woven into the very essence of the land and stars.

And far beneath the surface of the Earth,

something ancient stirred in acknowledgment.

CHAPTER SIX

THE MORNING AFTER THE STARS

The golden light of dawn crept slowly over the horizon, casting soft shadows across the canopy of Lumeria. Birds sang in gentle harmony, and the ocean's rhythmic hush echoed like a lullaby greeting the new day. The tropical air was warm and fragrant, filled with the sweet perfume of flowering vines and sun-kissed earth.

Inside the shelter woven from reeds and vines, Solei stirred. Her body was draped in soft light, her skin still tingling from the sacred energy that had moved through her the night before. Her hand rested over her heart, where a faint pulse of golden warmth still lived—steady, strong, and eternal.

Pehani lay beside her, his breath deep and peaceful, his arm gently wrapped around her waist. A single blossom had fallen during the night and now rested comically on the bridge of his nose, its soft pink petals rising and falling with each breath.

Solei stifled a quiet laugh, her eyes crinkling with warmth as she delicately brushed it away.

"Even the flowers can't resist you," she whispered playfully.

Pehani stirred, his voice a low murmur. "Were they watching? Should I have bowed first?"

Solei grinned and shook her head. "Too late now. You're officially consecrated by starlight and petal."

He smiled without opening his eyes, and his hand found hers beneath the woven cloth. In that simple, lighthearted exchange, joy danced between them—tender and true.

There was no question, no fear, no uncertainty.
Only the quiet, beautiful truth that they had chosen each other—not just now, but across lifetimes.

She traced her fingers lightly along the golden markings on his chest, feeling the soft thrum of his energy in response. Her heart swelled with a love that felt both grounded and transcendent. This was not the beginning of something new—it was the continuation of something sacred.

Solei exhaled slowly, closing her eyes for a moment to feel the warmth of his skin, the rhythm of his breath, the energy that still shimmered between them. It was soft now, subtle—but alive. Threads of light still wove gently through their bodies, connecting their hearts in a silent song.

She opened her eyes to the glowing world beyond their shelter. The island looked more alive than ever. The trees swayed with quiet joy, and the air sparkled as if carrying the memory of starlight.

Today, they would rise.

Together.

To begin their new life.

They rose slowly, savoring the softness of the morning air as it brushed over their skin. Solei wrapped herself in a woven shawl kissed with dew, and Pehani stretched, his muscles catching the golden light as he stood. For a moment, they simply looked at each other—no need for words, only the quiet thrill of presence.

Outside, the village stirred. A few Lumerians walked barefoot along coral-lined paths, carrying baskets of fruit or fresh herbs. The air was filled with birdsong and laughter—the gentle sounds of life unfolding.

As Solei and Pehani stepped out of their shelter, hand in hand, they were greeted with warm smiles and knowing glances. Their union had not gone unnoticed. The land had sung it. The stars had echoed it. And now the people welcomed it with unspoken celebration.

Zambia passed by carrying a bundle of glowing blue flowers. Her eyes sparkled with mischief and something more ancient—recognition. She paused, raised an eyebrow, and tilted her head.

"Ah, the newly consecrated rise. The whole island was glowing last night—you lit up the sky. It was almost as bright as when Luneia and I had our bonding. Almost," she added with a wink.

Her gaze briefly flicked to Pehani, and a subtle edge entered her voice—barely perceptible, but there.

"Did the stars give you permission to return to the world of walking?"

Pehani met her gaze with an easy calm, but Solei felt the flicker of tension pass between them like a shadow. Zambia and Pehani had always shared a silent friction—rooted in respect, but also in contrast. Her sharpness met his steadiness like fire meeting still water. They had never openly disagreed, yet something unsaid lingered beneath their exchanges.

Solei interjected with a smile, trying to soften the moment. "Only after the flowers tried to claim him for themselves."

"I am but a humble servant of the flora," Pehani bowed dramatically.

Zambia allowed a dry smirk, but her eyes lingered a heartbeat longer on him before she moved on, her bundle of flowers trailing stardust in her wake.

They all laughed, the lightness of the moment rippling outward.

And then the breeze shifted as Zambia walked away.

Solei turned her face into the wind, her smile fading slightly—not from worry, but from awareness. Something in the air had changed. It carried a new tone—subtle, stirring. A whisper from the land.

She felt it first in her chest—a gentle pressure, like the soft press of a guiding hand. The breeze carried a rhythm, faint yet familiar, a pulse that seemed to echo in her bones.

She looked to Pehani, who had already turned toward the trees as if listening to something distant.

"Do you feel it?" she asked.

He nodded slowly, the humor of moments ago melting into calm focus.

"It's subtle... but it's calling us inward. Deeper."

They shared a knowing glance. Their fingers tightened around each other's. The village continued to hum with life, but beneath it, something sacred was rising.

It wasn't urgent. It was invitational. A beckoning from the land itself—not for duty, but for presence. For listening. For remembrance.

Solei exhaled, steadying herself. Whatever was coming next, they would walk it together—just as they always had, in lives before and lives still to come.

The breeze curled around them like a whispered vow.
It was time to follow it.

Solei and Pehani moved quietly through the soft jungle paths, the earth warm beneath their feet and alive with the scent of blooming fruit and sun-drenched leaves. Golden shafts of light filtered through the canopy, and the sounds of the village faded behind them. In the hush of morning, the call of the land grew stronger.

They followed instinct more than direction—turning when the breeze shifted, pausing when a sudden stillness asked them to listen. The deeper they went, the more the trees seemed to lean in, guiding them with their silent wisdom. Beneath their steps, the ground shimmered faintly with luminescent moss that responded to their energy.

Finally, they came upon a hidden grove cradled deep within the forest's embrace.

The air shifted.

It was warmer here. Thicker. Alive with unseen memory.

The trees stood taller, their leaves flecked with light that shimmered like stars. Luminous vines hung in slow motion, swaying with a breeze that hadn't touched the outer woods. The moss-covered stones circling the grove glowed in soft pulses, as though the land had crafted a temple of breath and light—not built, but born.

Solei paused in awe.

"This place," she whispered, "it feels... awake."

Pehani nodded, voice reverent. "It's like the forest is dreaming... and we've stepped into its heart."

The grove responded.

Color shimmered softly around them. Energy moved through the air—not as wind, but as soundless song. They walked slowly, reverently, brushing vines that leaned toward them, curious and remembering.

Each living thing carried history. The leaves held echoes of laughter. The stones remembered sacred chants. And when Solei laid her hand upon a glowing tree, a wave of warmth rose up her arm—so familiar, it made her eyes brim with tears.

Here, in this enchanted womb of forest light, they remembered: the magic was not only within them.

It surrounded them.

It welcomed them.

It had waited for them.

They stood still as the ground beneath them began to hum—a deep vibration rising through their spines like a sacred chord tuning their bodies to Earth's heartbeat. Solei closed her eyes and let the frequency wash over her. It wasn't just sound. It was presence.

The grove pulsed with knowing.

Pehani stepped closer to one of the glowing trees, brushing the bark. Bioluminescent light rippled across it like breath. Solei followed, placing her hand beside his. Instantly, light moved between them—swirling and dancing, a luminous language of energy.

The glade darkened slightly. The canopy above flickered like starlight seen through emerald glass.

Then—visions.

Not in the air, but in their minds. Starlit corridors. Crystalline cities. Ancient beings tending to Earth with reverent touch. Threads of soul memory flickered across their inner sight like flame.

Solei gasped softly. These weren't dreams.

They were truths.

Echoes of what had come before—and what was to come.

She turned to Pehani. "We're being shown the way."

He nodded, his voice quiet. "And we're not alone."

A rustle in the brush broke the silence.

Solei turned, heart suddenly racing.

From the shadows, a creature emerged.

It moved like flowing water—graceful, powerful, impossible. Silvery fur shimmered with threads of gold and blue, and beneath it, faint scales glistened like crystal. Its form defied understanding—part feline, part serpent, part starlight.

An Elarian.

A mythical guardian species thought lost when the celestial realms fractured. Solei had only ever read about them—in the oldest scrolls, passed down in whispers. Yet here it stood.

Its emerald eyes shimmered with constellations. They held memory. And sorrow. And longing.

Solei stepped back, startled.

Pehani moved instantly, placing himself between her and the creature. His stance was steady, his energy grounded like a mountain.

"Stay behind me," he said calmly, not breaking eye contact with the beast.

The Elarian made no sound, no threat. It simply stood. Watching.

Solei's fear faded, replaced by wonder.

It blinked, and something passed between them—recognition.

Pehani exhaled, easing slightly. "It's not here to harm us," he murmured. "It's part of this."

The creature stepped forward, shimmering in the grove's soft light. Its coat rippled with ancient codes, and its heartbeat—visible in a faint glow at its chest—throbbed in rhythm with the forest's hum.

Solei knelt slowly, heart pounding. "You're not of this world," she whispered. "But you've come for us... haven't you?"

The Elarian lowered its head in affirmation. A gentle wave of light rose from its chest.

Solei reached out. Her hand hovered above its heart. The golden symbols on her skin glowed. A hum filled the glade.

She touched it—lightly.

Warmth surged through her palm. Not pain. Not fear. But ache. The ache of being remembered after an eternity.

She didn't heal it.

She *recognized* it.

And in return, it reminded her of the same.

The creature nuzzled her hand gently. Then, with a soft sound—half song, half sigh—it turned and vanished into the trees, leaving behind a faint trail of stardust.

Pehani stood in silence beside her.

"You didn't just heal it," he said. "You reminded it that it was never forgotten."

Solei nodded, eyes shimmering. "And it reminded me."

Solei stepped beside Pehani again, her hand slipping into his. "Thank you."

He looked at her gently. "Always."

The glade fell into a deep, velvety stillness, as if the land itself had bowed in reverence to what had just passed. Something ancient had been remembered. Something sacred had returned.

They turned slowly toward the trail, but they walked differently now—more rooted, more open. A deeper stillness moved between them. Solei felt more present in her body than she ever had before. The fear from moments earlier had softened into clarity. The Elarian hadn't come as a warning. It had come as a mirror.

She glanced at the glittering dust left behind in the undergrowth.

"We're not just here to remember," she said softly. "We're here to awaken everything that's been waiting to be remembered."

Pehani nodded.

"And to protect what is sacred. Even when it's forgotten."

The earth beneath them pulsed softly, a heartbeat echoing through the grove. The moss around their feet shimmered in hues of rose and violet.

Something had been activated.

Their journey—once luminous and tender—was now taking on a new shape.

It was no longer just about love.
It was about legacy.

—

Later that afternoon, as the sun dipped toward the west and the grove's golden glow softened to amber, Solei and Pehani returned to the village hand in hand.

They were met with warm glances and reverent smiles. No one spoke. They didn't need to. The land had already spoken through them, and now the people moved with sacred ease.

They sat together beneath a flowering canopy, beside a table carved from ancient driftwood and adorned with polished stones and fresh green leaves. Before them was a simple spread of nourishment: sliced starfruit and moonberries, golden mango and papaya, spiral greens with edible petals, and a pitcher of cool spring water infused with lemongrass and wild citrus.

Solei picked up a sunroot slice just as Pehani bit into an overripe mango, which promptly burst in his hands, dripping golden juice down his wrist.

"Divine blessings strike again," he said with mock solemnity, licking the nectar from his fingers.

Solei laughed, eyes bright.

"The fruit clearly approves of your dedication."

They ate slowly, savoring not only the flavors but the stillness—the presence. At one point, Pehani tried to feed Solei a slice of starfruit with dramatic flair, only to drop it into her lap.

Solei gasped.

"You've shared starlight and soul threads with me and still can't aim properly?"

He grinned, unbothered.

"Perhaps it was the fruit's idea. It wanted a closer connection."

She tossed a petal at him.

"Flirtation disguised as clumsiness—classic Pehani."

Leaning in, he dropped his voice just slightly, rich with devotion and mischief.

"If it brings you laughter, I'll drop fruit on you forever. And call it an offering to the most radiant being I've ever known."

Their laughter rose like a blessing, swirling through the trees. Even the leaves seemed to shimmer in response.

They didn't need ceremony.
This simple communion—shared fruit, soft smiles, the breath of the trees—was everything.

It was legacy in its simplest form: love, presence, and gratitude.

Solei leaned back against Pehani's shoulder, eyes to the sky.
"Do you think it will always be like this? The peace, the way the island sings around us?"

Pehani bit into a mango petal thoughtfully.
"I hope so. But even if it isn't... I'd still choose this. The quiet mornings. The glowing fruit. You."

She smiled, tracing slow circles over the back of his hand.
"It almost feels like a dream, doesn't it?"

He kissed her temple.
"Then let's never wake up."

Their eyes met, full of wonder. Whatever came next, this moment would live in them forever—pure, rooted, real.

And yet... as Solei rested her head on his shoulder, a flicker of unease stirred beneath her joy.

Not fear.
A knowing.

The harmony was undeniable. But so too was the quiet pulse of change, humming just beyond the horizon of awareness.

She closed her eyes and listened to the breeze rustling through the canopy.

And in it, she heard something new.

Not dark.

Not wrong.

Just... different.

As though the island, even in its song, had begun to ask a question.

CHAPTER SEVEN

THE ECHO BENEATH THE WAVES

The breeze that caressed the village that morning was not the same as the one that had danced through the trees the day before.

Yes, it still carried warmth—the soft breath of blossoming fruit, the earthy perfume of dew-kissed petals—but laced within it was something subtler. A hush. A wondering. A vibration just beneath sound that brushed against the soul like a silken veil stirred by the breath of ancient memory.

Solei stirred before the sun crested the horizon, not drawn by sound, but by sensation. A quiet calling pulsed beneath her breast bone—gentle, steady, sacred. It rose like mist within her, delicate and insistent, like the touch of the Great Mother brushing a dreamer's brow.

She rose with reverence, slow and careful, so as not to disturb the peaceful rhythm of Pehani's breath beside her. He slept still, his chest rising and falling in time with the earth's own lullaby.

For a brief moment, she lingered in the sacred stillness of their shelter, then stepped barefoot into the breath of dawn.

The forest wrapped itself around her like a prayer.

Mists drifted low across the land, luminous in the gold-tinged twilight. The world appeared untouched—verdant, breathing, tender in the light of morning. Yet within her, everything whispered: something has shifted.

As the soles of her feet met the damp earth, she felt it again—that soft, pulsing thrum rising from beneath the soil like a secret heartbeat. A song not meant for the ears, but for the body. For the womb. For the soul.

The trees swayed with knowing. The waters glistened as if remembering the stars. The island was not only alive—it was awakening anew.

Solei pressed her palm gently to her heart and closed her eyes. Her breath deepened.

"I'm listening," she whispered into the golden hush.

A moment later, Pehani stepped out behind her, wrapping a shawl over her shoulders. The gesture was silent and instinctual, an offering of presence, like the sun rising to greet the moon.

"You felt it too," he said, the words low and wrapped in understanding.

She nodded, her voice as soft as the wind stirring through the canopy.

"The island still sings," she murmured. "But the melody has changed."

Together they stood, side by side, wrapped in the holy stillness of a world waiting to speak. It was not the absence of sound, but a fullness of silence. One that held meaning, depth, prophecy.

Later that morning, the elders gathered—not summoned, but summoned still. Their hearts, attuned to the deeper rhythms of the land, had drawn them inward. Something sacred had moved beneath the roots of the island. A ripple had passed through the breath of the earth.

And the people of Lumeria, with open hearts and listening spirits, waited.

—

As the sun rose higher, spilling rivers of gold across the jungle canopy, Solei felt a call unfurling from within her.

It was not thought, but current—fluid and magnetic. A deep tide moving in her womb space. A pull not toward answers, but toward remembering.

And so she did not resist.

She followed.

Each step was a prayer—gentle, grounded, alive. The earth welcomed her bare feet with tender warmth. The breeze moved with her, curling around her limbs like a silken ribbon, guiding her forward as if the land itself whispered: this way.

She moved with devotion, letting the unseen lead.

The shoreline rose to greet her in stillness. The ocean breathed slow and steady, a sacred rhythm that mirrored her own. Its surface shimmered with silvery-blue light, rippling like a mirror of ancient truths not yet spoken.

Solei walked into the water until it embraced her legs. The tide curled around her like a memory made tangible—familiar, holy.

She closed her eyes.

She surrendered.

And let the sea hold her.

Then—

A tremble.

The water shifted.

The air thickened.

The horizon shimmered.

And from the far edge of the world... something rose.

It did not rush.

It emerged.

Like a temple breaching the veil of the sea.

Like a forgotten god exhaling beneath a sky of stars.

A towering form broke through the surface—slow, majestic, alive. Its head rose high, crowned in stillness. Its body followed—serpentine, massive, shimmering with tones of deep sapphire, glistening pearl, and shadowed silver.

Across its skin, sacred symbols pulsed in soft light—constellations carved not with hands, but by memory itself. Glyphs alive with breath and lineage.

And its eyes...

Its eyes were not simply eyes.

They were galaxies holding grief.

Tides filled with memory.

Depths untouched by time.

Solei gasped, her hands flying to her heart, stumbling slightly beneath the weight of awe. She had never felt anything so ancient, so deeply alive.

And then it spoke.

But not in language. Not in voice.

In feeling.

A song poured into her spirit—full of sorrow, deep as oceans, sacred as starlight.

"You hear me," it whispered. Not with sound, but through her cells. Her spirit. Her skin.

She pressed her hand to her chest, nodding through the core her throat.

"I do. I feel you. Show me what you carry."

The creature's luminous fins quivered, shimmering with alight not of this world. The waves around them stilled—as though the entire ocean held its breath—and then the vision came.

It unfolded like a dream made of water and sound.

A world beneath the sea.

Not distant, but deeply remembered.

A city of resonance and light. Coral towers that hummed with sacred frequency. Bridges woven of crystal and intention. Tunnels glowing with bioluminescence that pulsed in harmony with the ocean's song. It was a realm of peace, beauty, and soul-connected purpose.

But that beauty...

Was now buried in shadow.

The water thickened in her vision. Light dimmed. Harmony twisted into silence.

And through the broken sanctuaries... they came.

The Shadowed.

Not beings, but remnants.

Wounds made form.

Absences made flesh.

They slithered with grotesque elegance, eyes void of stars, mouths split open as if to devour everything sacred. Their skin writhed like oil, leaving behind trails of rot. They tore through coral, through song, through soul.

Solei's chest constricted. Her knees buckled beneath the weight of the sorrow.

"They do not take to live," the guardian's voice rippled through her.

"They consume. They unravel. They strip the light from memory and devour the sacred."

Tears welled in Solei's eyes, spilling freely down her cheeks.

She saw the children of the deep—soft-eyed, luminous beings—scattered, hunted.

She saw the elders—keepers of memory—falling into silence.

She felt the rupture in her bones.

In her womb.

In her spirit.

It wasn't only grief.

It was annihilation.

A lineage gone.

A song ended.

A light extinguished beneath the weight of hatred.

"They took my kin," the guardian wept.

"Those I once sang the oceans with. I am the last."

The ache in his voice wasn't just pain. It was emptiness.

The ache of being the final breath of a forgotten world.

Solei dropped to her knees, the water swirling around her. Her palms rested against the tide, grounding her to the Earth through her sorrow.

"They are coming," he said. "They feel your presence. They want what you hold. But for now... the veil still holds."

"Why?" she asked, voice trembling. "Why haven't they broken through?"

"Because hatred blinds them," he said. "Their rage binds them. Their fury anchors them to the reef they defiled. But the reef will not hold forever."

A flicker of courage lit within her chest.

"So we have time?"

"Yes. But not long. Use it wisely, daughter of the light."

Solei rose into the wind and water.

"Let me offer healing," she said softly. "Not to erase the pain—but to witness it. To honor what still pulses in your remembering."

The guardian bowed his massive head.

"For their memory... I accept."

She lifted her hands.

Golden light poured from her palms like a golden river weaving through ancient stone. It was not a force—it was a remembering. A lullaby. A soul-touch.

The grief did not vanish.

It softened.

It found a place to rest.

The glowing glyphs etched into the creature's form pulsed brighter, then slower—like a breath being exhaled after eons of holding.

Then—within that stillness—Solei heard the voice.

Not from the creature.

Not from the sea.

But from within.

It moved through her like a breeze through tall reeds. Like a hymn remembered in a grandmother's hum.

Lu Mai.

"Daughter of the tides, your light does not only soothe. It awakens. Through you, the sea remembers its song. Through you, the bloodlines long buried stir in the salt."

This moment was not only a healing.

It was a return.

She had always been of the water.

Of the breath between wave and womb.

She was not only priestess of Lumeria.

She was daughter of the sea.

As the light settled, the creature exhaled—a long, sacred sound.

"You reminded me," he said. "Of what peace once felt like."

He turned to the deep.

"I will rest tonight among the kelp. But at dawn, I return. If they stir... I will come."

Solei stepped forward one last time, voice like silk and fire.

"Then I send you back with love. With memory. And with the vow that we will rise."

He gave her one final glance.

Then vanished beneath the sea.

In his wake, the surface shimmered—not with sorrow, but with sacred promise.

Solei stood in the surf, water swirling around her ankles.

Her body hummed.

Her heart beat slow and deep.

Her soul trembled, not in fear—but in knowing.

The balance had shifted.

The veil had thinned.

The harmony had changed.

And something was coming.

Chapter Eight

THE LATTICE OF LIGHT

S olei ran.

    The vision still scorched behind her eyes, radiant and raw. Her skin burned with the imprint of what she had seen—not from heat, but from energy, coursing through her like fire laced with grief. The forest blurred around her, each step a prayer pressed into the earth, each breath an ache she couldn't name. Her heart pounded against her ribs as if it, too, was trying to flee the knowing.

Every sense was heightened. The scent of wet leaves. The sting of wind against damp cheeks. The pressure in her chest, heavy and pulsing. The grief of the sea guardian was no longer a story she had been told—it was a frequency she carried in her bones, his sorrow woven into the very rhythm of her breath.

The forest blurred around her, every breath ragged, her chest tight. The vision burned behind her eyes like a fire she couldn't unsee. Each step pounded with urgency—but it wasn't fear that drove her. It was sorrow. A sorrow too large to hold alone. The cries of the sea guardian echoed through her body, every note of his grief threading into her heartbeat.

Her legs trembled—not from exhaustion, but from the weight of knowing.

Knowing that peace was cracking.Knowing that the veil had thinned.Knowing that her people—her soul family—had to be warned.

Sunlight filtered gently through the canopy, warm against her tear-streaked face. Its beauty felt out of place beside the storm she carried within. Still, she didn't stop. She couldn't.

When the village came into view, she slowed, her breath catching.

She wiped her face, grounding herself. The grief of the sea creature clung to her—not as burden, but as calling. A call to rise. To protect. To remember.

At the village center, the elders were already gathered.It was as if the island had whispered to them, too.

Pehani stood among them, brow furrowed, stance grounded. The moment her form emerged from the trees, his gaze locked on hers. He moved to her side without hesitation.

"You saw something," he said, low and urgent.

Solei nodded. Her voice barely carried.

"Down by the sea... a guardian found me. A being older than time. He came from a city beneath the waves—once radiant, now silent. His kin... all gone."

Pehani's jaw tightened. Though a warrior through lifetimes, his strength was not in violence—it was in devotion. Stillness forged through fire. Love tempered through discipline. In his eyes, she saw the rising of something primal—disbelief, protectiveness, the first flicker of righteous fury.

He stepped closer, grounding her with the warmth of his palm at her shoulder, the firmness of his hand around her arm. His voice lowered.

"Zha'turim, -The Shadowed," he murmured. "They came?"

Solei nodded again. Her voice trembled, but did not falter.

"They overtook his people. Not for survival. Not for need. They devour light. They feast on fear. They consume their own. He's the last. And he came to me for help."

Pehani's grip tightened slightly.

"Did he say how close they are?"

"They're clouded by rage," she said. "Their hatred blinds them. They're trapped—on the reef they overran. But he felt them searching. He's afraid. And so am I."

Pehani looked into her eyes.

"Are you afraid?" he asked gently.

She held his gaze, and her spine straightened.

"Yes. But more than that, I'm ready. Something inside me... it's rising. The voice I've always carried—it's no longer whispering. It's calling me to lead. We must be ready. We must become the light they cannot extinguish."

In that moment, Pehani saw what the elders had long known but never spoken aloud. She was not becoming the High Priestess. She had always been. The truth of her soul was simply now rising to meet the time.

Whispers moved through the gathering like wind through trees. Elder Ama stepped forward.

"How much time do we have?"

"Not much," Solei said. "But enough—if we act now."

Elder Kalon's voice was firm.

"Then it's time. We awaken the old protections. The grid beneath the land."

Solei's eyes widened. She had heard the stories—of an ancient web of light woven into Lumeria's bones by the first ones. But it hadn't stirred in lifetimes.

"Do we remember how?" she asked.

Ama reached into her cloak and drew forth a crystal—etched with luminous glyphs pulsing faintly in the light.

"The Earth remembers," she said. "And so do we."

Pehani looked to Solei.

"Then we begin. Tonight. At moonrise. We gather every soul—every healer, every seer, every heart willing to protect the light."

And with those words, the village stirred—not with fear, but with purpose.

The Lumerians would rise.And the island would rise with them.

As twilight deepened into indigo, the village became a soft chorus of preparation .No one panicked. No one shouted. They moved as they always had—with reverence.

At the heart of the village, a great clearing was prepared—a sacred bowl nestled beneath the open sky. The soil had been cleared and swept with care, blessed with herbs and silent prayers. Torches made from sacred reeds lined the perimeter, their flames flickering in shades of lavender and indigo, casting dancing shadows that rippled like spirit across the ground. The air was thick with scent—jasmine unfolding in moonlight, lavender warmed by dusk, sea salt carried in from the breath of the bay. At each cardinal point, crystals were carefully placed upon hand-carved altars—earth stones the color of fertile soil, fire gems glowing amber-bright, airy quartz singing in high tones, and water-polished aquamarines that pulsed like the tide. Each one hummed softly, as if remembering their purpose. As if awakening.

Solei stood in the center, barefoot beneath the moon, her hair wild and free. Her golden markings shimmered under the lunar light. Around her body, she wore a wrap of ivory linen, braided with silver thread and petals blessed by the sun.

The High Priestess had arrived—not through ritual, but through remembrance. Solei could feel it coursing through her body—the ancestral breath rising in her lungs, the warmth of light curling in her belly, the quiet, unshakable knowing anchoring her spine. Her skin tingled as if kissed by memory, the golden markings across her arms glowing brighter with every beat of her heart. It wasn't ceremony that crowned her—it was the way the land responded to her presence, the way the people's breath shifted when she entered the circle. In that moment, she felt herself not stepping into a role, but returning to it. She was not becoming. She was remembering.

Pehani stepped beside her. His presence was the ground beneath her. He wore his mantle across his shoulders—marked with the triangle of the Protector. He said nothing. He only stood—anchored. Present.

One by one, the villagers joined them.Healers . Dreamweavers. Elders and children.They formed a great circle. Hands joined. Hearts attuned.

As the moon reached its apex, Elder Ama stepped forward, raising the crystal.

"The grid sleeps beneath us," she called. "But the Earth never forgets."

Then she turned to Solei.

"And neither does she."

Solei stepped forward. She raised her hands. Her eyes closed.

The ground stirred.

A pulse rose from beneath her feet—soft at first, like the hush of breath before a cry. Then stronger. Steadier.

The ancient lattice of light—woven by ancestors, seeded by stars—began to awaken.

Threads of light burst from the soil—thin and gold, weaving sacred geometry through the clearing like a living mandala. The symbols of Lumeria shimmered back into life.

Gasps rose from the circle. The air shifted. The trees leaned closer. The wind stilled.

Solei arched slightly as the energy moved through her spine. She could feel them—her ancestors. Priestesses. Guardians. Voices of wisdom rising in her blood.

Her lips parted, and a chant emerged—not taught, not learned, but remembered.

Others joined her, their voices layered and low, the harmony growing in waves. The land vibrated beneath them, pulsing with sacred purpose.

Then—vision.

A wave of warmth surged up from the ground beneath Solei, rushing through her feet and rising into her spine like a golden flame. Her breath hitched. Her body stilled. And in an instant, her inner vision cracked open like the petals of a sacred flower.

Light poured through her consciousness—brilliant and fast, painted in tones of sapphire, silver, and burning gold. Her senses expanded beyond the physical: she could hear the hum of the stars, feel the breath of the ocean touching the shores of distant lands. Her heart beat in time with something vast and ancient.

The energy moved through her like a remembering. Her body trembled with the weight of it, her fingers curling as she anchored herself in the now. Her skin glowed with reverent heat. She could smell salt and the faint tang of minerals rising from ancient stone, taste wind and starlight It was not simply vision—it was immersion. Revelation.

Solei's inner sight expanded. She saw the Shadowed creeping over dying lands, their shadows unraveling color from the earth.

But she also saw light—a dome of energy rising over Lumeria, woven from heart and unity.

She saw choice.And destiny.

The chant softened. The pulse slowed. The grid stabilized—anchored into the land once more.

Solei opened her eyes, glowing faintly gold.

"The lattice of light is awake," she said, voice steady.

"But this... is only the beginning."

The circle remained still, reverent.

Then Elder Kalon stepped forward, his long cloak trailing behind him like a river of dusk. His greenish-blue skin shimmered beneath the torchlight with a soft opalescent glow, etched with luminous glyphs that ran in elegant lines across his collarbone and down his forearms—symbols of the Orin'thal, the ancient Lumerian order of wisdom keepers and star-rememberers. His face, carved with the grace of many lifetimes, bore the softness of compassion and the sharpness of clarity. His silver hair, braided with strands of crystal thread, cascaded over one shoulder like a woven stream of moonlight. His eyes, wide and almond-shaped, held galaxies within them—soft pools of indigo flecked with stardust, now lit with a fire that had not been seen in generations.

He clasped his hands behind his back, the soft rustle of woven crystal fibers brushing against his palms. He walked slowly into the center, each step reverent, the flickering flames casting shifting shadows across the worn but regal lines of his face. When he spoke, his voice was low and deep, vibrating like thunder beneath sacred soil, echoing with the gravity of lifetimes remembered.

"We've known peace so long, we forgot what it meant to prepare for what does not understand peace."

Zambia followed, fierce and graceful, her eyes gleaming.

"We must do more than remember the old ways. We must live them. Teach them. Especially to the young."

Solei nodded.

"Tomorrow, we begin training—not just of body, but of soul. We learn to shape energy through stillness, to channel strength through breath, and to anchor light through presence. We protect not with force, but with frequency. Not through war, but through truth—the kind that hums through the bones of the Earth and remembers who we are even when we forget."

Pehani placed a hand on her back, his palm warm and grounding, like the steady heartbeat of the Earth itself. The touch was not just comfort—it was a vow. A silent transmission of strength, a promise that no matter what came, she would not carry this alone. His presence wrapped around her like a protective field of light, anchoring her in love, in unity, in sacred remembrance.

"Let this night be remembered—not as the moment fear touched our threshold—but as the moment we stood in the fullness of our light. Let it be known as the breath where we chose remembrance over retreat, resonance over reaction. When the Earth heard our voices, and our ancestors rose within us like a choir of starlight. When unity became our weapon, and love, our lineage."

A ripple of energy moved through the circle, rolling like a golden wave through each linked hand and open heart. It was more than energy—it was remembrance in motion, a frequency of ancient unity rising again. Their breath synced, their glyphs glowed brighter, and for a breathless moment, it felt as if every soul there had become one body of light, pulsing in time with the awakened grid. A prayer of unity passed not through words, but through the space between them—soft, sacred, unbreakable.

And from beyond the village, the wind carried a soft melody—a sound like silver rain falling on ancient stone, wrapped in the breath of lullabies sung long before time. It rose from the sea like a murmur of memory, too distant to name, yet woven into the marrow of every soul present. It stirred something beneath the skin—a knowing, a promise, a prayer. And those who heard it, even in sleep, turned their hearts toward the shore, their spirits tilting gently toward the sacred pulse that lingered beyond the veil.

That night, the village did not sleep.

The moon hung high and full, casting silver light across every thatched rooftop and flowering vine. A hush draped the land, not in fear, but in reverence. The wind had quieted to a breath, and the air carried the weight of prophecy. Crystals embedded along paths shimmered faintly, responding to the charge in the atmosphere. The trees stood like sentinels, their leaves glinting with moonlight, as if leaning in to listen.

All of Lumeria pulsed in one rhythm—an ancient thrum beneath the surface, alive, alert, and listening. It echoed through root and river, through crystal veins and canopy breath. The vibration was not just heard but felt—a subtle resonance moving through every stone and every soul. It was the heartbeat of remembrance itself, stirring awake the deep codes buried in the land. Every tree stood a little taller, every breeze carried a whisper of sacred alignment. The island was not just watching. It was awakening with them.

Healers gathered in shimmering clusters, their hands tracing luminous patterns through the air as they passed ancient rites between them—rites not taught, but remembered in vibration. Their chants hummed through the clearing like a living heartbeat, wrapping the space in a veil of harmony. Warriors moved through sacred forms, blades gleaming with protective energy, their bodies weaving strength and grace into motion. Zambia and Pehani led with effortless synergy, each movement a dance between divine fire and grounded presence. Meanwhile, the elders sat with the children beneath the twilight trees, their voices soft and rhythmic, guiding young minds back into their soul memory. The children listened with wide, glowing eyes, as if stars had opened inside them.

Each soul stepped into their place.

This was no longer Solei's burden to carry alone.

The people of Lumeria were rising.

And with them, the light.

CHAPTER NINE

THE GATHERING FLAME

The sun crested the horizon with quiet reverence, casting a warm golden glow across the lush hills of Lumeria—as if the dawn itself bowed to the guiding light of Solei, High Priestess of the land. The golden rays shimmered in soft halos, mirroring her presence, signaling a new day shaped by wisdom and sacred purpose. The air carried a gentle stillness, yet beneath it, a subtle tension pulsed—as though the land itself held its breath.

Solei stood atop a ridge just beyond the village, her gaze sweeping across the glistening ocean with a regal stillness. As her eyes touched the horizon, a gentle breeze rose from the sea, carrying with it the scent of salt and blooming lilies—answering her presence like a lover returning home. The ocean shimmered as though recognizing her, waves glittering under her gaze. The wind curled around her ankles and rose through her hair, weaving through the golden symbols on her skin with reverent grace. It was as if the elements themselves were in communion with her spirit—honoring her role as the heart of the land's sacred rhythm. She was the embodiment of divine feminine presence—regal, graceful, and radiant with an inner light that seemed to speak directly to the soul. The golden symbols etched across her arms and collarbone shimmered in the morning sun, glowing with the quiet power of lineage and purpose. Solei did not just lead—she healed with her presence, offered wisdom in her stillness, and exuded a calm strength that wrapped itself around her people like a blessing. The wind wrapped around her like a silken ribbon, lifting strands of her hair and whisper-ing through the folds of her robe. Her bare feet pressed into the cool, damp earth, grounding her in the heartbeat of the land below. She could feel every breath of the island—the pulse of the trees, the silent hum of the soil, the deep memory held in the stone beneath her. Her chest ached with awe, with reverence, and a weight she could not name. It was as if the whole island had placed its trust in her hands, and she held it there gently, like a flame cupped in palms. She closed her eyes briefly, inhaling the salt-laced breeze, and in that moment, she felt not alone, but profoundly woven into the soul of the land—its memory, its ancestry, its pulse. This connection was not simply spiritual, but ancestral, etched into her very being as part of the priestess lineage she carried. The earth knew her not just as guardian, but as a daughter returning to fulfill an ancient vow. The events of the night still lived in her body, her skin buzzing faintly with the lingering frequency of the grid. Though the island now pulsed with renewed protection, her heart knew this was merely the beginning.

Pehani joined her in silence, his steps soft over the dewy grass. As he neared, his eyes settled on her, and for a breath of time, he didn't see just the High Priestess—he saw the woman he loved wrapped in morning light, rooted to the earth like a sacred tree. Solei radiated strength, serenity, and something untouchable, and it stirred both awe and tenderness in him. Her mere presence calmed the turbulence within him, as though the threads of his worry unraveled in the soft pull of her aura. Every time he looked at her, he felt as though he were seeing the soul of the island itself—ancient, luminous, and unshakably wise. A quiet reverence stirred within him, along with a fierce devotion—to her, to Lumeria, to the light they had vowed to protect.

He didn't speak right away. Instead, he stood beside her and followed her gaze toward the sea. His presence, as always, steadied her. When he finally spoke, his voice was low and sure.

"You feel it too," he said.

Solei nodded, her voice calm and melodic. "The air has changed. It's subtle, but it's there. It moves through the roots, the sky, and our bones. The earth is whispering to us—preparing us."

They stood together, listening—not just with ears, but with spirit. The silence between them was thick with understanding. It was not absence of sound, but presence—of tension, of messages unspoken, of nature murmuring through its rhythms. From the forest, birds sang, but their calls were short, clipped, uncertain, like questions left unanswered. The ocean, ever a constant companion to the island's breath, moved with a strange hesitation. Waves that once rolled in melodic cadence now broke in irregular intervals, as though something beneath disturbed their harmony. Even the wind, usually playful and melodic, had changed—its tone lower, heavier, brushing past them like a warning wrapped in whispers. It tugged gently at their clothing, rustling the tall grass with a kind of restless urgency, as though searching for something—or someone—to speak through.

The island was speaking.

A rustle behind them signaled Zambia's arrival. She approached with her usual grace, though her sharp eyes were narrowed in concentration.

"Something stirs in the far cliffs," she said. "A flicker. Not light, not shadow. Movement that feels... displaced."

Solei turned toward her. "Have you sent scouts?"

"They're already on their way," Zambia replied. "And I've called the dreamweavers. If anything is approaching, it may appear to them first—between the veil of sleep and vision."

Solei breathed deeply, letting the sensations wash over her. Though she had long carried the sacred mantle of High Priestess of Lumeria, Solei didn't just observe the energies—she listened to them with her whole being, interpreting their whispers like sacred songlines passed through the elements. Her role wasn't only to guide, but to embody the heart of the colony—a living temple of grace, strength, and unconditional love.

"We hold the light, but we must see through the dark," she said. "We must be ready for what stirs in the wind."

The three stood atop the ridge, guardians of peace on the edge of change. And below, in the heart of Lumeria, the people continued to train—not in fear, but in remembrance of who they were, and the legacy they vowed to protect—a legacy deeply rooted in the sacred guidance of Solei, whose presence held the vision and heart of their mission like a living flame.

By midday, the village stirred with purposeful activity. Builders began constructing larger, stronger structures near the heart of the village—reinforced halls crafted from stone, crystal, and living wood. These would serve as protective sanctuaries, meant to withstand not just the elements, but energy itself. Each beam placed was infused with grounding frequency, and at the center of each foundation, a stone of memory was laid to hold intention for harmony and strength. Builders reinforced the communal shelters with stones infused with intention and healing. Gardeners expanded the fields, sowing new medicinal plants and fruit-bearing trees, whispering to the roots as they worked. Healers opened sacred spaces to anchor new energy centers, marking the earth with swirling glyphs drawn from powdered crystals and flower petals. They sang ancient harmonic tones that vibrated through the air like threads of light, calling in protection and clarity. Each healer moved with intention, hands tracing invisible patterns, guiding streams of energy into woven grids beneath the surface. Their voices blended like rivers merging into a sacred sea—low and resonant, echoing the heartbeat of the island itself, while dreamweavers gathered in shaded groves to deepen their connection to the veil. Artists carved protective sigils into stone and wood, each symbol glowing faintly as it was placed around the village's perimeter. Even the animals seemed to respond—birds hovering close, wild deer watching from the trees.

Lumeria was becoming more than a sanctuary. It was evolving into a massive, magnificent colony—an embodiment of unity, wisdom, and sacred intention. Pathways lined with flowering vines and polished stones now stretched between structures, connecting the community like veins pulsing with light. Towering trees formed natural archways, their canopies shading open-air gathering spaces where wisdom was exchanged like sacred breath. Elevated walkways of crystal-bound wood linked new lookout towers, while vibrant gardens spiraled in geometric patterns that resonated with the frequency of the land. Everything was alive with purpose. From the tallest carved totem to the smallest luminous seed, every detail was built with reverence for the Earth and the cosmos. The village was expanding in all directions—upward, outward, and inward—becoming a radiant reflection of the Lumerians' devotion to harmony, healing, and the preservation of light.

And in the quiet hours of rest, the dreamweavers began to speak of visions—haunting yet prophetic glimpses from the spaces between sleep and starlight. They saw tendrils of darkness sliding through the ocean's floor like veins of shadow, reaching outward. Among these visions came a grave and sorrowful glimpse—a great war, not just of weapons but of spirit. They saw fires burning across once-sacred lands, and cries echoing through valleys where once there had only been peace. A great sadness blanketed their visions, thick and suffocating, as buildings crumbled and bonds were torn asunder. The devastation wasn't just physical—it was emotional, spiritual. A test of light against a storm of despair.

Yet even through that vision of destruction, they also saw threads of golden light weaving around Lumeria, forming a radiant lattice above the land.

Some dreamweavers described a great storm approaching—not just of wind and rain, but of emotion, memory, and time itself. And within these visions, many saw Solei herself—standing as a radiant pillar of light amidst the darkness, a spiritual guide who anchored the collective through the tempest. Her presence pulsed like a lighthouse in the storm, reaffirming her role as the High Priestess whose lineage stretched far beyond this realm. They felt pulses of power moving beneath the island, ancient and intelligent, waiting to be remembered. A voice—neither male nor female—whispered in unspoken language, resonating through their chests: "Hold the light, anchor the truth."

There were also visions of triumph. Of Solei standing in a circle of firelight, her hands lifted to the heavens, surrounded by a rising chorus who chanted in tones that echoed across dimensions. In their eyes, she was more than a leader—she was a divine conduit, a bridge between the earthly and celestial realms. Light streamed from her fingertips as if guided by the heavens themselves, and the land beneath her pulsed in rhythm with her breath. Her presence in the vision was luminous, sovereign, and eternal—a true embodiment of sacred feminine power. Of Pehani deflecting a wave of shadow with a single pulse of golden energy. Of Zambia, guiding others across a trembling bridge of light through swirling mists.

Something was coming—but so too was a radiant force rising in them all.

Lumeria was preparing. Together.

And as they worked in harmony, something extraordinary began to unfold. The more they aligned, the more their gifts evolved. Healers discovered new frequencies in their hands, unlocking healing tones that pulsed deeper into the earth. Dreamweavers saw farther through the veil, glimpsing timelines they had never touched before. Builders became attuned to the materials they used, shaping stone and wood not only with their hands but with their hearts. Warriors like Pehani and Zambia moved with a new fluidity, as though time slowed around them when they acted with pure intent. Yet, even as their skills sharpened, challenges stirred within the warrior circle. Pehani and Zambia, though both revered and powerful in their own right, often found themselves at odds over how best to defend the colony. Their approaches clashed—his grounded and strategic, hers swift and instinctive. Training sessions grew tense, voices rose, and plans unraveled before they could be agreed upon. Other warriors looked on with uncertainty, caught between the wisdom of both leaders. Despite their deep mutual respect, Pehani and Zambia's constant bickering fractured the cohesion of their efforts. It was as if the very harmony they sought to protect resisted being forged through disharmony. They needed to find alignment—fast—before their dissonance became a weakness Lumeria could not afford.

Later that evening, as the last light of day faded into indigo twilight, Pehani found Solei beside the central well, her fingers trailing the rim as if drawing wisdom from its still waters.

Later that evening, under the golden glow of twilight, Pehani found Solei beside the central well, her fingers trailing the rim as if drawing wisdom from its still waters. His shoulders were tense, his eyes shadowed with frustration. He paused before her, reluctant to speak, as if holding the words too long had made them heavier than they should have been.

"Solei," he said, his voice low and burdened, "I need to tell you something. It's about Zambia and me."

Solei turned to face him fully, her expression open and gentle. But inside, her heart ached. She had never seen Pehani so troubled—his usual calm now cloaked in weariness, his voice edged with doubt. Seeing the strain in his eyes stirred something fierce and tender in her. He had carried so much, not just as a warrior, but as her beloved, as a protector of their people. The heaviness he bore pressed against her own spirit. She wanted to wrap him in light, to transmute the storm within him through the grace of her divine feminine energy—the same serenity he so often gave to others. Her presence as High Priestess was not only comforting, but alchemical, turning ache into clarity and doubt into sacred remembrance.

"We can't seem to find a way forward. Every time we try to make plans, we hit a wall. She rushes ahead, I hold back. She trusts her instincts, I need structure. It's like we're dancing to different rhythms, trying to lead the same movement. And the warriors... they're starting to feel it. They don't know who to follow. I worry we're failing them. I worry I'm failing."

He let out a breath and looked away. "I respect her. I do. And I know she has the colony's best interest at heart. But I can't get through to her. She challenges everything I say, and instead of clarity, all we find is discord."

Solei reached for his hand, holding it with a calm strength that radiated grounding energy. Her touch, infused with the quiet power of the High Priestess, moved through him like a balm—centering his breath, softening the sharp edges of his doubt. In that moment, her presence became an anchor, a sacred tether to everything steady and true.

"You're not failing, Pehani. But perhaps it's not clarity you need to give each other. Maybe it's trust. Let me speak with her. Let me help her see the unity that lives beyond the difference."

Pehani nodded, his eyes softening. "Thank you. I don't want us to be divided. Not when we need each other the most."

Solei listened quietly, her hand finding his. "Then perhaps it's time I speak with her."

That night, Solei made her way to the edge of the village, where the flowering archways gave way to a crescent grove woven with soft lights. Zambia's home stood within, made of pale crystalwood and draped with layers of embroidered fabric that shifted like water. The structure rose in a graceful arc, formed from living trees whose trunks had been gently shaped over time to create protective curves. Vines bearing star-shaped flowers curled around the beams, glowing faintly with bioluminescent hues. Crystals were embedded in the walls—clear, amethyst, and deep aquamarine—catching the moonlight and reflecting it across the interior in soft prismatic patterns. Wind chimes made of woven seashells and polished stones hung from the eaves, their tones soft and melodic, creating a perpetual harmony with the wind. Inside, the air was fragrant with dried herbs and oils, and the floor was covered in soft woven mats. At the center of the space, a small circular fire pit was ringed with carved stones etched in protective sigils, creating a sacred hearth for gatherings and quiet rituals. As she approached, a gentle figure appeared in the doorway.

Luneia.

She was ethereal—tall and willowy, with luminous greenish-bluish-grey skin that shimmered like water kissed by moonlight. Her eyes, a striking shade of sea-glass green, held galaxies in their depths—kind, curious, and filled with the wisdom of many lifetimes. Her long, flowing hair was dark bluish-black, woven with intricate braids that sparkled faintly with tiny threads of gold and silver. Like the rest of the Lumerians, her body bore radiant golden symbols that glowed softly with her energy—etched across her arms, collarbone, and down the sides of her face in beautiful swirling patterns.

She wore a flowing wrap of deep lavender and soft beige, embroidered with shimmering lines that resembled the sacred geometry of the stars. Her fingers were strong and graceful, calloused from her craft. Luneia was a braider—of hair, yes, but also of vines, reeds, cloth, and energy itself. Her hands created woven wonders imbued with subtle enchantments of harmony, strength, and renewal—objects that pulsed with memory and magic.

She smiled gently as she welcomed Solei inside. "We felt you coming. Zambia is just finishing her sacred alignment rite."

Zambia emerged from a curtain of woven shells, her eyes tired but alert. Solei greeted her with calm warmth.

"Zambia," she said, her voice soft but full of knowing, "you've always been the fire that clears the path. But I wonder... have you forgotten that the path doesn't need to be walked alone?"

Zambia arched an eyebrow, her stance still guarded. "You think I'm pushing too hard."

"I think you're holding too much," Solei replied, stepping closer. "Pehani's not against you. He's beside you. The people see two leaders in conflict—but I see two lights that haven't yet remembered how to burn together."

Zambia looked away for a moment, then back. "Sometimes I don't know how to slow down. I see danger, and I react. It's what I've always done."

Solei smiled gently. "That instinct has saved us before. But now, Lumeria needs us to lead not just with instinct, but with heart. That's the hardest part—trusting someone else to hold what you care about so fiercely."

There was a silence, then Solei's voice dropped to a more intimate tone. "Do you remember those nights by the sacred spring? When we were still learning these bodies, and you would braid wildflowers into my hair, telling me the names of stars?"

Zambia chuckled softly, the edge in her eyes dimming. "You always asked me to use the purple ones. Said they matched your soul."

"And they did," Solei said, her smile widening. "Because you placed them there. We led with love then. Before titles, before roles, we were just us."

Zambia nodded slowly. "I miss that simplicity."

"Then let's bring some of it back," Solei said. "We don't need to change who we are. Just remember who we were—together."

Zambia's breath caught, and she looked into Solei's eyes, her own softening further. "I don't want to let him down. Or you. But sometimes... I don't know how to slow down. I see what needs to be done and I charge ahead. It's how I've always been."

Solei nodded. "And it's what makes you powerful. But Pehani—he's not trying to control you. He's trying to walk beside you. You don't have to carry it all on your own."

Zambia reached for Solei's hand, squeezing it gently.

"Thank you. For reminding me who I am beneath all this fire."

Luneia stepped forward then and gently placed her hand on Zambia's shoulder, a silent tether of love and grounding.

"You don't have to lead like anyone else," Solei continued. "But you do have to lead with love."

For a moment, silence stretched between them. Then Zambia nodded, her eyes meeting Solei's with softened resolve. The quiet grace of the High Priestess lingered in her chest, a balm to the fire that often raged unchecked. In that still moment, she felt her own heart shift.

"For Lumeria," she said, her voice low. "I will try."

The following morning, the warriors gathered at dawn beneath the great canopy trees, whose broad emerald leaves arched high overhead, forming a cathedral of green and gold. Vines heavy with vibrant blossoms dangled like living chandeliers, swaying gently in the warm, fragrant breeze. Shafts of sunlight filtered through the foliage in iridescent beams, casting soft rainbows that danced across the forest floor. The trees, ancient and wise, exuded a gentle hum—an energetic pulse that wrapped around the warriors like a blessing from the land itself. The earth beneath them was soft and damp, a mosaic of moss, wildflowers, and sacred roots woven in intricate spirals. This was no ordinary forest—it was a living sanctuary, a sacred circle of magic and memory that held their training like a sacred rite of passage. The energy was different—calmer, more focused.

The tension that once crackled between Pehani and Zambia had softened into something fluid, like the rhythm of ocean waves finally syncing with the tide.

Zambia entered first, flanked by two younger warriors, her expression steady and grounded. Pehani followed soon after, his steps confident yet humble. They met in the center of the circle—not as rivals, but as allies. A hush fell over the warriors as the two locked eyes.

"We lead as one," Zambia said, voice firm and clear. "Different flames, same fire."

Pehani nodded. "Together, we become something stronger than either of us alone."

The warriors formed a wide circle, and the training began—not with weapons, but with breath. Pehani guided them through grounding movements—rooting their energy into the earth, syncing their breath with the pulse of the island. Zambia followed, flowing into combat forms laced with intention and grace. Where once they clashed, now they danced.

They practiced shielding not only the body, but the spirit—projecting energy fields, deflecting dark frequencies, drawing from the island's life force without draining it. A new technique emerged as they trained: white energy rings began to form around their bodies, flowing outward from their core fields in pulsing waves. These radiant rings, channeled with focused breath and intention, held a powerful force—so potent that when released, they could shatter the largest boulders embedded deep in the earth. The ground trembled with their resonance, the air humming with the sharp clarity of pure light unleashed. Each warrior learned to control this energy not with brute strength, but with balance, breath, and heart. Warriors paired off, helping each other attune to subtle energy shifts. For the first time, they moved as one body, one rhythm.

Above them, the trees swayed gently, and the light filtered through the leaves in golden beams that kissed the warriors' skin like blessings. The land, too, responded—vibrating faintly with every stomp, every shout, every exhale of strength.

And when the training ended, Pehani and Zambia stood together, shoulder to shoulder, their energies no longer colliding, but interwoven like braided light.

Yet beneath the triumph of their newfound unity, a troubling pattern began to emerge. The more they practiced channeling the white energy rings, the more the warriors found themselves growing depleted. After each release, their breath shortened, their limbs trembled, and their light dimmed. Even the strongest among them fell to their knees in exhaustion, needing hours—sometimes a full day—to recover.

They tried everything. Rest. Re-centering rituals. Sacred herbs. Water from the highest spring. But nothing seemed to replenish what was lost. The energy they called upon was potent—otherworldly—and with each summoning, it asked more than they were prepared to give.

Pehani and Zambia stood watching one afternoon as a promising young warrior collapsed to the ground, the energy rings still echoing around him like fading whispers.

"We're drawing from a well that wasn't meant to be touched this often," Zambia murmured, her brow furrowed.

Pehani nodded grimly. "Or we haven't yet remembered how to fill it."

The wind moved through the trees with a quiet hush, as if echoing the weight of the moment. Doubt settled like mist around the warrior circle, thick and clinging.

And for the first time since the training began, it didn't just feel uncertain—it felt as if even the light itself might falter.

That evening, as twilight draped the island in violet hues, Solei stood alone on the cliffs above the ocean. The rhythmic crash of the waves echoed her thoughts—steadily rising, then pulling back, as if something below was trying to surface.

She closed her eyes and reached inward, into the stillness between her breaths. Her awareness stretched through the roots of the island, down into the layers of stone, into the ancient memory embedded in the bones of the land.

And there it was—a flicker.

Not a voice, not quite. But a feeling. A subtle pulse beneath the ground. Not malicious... but vast. Dormant. Watching.

She felt the resonance that matched the white energy rings the warriors had begun to wield. It was the same frequency, but deeper—like an ocean echoing back a song that hadn't been sung for centuries.

Her heart shivered. Whatever it was, it was tied to their gifts. But it wasn't just energy.

It was consciousness.

"Something remembers us," she whispered to the wind. "And it waits."

CHAPTER TEN

REMEMBERING THE FLAME

C enturies moved like sacred songs, carried by the breath of wind. Though time continued its eternal flow, the Lumerians did not age as mortal beings do. Their bodies, nourished by light, energy, and purpose, remained ageless—radiant, strong, and imbued with the essence of eternity. Time shaped them, but never wearied them. Their faces held the grace of ageless wisdom, and their movements—fluid, sure, and graceful—seemed to echo with the pulse of the cosmos itself. They were the embodiment of an eternal dance, where the soul was both ever-present and infinite.

Under the twin suns of Lumeria, warm and golden, the island hummed with vitality, and the rhythm of the sea sang its eternal lullaby. The colony bloomed, surpassing the dreams of the ancients. With every cycle of seasons, they wove themselves more deeply into the fabric of the island, blending with nature's heartbeat, building a civilization of breathtaking beauty and radiant, sacred brilliance.

The city unfolded like a living mandala, rising in layers, each structure a prayer, each path an energy line, spiraling outward in sacred geometry. At the center of it all stood the Temple of Harmonic Light, its towering spires reaching toward the heavens, where Solei and the High Council would commune with the whispers of Lu Mai.

Among the builders who crafted this divine masterpiece was Kaelion, a man whose strength was as gentle as the ocean's pulse. His skin shimmered like sea-glass—soft opalescence with glowing golden markings that danced like sacred constellations down his arms and collarbones. His eyes, deep emerald flecked with radiant light, mirrored the land's energy, calm and boundless. His hair, midnight blue like the ocean's depths, cascaded in thick waves, often adorned with crystal threads or vines, marking his connection to the earth. His movements were like those of the land itself—fluid, grounded, attuned to the island's breath. Where Kaelion stood, the earth seemed to listen, bending to his gentle touch.

Elina, too, wove the fabric of their world. A seer with silver hair that shimmered like moonlight upon water, her beauty reflected the essence of Lumeria itself. Her skin, a luminous silvery-aqua, glowed faintly beneath the stars, while golden glyphs flowed across her temples, tracing down her neck and arms in a delicate dance of light. Her long hair, spun of pearl, tumbled in soft waves, adorned with blossoms and quartz beads gifted by the wind. Her voice, soft as the ocean's tides, carried the resonance of deep, ancient wisdom, while her crystalline lavender-blue eyes seemed ever-distant, as if they were always gazing beyond the veil.

Together, the council stood as living prisms—embodiments of Lumeria's evolution, each a thread in the sacred tapestry of remembrance.

In the Temple of Harmonic Light, Solei stood upon the sunlit terrace, her dark hair lifting like a veil of midnight silk, carried by the caress of the breeze. She gazed beyond the city, over the golden rooftops and toward the distant sea. The island's pulse still sang within her bones—soft and rhythmic, like the gentle heartbeat of the earth. But something had shifted. The harmony was still there, but now it carried a faint, dissonant note.

Behind her, the soft echo of footsteps broke the stillness.

"You're up early," Pehani's voice was warm, carrying an edge of awareness, like the stirrings of a quiet storm.

"You mean I beat you for once?" Solei's voice was playful, though her eyes remained distant.

"Barely." Pehani's smile was a wisp of light, fleeting but sharp. "I was going to bring you tea, but I figured you'd already brewed half the island's thoughts by now."

Her laugh, soft and radiant, rose like a ripple across the stillness. But then, like a cloud passing over the sun, her smile dimmed, just slightly.

"They're watching again," she murmured, her voice low, threaded with unease. "The Shadowed. I can feel it in the wind."

Pehani moved beside her, his jaw tense, his presence a steadying force in the thickening air.

"You think they'll try to take it all?"

"Not just what we've built." Her gaze turned inward, soft but fierce, like a flame caught in the breeze. "They want the light that made it."

The silence between them stretched for a heartbeat, then he leaned against her lightly, his arm brushing hers with tender reassurance.

"Then we don't just guard walls. We protect the heart of it all."

Solei turned to meet his eyes, the gold in hers softening, tender with the weight of what they carried together.

"You always know exactly what to say when I wonder if I'm alone in this."

"You're not," he whispered, his voice low and steady. "You never were."

A breeze curled between them, carrying with it the scent of sea and earth. Together, they stood in the sacred silence, watching the sun rise, its light spilling like liquid gold across the sea, flooding the world with warmth and promise.

Below them, the streets of Lumeria stirred with light. And deep beneath the soil, an ancient pulse waited—quiet and still, as if the earth itself drew in a breath before the storm.

That evening, the High Council gathered beneath the mirrored dome of the Temple of Harmonic Light, where the air shimmered like a caress before a storm. Solei sat at the center, her gaze steady, as Kaelion, Pehani, Zambia, and Elina encircled the sacred flame.

"They're coming," Elina's voice was barely a whisper, the tremor of prophecy threading through it. "I saw them in the dreamscape—shadows beneath the flame, their hunger so vast I could taste it."

Kaelion's deep, steady voice followed, like the hum of the earth itself. "They've always watched... but now the light they crave has grown stronger. Now it calls to them."

Pehani rose, pacing slowly across the crystalline tiles, the silence of his movements filled with thoughts too heavy for words.

"We must be ready, but the warriors... we still can't find a way to protect ourselves without draining our essence. The training we've built, it wears us down before we even face them."

Zambia leaned forward, her arms crossed tightly, her golden glyphs glowing faintly, like embers in the twilight. "It's like fighting a wave with fire. We burn so bright, but it's not enough. We fall before we can rise."

Her words crackled with frustration, sharp and fiery, and the room tensed with the weight of her truth.

"It's more than just our training," she continued. "It's deeper. Something in the energy rejects us when we push too hard."

Pehani's voice broke the stillness, soft yet firm. "Because we're trying to wield it alone."

Solei's gaze softened, the knowing rising within her like a warm tide.

"The answer isn't strength alone," she whispered, "It's harmony."

Zambia exhaled sharply, a sharp breath that could split stone.

"Don't speak to me of harmony when our warriors are already fracturing." Her voice was rough, tinged with urgency. "We need solutions—not songs."

Kaelion's voice was gentle but strong, like the steady lapping of waves upon the shore. "Perhaps the solution is not in resistance, but in remembrance."

A long silence followed, stretching across the room like a breath held in anticipation. Outside, the wind howled through the open archways, rattling the vines that clung to the temple's edge. The sky burned with deep orange and violet hues, like the afterglow of an ancient wound.

Zambia stood and turned toward Pehani, the resolve in her eyes solid as stone. "We'll try again tomorrow. And the day after. Until we find the rhythm. Until we stop tearing each other down."

Pehani's jaw relaxed, his posture softening with a subtle nod. "Agreed. No more division."

Solei watched them, her heart swelling with a mix of hope and warning. The Shadowed were near, and the light they carried would need to burn brighter than ever before.

That night, Solei walked alone beneath the canopy of biolu-minescent trees, their branches heavy with glowing petals that drifted like stars in the darkened sky. The soft light kissed her skin, but her thoughts were heavy, wrapped in the echoes of the council's voices—Zambia's fire, Pehani's resolve, Kaelion's stillness. But still, the answer remained elusive.

She pressed her hand to her chest, over the golden glyph that marked her as High Priestess.

"What am I not seeing?" she whispered, her voice a prayer, a plea.

She sank to her knees by the sacred stream, its waters shim-mering like starlight in motion. The reflection that met her eyes was not just her own—it was the face of her soul, ancient and burdened with a responsibility greater than the stars themselves.

"Lu Mai," she breathed, her voice trembling with reverence. "If there is something we've forgotten... show me."

The stream pulsed beneath her touch—not with water, but with memory. The images flooded her mind, vivid and wild—visions of the first landing, white light crashing into earth like a burst of divinity. Warriors standing in perfect rhythm, their energy braided together like a symphony of light and sound. She saw no separation. Only unity.

And in that moment, it was clear.

The warriors were never meant to fight alone. They were meant to link, to weave together in perfect harmony.

Solei gasped, her heart racing, her skin glowing brighter in the moonlight as her glyphs hummed with the urgency of her discovery.

She turned, her voice trembling with awe and newfound resolve.

"They were never meant to fight as individuals... but as one."

And deep in the forest, beneath the canopy of ancient trees, the leaves stirred.

The Shadowed had crossed into the outer fields.

The time of waiting was over.

CHAPTER ELEVEN

THE SILENT INVASION

The morning after Solei's vision, a golden mist curled softly over the treetops, casting a serene, ethereal glow over the land. The air was thick with the scent of dew-drenched earth and the subtle hum of the island's pulse. Yet, despite the beauty surrounding her, Solei's heart beat with an unsettling unease. She awoke with a heavy weight in her chest, as if something unseen—something waiting just beyond the veil of mist—was calling to her. Deep within the eastern forest, the stillness did not feel sacred. It felt observed, haunted by an energy that did not belong.

With every step she took beneath the towering, ancient trees, her breath remained shallow, and her feet moved as though on instinct, treading softly on the mossy earth. The golden glyphs on her skin flickered faintly, like quiet beacons, as her senses extended outward, attuned to the world around her. Suddenly, a sharp rustle of underbrush sliced through the silence.

Her body tensed, every muscle coiled in quiet alertness. She crouched low, her breath caught in her throat. Again, the rustling came—closer this time, urgent and unnerving. Then a growl, low and guttural, rumbled through the ferns, its sound twisted, alien.

Her heart surged, thudding violently in her chest. The Shadowed, she thought. They've come.

She turned toward the sound, expecting to see a shadowed figure cloaked in dark mist, but what emerged from the underbrush was no mere phantom.

It was a creature.

Wild. Twisted. Infected.

A feral thing, driven by a force far darker than instinct. It lunged toward her.

There was something else in the air—a presence, ancient and watchful. The forest itself seemed to hold its breath.

A branch snapped sharply in the distance.

Solei froze. The hairs on her arms stood at attention, her senses flaring with heightened awareness. She strained her ears, her heart racing faster. The rustling grew closer, more deliberate—urgent and unnatural. The symphony of the forest had fractured, disrupted by a presence that did not belong.

Stepping carefully between the thick roots of an ancient tree, she felt the golden glyphs along her arms pulse, a silent heartbeat of power. Every instinct told her to remain still, to listen. To understand.

A growl echoed again—a low, guttural sound that vibrated through the air like a warning torn from another world.

Solei turned, her breath held in her chest, her gaze sharp and focused. Could it be the Shadowed? Could they have sent this beast?

She stepped forward—then another step, careful but resolute—until the world erupted in a violent explosion of movement.

A massive creature burst through the brush. Its body, twisted and grotesque, snarled with fury, its black eyes void of any soul. Jagged, glistening teeth bared in a twisted snarl, dripping with malice.

It was unlike anything she had ever seen.

Its matted fur was streaked with a black, oily sheen, as though the very light recoiled from it. Once soft amber eyes were now empty, deep pools of pitch black, devoid of warmth. The creature's breath was ragged, and sickly vapor rose from its skin like an ethereal, dark mist. It was no longer of the earth. It had been consumed, its very essence corrupted.

And it lunged.

But Solei did not flinch.

With the grace of a goddess, she raised her hand, palm facing the beast, and golden symbols flared across her skin like a beacon of pure light. A pulse of radiant, healing energy burst from her heart, expanding outward like the dawn's first rays.

The creature collided with her palm, the force of its strike reverberating through the air. Time seemed to still, as if the very earth held its breath.

Then, light.

A blinding, radiant wave of energy consumed the creature, lifting it from the ground and suspending it in midair. It trembled, its body quivering under the weight of the light that poured from her, and the snarl faded into a soft, confused whimper. The blackness in its eyes flickered, its twisted form beginning to soften.

The dark mist that had clung to it evaporated, dissipating into the ether, leaving behind only the creature's broken form.

It collapsed to the ground at her feet, its chest heaving in confusion and exhaustion. Slowly, the once-black matted fur began to shimmer—first faintly, then glowing with an iridescent hue. Soft lavender and deep sapphire streaks rippled across its form like moonlight diffused through water. The jagged edges of its body softened, its features relaxing as though it had awakened from a long, tortured nightmare.

It stared up at Solei, no longer with rage, but with confusion and a deep, aching shame.

Solei knelt beside the creature, her hand gently brushing over its fur, the golden light in her body now dimming to a soft, steady glow. The warmth of her energy enveloped the creature like a soft embrace.

"It's not your fault," she whispered, her voice tender and full of compassion. "You were taken."

The creature let out a soft groan and curled into itself, shivering, as if the weight of its torment was too much to bear.

Solei lingered, watching it closely, her pulse slowing as the last remnants of the healing energy hummed through the air. But her mind raced. A sudden realization struck her, cold and sharp, like a storm crossing still waters. This was no accident.

This creature, once pure and gentle, had been twisted. Not to destroy her. Not to feed. But to spread the corruption. It was a vessel, a silent messenger of darkness. If it had bitten her—or anyone in the colony—the curse of shadow fire would have spread through their veins, infecting Lumeria with a plague of despair.

Her hands trembled—not with fear, but with the weight of what could have been.

The Shadowed did not come with armies. They came with subtlety. With corruption. They sought to breach the sanctuary, not through force, but through the unsuspecting. Through those they loved.

She looked down at the creature, now curled in exhaustion at her feet, and felt a wave of deep compassion rise in her chest. It was not evil. It was a pawn—an innocent swept away by darkness. A whisper of shadow sent to weaken their light.

But they had failed.

Solei stood slowly, the golden glyphs on her skin still faintly glowing in the misty morning light, like a beacon of hope amidst the shadow. Her breath came in steady waves as the forest around her began to still.

"They'll try again," she whispered, her voice firm and resolute, but gentle, as if speaking to the trees themselves. "And we will be ready."

The forest around her seemed to exhale, as if releasing the heavy breath of what could have been. The warning had been given.

The Shadowed had not yet arrived—but their influence had already begun to creep across the land.

The wind shifted, carrying with it a distant whisper.

Solei turned, and there he was.

Pehani emerged from the trees, breathless, his eyes wide with panic. His glyphs were alight, his hands trembling slightly as he reached for her.

"I felt it," he said urgently, gripping her shoulders. "I felt you... and something terrible. Are you hurt?"

Solei shook her head, but her eyes were glassy, her breath still catching in her throat. "It was an animal," she whispered, "but not like any I've ever seen. It was infected. Its eyes—its soul—it was hollow. Twisted."

She recounted everything—the way it had lunged at her, how her healing energy met its darkness, and how the light had stripped away the corruption. And what it meant for them all.

"They tried to send it to infect me, Pehani," she said, her voice steady now, the weight of truth anchoring her. "Not just to harm—but to spread the darkness. Through me... through all of us. It was a silent invasion."

Pehani's expression shifted from concern to a quiet fury, his jaw tightening, his fists clenching in silent rage. "They wanted to use you. To use anyone. This is how they plan to take Lumeria—from the inside out."

"We have to warn the others," Solei said, her voice firm with purpose. "This was a test. A whisper. The next one won't be so small."

Together, they turned and ran, the trees parting for them as if guided by some ancient instinct. Birds scattered overhead, their wings a soft, chaotic rhythm. The forest, once serene, now pulsed with tension, as though the land itself sensed the growing storm.

When they reached the village, Solei called the council together, her voice a clarion call. She and Pehani stood at the center of the gathering circle, breathless and golden, the weight of their discovery pressing on them.

"The Shadowed are using creatures," Solei said, her voice ringing clear, steady. "To carry their infection. They'll try to send more."

The colony stood in stunned silence, the gravity of her words sinking in. Then, movement rippled through the crowd—builders, healers, warriors, all standing tall, their resolve hardening like stone.

"We fortify the edges of the island," Pehani ordered. "We'll set up energy wards, watchers, sacred thresholds. Nothing gets through unseen."

"And if they do," Zambia added, stepping forward, her golden glyphs glowing with fierce determination, "we'll be ready to burn their shadow away with light."

The days that followed were a flurry of activity. The warriors took their positions at the island's edges, forming a protective web of energy, their focus unshakable. Watch posts were established at every natural boundary—waterfalls, mountain passes, hidden paths through the jungle. The warriors rotated in pairs, their eyes sharp, their energies pulsing in perfect rhythm with the land. But beneath every movement, tension simmered like an impending storm.

"I don't like this waiting," Zambia muttered to Pehani one evening as they stood high on a ridge, gazing out over the eastern coastline. "It feels like something is always just beyond the trees."

"I know," Pehani replied, his jaw clenched in silent frustration. "But every moment we train, we grow stronger. Every boundary we set makes it harder for them to reach us."

Zambia nodded, though her golden eyes scanned the horizon, filled with unease. "We have to protect them. All of them."

Meanwhile, Solei gathered the healers beneath the silver-leafed canopy of the temple grove, where the air hummed with ancient power.

"The infection is not like anything we've seen before," Solei told them, kneeling before the glowing glyphs etched into the earth. "It's a vibration—sharp, jagged, hollow. But our healing energy can meet it. Shift it. Clear it."

The healers practiced, their energy flowing through sacred stones, learning to redirect the foreign energy without absorbing it. Some wept when they succeeded, feeling the weight of the sorrow that clung to the infected creatures.

Solei stood among them, her voice a calming current. "They don't know what they're sending, but we will know how to receive it. Not with fear, but with truth."

Still, the island pulsed with tension. The air felt heavy, the trees whispered more urgently, the birds flew lower. The Shadowed had not yet come, but their presence had already begun to unfurl like smoke in the wind.

No one knew exactly what was coming.

But they would be ready.

They had to be.

That night, as the last embers of the watchfires dimmed, Solei returned alone to the highest terrace of the Temple of Harmonic Light. The sky had turned a bruised violet, and stars pierced the heavens like the eyes of ancient beings watching over them.

She knelt, pressing her hands to the smooth crystal floor, her eyes closed. The warmth of the land answered her touch—steady, but strained.

From the horizon, a streak of violet light split the sky, silent and ominous. The wind stilled. The island seemed to hold its breath.

Solei opened her eyes, her heart pounding in rhythm with the earth beneath her. "Lu Mai," she whispered into the stillness, "is this the beginning?"

And somewhere, deep beneath the earth, far below the roots of even the oldest tree, something ancient stirred.

CHAPTER TWELVE

THE HARMONIC LIGHT WEAVE

The sky over Lumeria remained clear, but the people could feel the weight of something pressing in from beyond the veil of light. The island's gentle rhythm—the winds, the waters, the crystalline heartbeat of the land—had shifted. What once sang in harmony now pulsed with urgency, as if the very earth itself was bracing, holding its breath for a moment yet to come.

On the southern cliffs, Pehani stood beside Zambia, both of them watching the horizon where the ocean kissed the sky. Their expressions were as solid as the rocks beneath their feet—resolute, yet heavy with unspoken questions.

"I don't like the silence," Zambia muttered, her hands resting lightly on the twin daggers at her hips—blades forged from silvery auricite, etched with sacred glyphs of El'Suvai, the Lumerian sigils of protection and clarity. The hilts were wrapped in woven obsidian leather, each adorned with a single moonstone at the base, softly humming in tune with Zambia's energy. "It feels like a lie."

Pehani nodded, his gaze never wavering from the distant sea. "They're waiting. Measuring us. Testing. The creature was only the first breath of their plan."

Zambia's violet eyes flickered toward the jungle, her body instinctively tightening, alert. "They'll try again. With more. With worse."

Back in the temple grove, sunlight filtered through the wide, iridescent leaves of the yelurai trees, casting golden patterns across the soft moss floor. The air was rich with the fragrance of kinari blossoms, mingling with the earthy scent of sun-warmed stone. The grove was alive, sacred in its stillness.

Solei moved through the circle of healers, her long robe whispering against the earth as she passed. Each step she took was infused with grace, a fluid dance with the land beneath her feet. With every touch, she offered not just comfort, but transference—an offering of herself, a steadying breath of energy flowing from her heart into theirs. Her fingertips glowed with soft golden light, the ancient symbols of Suvhari'el—light, compassion, remembrance—illuminating briefly with each movement, flickering like distant stars.

The healers had grown stronger, more attuned to the harmonic codes of the land, yet their energy still rippled with uncertainty. It was as though they were water still remembering the calm after a storm—steadying, but not yet still. Solei felt it in their auras, the way some of them leaned inward, bracing themselves for an unknown force, an unseen wave.

She paused before a young healer named Liora, who looked up at her with wide violet eyes—uncertain, but brimming with quiet determination. The girl's hands trembled slightly in her lap, but her aura shimmered with the unmistakable glow of awakening potential.

Solei knelt beside her, the folds of her robe pooling like starlight on the moss. She took Liora's hands gently into her own, her touch light as a breeze, steady as the earth beneath them. Her voice flowed softly, like a sacred lullaby meant only for the soul it sought to reach. "Come, sweet one. Let's walk the breath of light together. Inhale with the earth... and exhale into your power."

They both inhaled slowly, their energy synchronizing. Liora's palms began to shimmer, faint and flickering, like the first starlight of evening. Solei guided her with words that wrapped around her heart, tender and knowing. "There is no force in light, only remembrance. Let the energy rise like a tide returning to its shore—soft, inevitable, divine."

Liora closed her eyes, her lips parting with a silent gasp as her hands began to glow more brightly. The golden light rippled outward in concentric circles, as if the surface of a sacred pond had been stirred by truth. The warmth radiating from her palms became visible, sparkling with flecks of rose and opal hues.

"Now listen to the energy," Solei whispered. "Let it guide you—not just where to go, but how to love."

Liora's breath deepened, and tears shimmered on her cheeks—not from sorrow, but from the overwhelming beauty of what she felt. She could sense the pain of the infected creature, as though it were a part of her own memory. But instead of recoiling, she sent her light there—soft, radiant, unwavering.

"I feel them," she said, her voice trembling, soft as a prayer. "I feel the pain leaving... like it's been waiting for this moment."

Solei gently released her hands and rose, moving with serene elegance. Her presence radiated timeless strength and quiet knowing. She gave Liora a warm smile, her eyes twinkling like distant stars. "You've just graduated from trembling star to rising sun. Go share your warmth—and maybe try not to glow too bright unless someone asks for it first."

Then, softer, her tone wrapped in reverence, she added, "You have returned to the truth of your light. Now, beloved, go and awaken that truth in others. Not with force—but with your remembering."

Moved by what they had witnessed, the rest of the healers slowly stepped forward, forming a wider circle around Liora. One by one, they extended their palms, golden and rose-tinted light blooming between them like an unfolding lotus. Their energies began to link—not overpowering, but flowing, weaving like silk threads through sacred fabric.

Solei stepped into the center, her movements fluid and graceful, like a breeze stirring sacred waters. She raised her hands above her heart, her eyes soft with compassion, her voice a gentle melodic current that wrapped around each soul present. "Let it move between you," she said, her voice carrying warmth and tenderness. Then, with a playful smile, she added, "Don't overthink it. Light doesn't need choreography. Just trust it to dance."

Her tone softened once again, reverent and knowing. "Let the light speak its own language—the language your soul already knows. Let it remember. Let it return."

The grove shimmered with healing resonance. The ground beneath them pulsed gently with the island's heartbeat, and the chimes hanging above them harmonized with the rising energy field, creating a dome of warmth and connection. Each healer's aura expanded, colors mingling—soft blues, warm pinks, vibrant ambers. Some wept silently, others smiled with awe, feeling the truth of the divine light flow through them.

Together, they held that resonance—strong, sacred, whole. No longer individuals learning a craft, but a collective remembering their divine task.

Solei turned back to the circle of healers and offered a light laugh that melted the lingering tension. "Well," she said softly, "that was much better than the first time I tried to hold resonance. Let's just say there was less grace and more... accidental levitation." The healers chuckled, their laughter mingling with the last shimmering notes of the chimes, grounding them in the present moment.

The levity rooted them deeply in the now. They were warriors of light, yes—but also people, real and alive, growing in courage, kinship, and the beauty of their shared purpose.

Solei, watching them, murmured with a wink to the wind, "Now that's what I call a harmonic light weave. If we can hold that in battle, the Shadowed won't stand a chance."

And high above, in the branches, the golden leaves trembled—not from fear, but from recognition.

As Solei rose again, the wind picked up—stronger than before. Chimes hanging in the temple trees began to ring, their song warping, distorted by the intensity of the shift.

Solei turned toward the sea, her heart echoing with the pulse of the island. She felt it. Not in her mind, but in her bones.

The Gathering had begun.

In the village center, the council convened once more. Word had spread of the changing winds, the strange patterns in the birds' flight, the unease rolling through the roots of the land.

"We'll activate the glyph grids," said Kaelion, his voice steady and resolute. "All of them. Even the old ones—especially the ancient Ma'hala line that runs beneath the obsidian ridge. We can't take chances."

"And the dreamweavers?" asked Elina, her voice tinged with concern.

"Their visions are unclear," Solei replied, her voice distant, yet anchored. "But the feeling is strong. Whatever is coming... it's close."

Pehani entered the circle, his presence grounding the energy. He placed his hand briefly on Solei's shoulder as he passed—a silent gesture of shared purpose. His stance was firm, and the faint glow of his warrior glyphs pulsed beneath his skin, a steady drumbeat.

"We don't have the luxury of waiting. Every hour we hesitate is another opening they can use."

Solei looked at him, the light of the fire reflecting in her eyes, a soft smile curving her lips with gentle reverence. As she stepped forward, she planted the base of her radiant staff—Etari'sha, the staff of sacred convergence—into the earth beside the flame. A subtle hum of energy pulsed outward in a soft ring of light. Her voice resonated with sacred knowing, a glint of wry humor dancing in her tone.

"Then we prepare not just to defend. We prepare to remember who we are—and we do it with grace, guts, and a little bit of sparkle."

A hush fell, as if even the wind bowed to the circle's resolve. It was not fear that held them, but readiness—readiness forged through kinship, trust, and a collective vow born in light.

Beyond the island, the sea darkened.

The storm was gathering.

And it would not ask for permission to arrive.

CHAPTER THIRTEEN

WHEN THE VEIL TREMBLES

The days that followed were rich with movement, preparation, and an undercurrent of invisible pressure that touched every edge of the island. Though the skies over Lumeria remained golden and the ocean lapped gently at the shores, their waves shimmering like ribbons of sapphire light, something deeper had begun to stir. The jungle canopy, usually alive with the songs of crystalline birds, had quieted. Vines draped from the trees like emerald silk, glistening with morning dew, while the scent of blooming star-fruit flowers perfumed the breeze. The stillness between each gust of wind seemed longer. The pulse of the island had shifted from serenity to something that felt... alert.

Solei stood on the crest of the western ridge at dawn, wrapped in a pale cloak that shimmered like water touched by moonlight. Her gaze drifted over the vast expanse of jungle and sacred lands—the winding Lira'kai river that shimmered like a silver serpent, the cascading Maihara waterfalls spilling over crystal cliffs, the tall blossom-trees with petals glowing softly under the morning light. Her breath aligned with the rhythm of the island. As High Priestess, she had learned long ago that it wasn't the loud warnings that spoke truth—it was the subtleties. The softened glow of the flowers. The tremor in the roots. The way the air, even in stillness, felt restless.

Behind her, soft footsteps approached. "You sense it too," Zambia said, coming to stand beside her. Her violet eyes carried no fear, only a fire tempered by clarity.

Solei nodded slowly. "The veil between our world and theirs is thinning. I can feel the pressure pressing through... like the air is being exhaled by something watching."

They stood in silence, and then Zambia asked, "What will you do when they breach it?"

Solei turned to her, her eyes reflecting both the rising sun and her inner knowing. "I will do what I was born to do. I will stand in the light and speak its truth."

Far below, the village stirred into motion. The colony appeared strong, thriving in preparation. Builders reinforced sacred grid stones at the base of each energy temple, and dreamweavers etched updated protective codes in flowing Telari'en script across thresholds. Children—still too new to understand what it meant—watched with wide eyes as elders taught them chants and breath rhythms that kept the body and soul aligned in vibration.

Yet as Solei observed from the ridge, a whisper of concern nestled in her heart. Something was... missing. On the surface, Lumeria pulsed with radiant function, but the deeper current—the soul-thread of communal unity—felt frayed. The colony moved like individual flames, flickering brightly but disconnected from the great fire.

Later that day, Solei called a village-wide gathering beneath the Great Canopy of Kurell'iah trees. Word spread quickly, and by sunset, the entire colony stood in quiet anticipation.

"We are luminous," Solei said, her voice rising like a song carried by wind, "but even the most radiant light must be remembered—together. I see how we've grown, how we've prepared... and I also see how quiet our cords to one another have become. Let us weave them anew."

She stepped into the center of the clearing and raised her arms. A current of golden energy spiraled from her palms, expanding like a flower in bloom. "This is not a correction—it is a remembering. A homecoming for our souls."

One by one, the Lumerians placed their hands on the person beside them, forming a great circle. The energy threaded from one heart to the next, not rushing, but resonating—soft and sure. Colors bloomed in the air: warm gold, crystalline aqua, lush green, radiant lavender. The land responded, its pulse rising in harmony. The trees shivered gently, their leaves whispering in hues of aquamarine and rose. The moss beneath their feet brightened, casting a faint glow like bioluminescent embers. Even the air itself sparkled faintly, as if threaded with stardust.

Some wept openly. Others sighed as if releasing burdens they hadn't realized they were holding. The light moved through them—not just as individuals, but as one radiant breath.

When the energy settled, the air shimmered with peace, thick with the scent of blooming orchids and ionized mist. A stillness fell over the gathering—not empty, but sacred. The heaviness that had weighed upon so many hearts began to dissolve. Anger softened. Anxiety uncoiled. Grief lightened like fog kissed by morning sun. Where there had been isolation, warmth now bloomed. Where uncertainty had lingered, a quiet strength took its place.

The Lumerians stood in silence, eyes closed, breathing in harmony. For many, it felt like coming home to themselves—and to each other. A deep sense of belonging anchored into their bones, syncing once more with the island's sacred pulse.

Solei opened her eyes, her voice tender. "Now we are whole again. Not just luminous—but connected. Not just surviving—but alive."

Lumeria exhaled as one.

And the flame of their unity burned brighter than ever before.

Kaelion moved like thunder through the village, his silhouette backlit by the firelight dancing from the village braziers. He directed workers with sweeping gestures of purpose, his voice rising above the chorus of rustling palm fronds and the low hum of elurai stones embedded in the foundations of every building.

Pehani stood on the eastern rise, observing the sentries. He had barely slept in days, not out of worry, but readiness. His glyphs were beginning to glow even when he wasn't calling on them—a sign the energy of the island was no longer resting.

That evening, Solei gathered the inner circle beneath the Temple of Harmonic Light. Flames flickered in the sacred lanterns, casting fluid shadows on the glowing stones beneath them.

"The Shadowed will not come in a way we expect," she said. "They do not strike with strategy—they move through fear, distortion, decay. But Lumeria is not made of such things. We are harmony made manifest."

She placed her palms on the altar stone—smooth, ancient, and humming with ancestral memory. A soft chime echoed from nowhere and everywhere at once. As her fingers made contact, golden light flared beneath her touch, not harsh but like liquid sunlight spilling into sacred lines. The spiral that emerged moved slowly at first, curling like smoke, then expanded outward with growing brilliance, trailing celestial patterns across the glowing stones. It pulsed in rhythm with her breath and heartbeat, weaving through the soles of everyone present, grounding them in a resonance both timeless and divine.

"I am calling forth your deepest truth," she said, her voice soft and resonant. "Not your perfection—but your alignment. Whatever comes, remember: they cannot take what you do not surrender."

Zambia stepped forward next, her twin daggers shimmering in their sheaths. "Then let them find us radiant," she said. "Let them break themselves against what cannot be broken."

A murmur of agreement spread through the circle like wildfire through still grass.

After the ritual, as the others slowly filtered out beneath the lantern glow, Zambia remained behind. She stood in the quiet clearing, watching the shadows flicker like memories against the stone walls. Solei stepped beside her, sensing the weight of something unspoken.

Zambia spoke softly, almost reverently. "Luneia is with child."

Solei turned toward her, surprise softening into joy. "Zambia... that's beautiful. Truly."

Zambia's fierce exterior faltered, her eyes glistening with rare vulnerability. She looked down, then back up at Solei, her voice breaking slightly. "When she told me, I laughed. Then I cried. I've fought so long, so hard—for this land, for our people. But this... this is something I've never prepared for. It's terrifying, Solei."

Solei reached for her hand, her touch steady and warm. "You don't have to be prepared. You just have to be present. That's what love asks of us."

Zambia nodded, a tear slipping down her cheek. "It feels like a spark of hope, like something untouched by the darkness trying to breach our world. But it also terrifies me. I've faced shadowed beasts, storms, and the unknown. But this... this is the future resting in her body. Our future."

Solei squeezed her hand. "And she—and the child—couldn't have a fiercer protector. Nor a softer one. You've always carried both the sword and the heart, Zambia. This only deepens that power."

Zambia let out a soft, breathy laugh, brushing the tear away. "I needed to hear that. I feel everything more now. The ground under my feet. The air. Every tremble of the veil. I don't just want to defend Lumeria—I need to. For Luneia. For the life growing within her."

Solei's voice was low, full of sacred knowing. "Then we fight not just for what we are—but for what we dream to become."

They stood close, wrapped in quiet love, the firelight cradling their shadows like sisters embracing.

As Zambia slipped into the trees, her presence lingering like a pulse of starlight, Solei remained.

Her hand moved slowly to her abdomen, not out of reflex but reverence. The fabric of her robe felt like silk and memory beneath her fingers. She exhaled, but it trembled—because something inside her was rising.

A longing she had pushed away, silenced beneath sacred duty, returned like a tidal wave of knowing. She had been the flame-keeper, the path-holder, the guide. But now—now she yearned to become the seed-bearer of her own future.

Tears stung her eyes, and for a moment she let them fall freely. Not from sorrow, but from the overwhelming presence of something sacred pressing through her. She did not just want to defend this land—she wanted to birth into it the next light. A child. A future. A living extension of the love that had bloomed in her soul and taken root in the arms of Pehani.

The wind curled around her like a ribbon of prophecy. She felt the presence of Lu Mai, ancient and warm, like moonlight pressed against her spine.

She dropped to her knees, overcome.

"I want that too," she whispered—not to the night, but to the universe. "I want life to move through me. I want to create. I want to love so fully that the stars remember."

She pressed her forehead to the moss, anchoring herself into the pulse of the land. The cool, earthen scent filled her lungs, and she could feel every heartbeat of the island matching her own. It was as if the island held her in its arms, whispering its support through the roots, lifting her grief, and amplifying her desire. The tears came harder now, not from sadness, but from the immensity of wanting—of knowing.

She could see it. A child in her arms, laughter in the grove, tiny fingers curled around hers. She imagined Pehani's eyes looking down in awe, his warrior's heart undone by softness. A family. A continuation. A new flame born of their bond.

The moss beneath her pulsed once with warmth. Lu Mai's presence enveloped her, not as a voice but a sensation, as if the goddess had laid her hand over Solei's chest and whispered, "Yes."

The moment swelled inside her like a sunrise. Solei rose slowly, trembling with something more than emotion—transformation. She looked toward the path that led to Pehani.

But before she could take a step, the wind changed.

It came not as a breeze, but as a force—a ripple that sent the branches overhead into a wild dance. The bioluminescent moss dimmed briefly, and the pulse of the island faltered, like a skipped heartbeat.

Solei stood upright, heart racing. From deep within the jungle, a low hum began to rise—a sound not made by nature but by something foreign. Something wrong.

The air shifted.

And in the distance, the birds went silent.

Solei's hand hovered over her heart, the radiant glow returning to her fingertips.

Whatever had passed through the veil... had not come alone.

As the ritual concluded, a wind swept through the grove—this time not uneasy, but sharp, electric, like the intake of breath before something is spoken.

And far beyond the eastern cliffs, unseen by Lumerian eyes, a rift shimmered briefly in the sky like heat over water. Then it vanished.

But the veil had been touched.

And it would not remain whole for long.

Chapter Fourteen

THE LIGHT-BORN FLAME

S olei ran through the jungle, her cloak trailing behind her like the wings of an unseen goddess, brushing against glowing roots that pulsed with the ancient heartbeat of the earth. The moss beneath her feet, soft and alive, seemed to whisper secrets of the land as she moved swiftly, her body a vessel for the sacred urgency within her. Her heart thundered—not from fear, but from the weight of revelation. Each beat resonated with the pulse of the island itself, as if every step was a step closer to her destiny, unfolding in the sacred rhythm of the universe.

The air was thick with the breath of the island, warm and fragrant, as though the very land was reaching out to kiss her skin, to enfold her in its embrace. She moved with urgency, but there was a longing too—an aching desire to return to something forgotten, a longing she didn't fully understand but that vibrated through her bones.

Her golden glyphs pulsed on her skin, glowing softly with the sacred language of the earth. The ancient symbols hummed in a rhythmic dance, like the whispers of the wind speaking through her body, channeling the messages of long-forgotten ancestors. Each pulse of light illuminated the path ahead, tracing the lines of fate, calling her forward as the jungle seemed to breathe with her.

Through the dense foliage, Pehani appeared—a flash of light amidst the dark green shadows. His presence was a beacon, his eyes wide with concern, his body radiant with the light of Sael'toran, the divine warrior energy that flowed through him like a river of fire. The markings on his arms, once soft and faint, now blazed with the power of their shared mission, a divine protection woven into his being.

"Solei!" he called, his voice thick with relief, breaking through the tension in the air like a melody of sacred reunion.

Without hesitation, she moved into his arms, and the world seemed to still. Their embrace was a collision of light and energy, so powerful it nearly drew them both to the earth. In that instant, time itself seemed to suspend, holding them in a space where only love and sacred truth existed.

"I felt you," Pehani whispered into her hair, his voice a sacred hum, a promise made long before this moment. "Something told me you needed me."

Solei pulled back just enough to meet his gaze, the sacred truth of what she was about to share shimmering in her eyes.

Her breath trembled with the weight of it, a divine longing that had awakened deep within her soul.

"Zambia told me... Luneia is with child," she said, her voice breaking with awe, reverence, and a tender joy that flowed like a river through her words.

Pehani's eyes widened, softening into something more profound than surprise—something ancient, something divine. The light within them flickered with the reflection of the eternal, and for a moment, it was as though they were gazing not at each other, but through the veil of time itself.

Solei pressed his hand to her chest, over the glyph of Ahri'el—the mark of divine creation, the sacred seal of life itself. "And something awakened in me. Something I didn't know I had, tucked away beneath everything else we are called to do. I want that too. With you."

A breathless pause hung in the air, suspended in the sacred space they had created between them. The jungle held its breath, the world paused, and in that moment, the stars themselves seemed to align.

Then Pehani's face broke into a radiant smile, a light so pure and so filled with love that it illuminated the very air between them. "Yes," he said, his voice thick with the weight of eternity. "Yes, Solei. If a soul chooses us... I will honor it forever."

Hand in hand, they turned, and the sacred journey continued. Their steps were in harmony with the heartbeat of the land, their connection a deep, unspoken prayer to the earth beneath them. The jungle responded. Luminescent vines stretched toward their path like welcoming arms, the fragrance of El'thera blossoms—a heady mix of sacred nectar—carried on the wind, wrapping them in its divine embrace. The trees bowed slightly, their leaves shimmering in hues of emerald and silver, as though the very earth was acknowledging the sacred union unfolding in their midst.

The path opened to a clearing bathed in the soft glow of twilight. Towering obsidian stones rose like ancient sentinels, their surfaces veined with golden threads that pulsed gently, as though the rocks themselves were alive, breathing in rhythm with the earth. Bioluminescent flowers bloomed like sacred hands, casting light in hues of indigo and rose. The moss beneath their feet throbbed with energy, responding to their vibration, to the frequency of their love.

They stepped onto the central terrace, where the earth had been etched with the sacred glyphs of Ma'riel—symbols of union, lineage, and soul invitation. The twin moons above bathed the space in a silvery glow, their light sacred, eternal, as the heavens themselves seemed to bow in reverence. The air was thick with expectation, the sacredness of the moment unfolding like the petals of a flower.

In perfect stillness, they stood facing each other. The world outside them ceased to exist. All that remained was the sacred union they were about to invoke, the eternal bond they had chosen to honor. Pehani placed one hand over her heart, and Solei mirrored him, her touch a gentle flame. With their other hands, they reached toward the earth, channeling the energy of

Elar'kai—the sacred life-thread that bound them to Gaia, to the stars, to all that was.

The stones responded. A warm, rose-gold spiral of light rose up around them, weaving in delicate patterns, enfolding their bodies in a sacred cocoon of energy. Their breaths synchronized, their hearts beat as one, and the energy between them intensified. A luminous sphere bloomed between them—not conjured, but revealed—an orb of pure divine light formed by devotion, by love, by the remembrance of all that they were.

Solei's eyes welled with tears, tears of sacred longing, of a deep, timeless knowing. She felt it—felt the earth, the sky, the very stars, holding their breath. Pehani trembled, his strength softened by the sheer beauty of the offering, by the light of their shared divine purpose. Around them, the energy of the earth itself danced—radiant spirals of starlight and love weaving new possibilities into the fabric of the universe.

They offered their love. Their lineage. Their light. And the jungle, the land, the very universe itself, bore witness.

But deep in the earth, something stirred.

As they turned to leave, a gust of wind tore through the trees—no longer a gentle breeze, but a slice, a cutting, as though the very veil between worlds had frayed. The moss beneath their feet dimmed, the light of the flora flickering, fading. A single blossom, vibrant a moment ago, wilted into shadow, as if the land itself mourned.

Solei stopped, her glyphs flaring with a sudden pulse of light, a warning that came from deep within her bones. Her heart pounded, and the air around them cracked, as if reality itself were trembling.

"Something's wrong," she said, her voice a whispered prayer to the earth.

The air groaned—a sound not of beast or branch, but of the veil itself—bending, breaking under the weight of something dark, something ancient.

A roar rose—a deep, unholy frequency, rattling the treetops, sending a tremor through her soul. The sound was pure chaos, vibrating through the land like a force of nature.

"The veil," Solei whispered, her voice carrying the weight of a prophecy that had been whispered for eons. "It's been breached again. But this time... something's entered."

A violet pulse flickered in the sky, like a dying star, and cold air swept through the jungle—unseen, but felt, like the chilling presence of something ancient stirring in the shadows.

The Shadowed had not yet arrived.

But their harbingers had.

Solei's breath caught, but she steadied herself, grounding her energy in the sacred knowing that this was only the beginning.

"We must go to the council. Now."

As they neared the village, a shriek cut through the stillness—twisted, unholy, the sound of a soul in agony. Then another. Then many, a chorus of anguish.

A flood of infected beasts poured from the jungle—once-gentle creatures now mangled and corrupted by shadow. Their eyes burned black, voids of nothingness, their movements erratic and unnatural, pulsing with the corrupted frequency of Esh'ravin—the signature of distortion.

Solei raised her palms, and golden light exploded from her, forming a radiant barrier between the villagers and the oncoming tide of darkness. Pehani roared beside her, his glyphs ablaze with sacred fire. From his solar plexus, a surge of pure light emanated, cutting through the air like a sword of divine will.

The battle had begun.

The first wave shattered the stillness. Trees splintered, their ancient trunks torn from the earth. Claws raked through sacred ground, the earth itself crying out in agony. The sky darkened beneath the wings of corrupted beasts, and the land groaned under the weight of the invasion.

Solei stood at the center, her arms outstretched, a living conduit of divine energy. Her glyphs expanded, covering her skin in swirls of golden flame. Each pulse of energy she released thinned her essence, yet her resolve solidified, her connection to the earth deepening. Her voice became mantra, her breath the rhythm of restoration, a prayer sung in every heartbeat.

Pehani was the storm, an embodiment of pure force, a living manifestation of divine will. His staff, charged with radiant current, swept through the air in arcs of blinding brilliance, scattering the corrupted creatures in waves of sacred light. Each movement was a prayer, a sacred invocation of balance and protection. Beside him, Zambia danced like a force of nature, her twin daggers slicing through the air with the grace of a goddess weaving her own sacred thread through the fabric of the universe. Each strike was a prayer for the earth, a fierce plea for restoration. The warriors, united in purpose, moved in sacred synchrony—each step, each breath, a reflection of the ancient rhythm of the land. Their energy rings pulsed with a steady, unwavering beat, harmonizing with the heartbeat of Gaia herself.

The light-beasts arrived—not with the deafening roar of thunder, but with the soft, resonant song of the cosmos.

Silver-antlered stags, their eyes burning with the fire of the stars, emerged from the shadows. Winged pantheras, their bodies cloaked in stardust, flowed through the air like celestial rivers. Serpents of living light spiraled between the branches, their undulating forms like water through the air, an embodiment of fluid grace and cosmic wisdom.

Their arrival was not a surge of destructive force, but a gentle, radiant wave—a ripple of harmony that swept over the battlefield, unraveling the chaos in its wake. The corrupted creatures faltered, their once-malignant eyes flickering in the presence of the light-beasts, as if the very essence of their shadow began to dissolve in the luminous embrace. The light of the beasts touched them, a divine caress that unraveled the dark thread that had woven itself into their souls.

Lumerians and light-beasts became a symphony of grace, power, and divine unity. Warriors, once caught in the frenzy of battle, found their rhythm again, their movements flowing with the sacred pulse of the earth. Healers wept—not in sorrow, but in gratitude—as the tide of darkness began to recede. With each breath, the world grew clearer, lighter, as the energies of the light-beasts and warriors intertwined.

The infected creatures, once frenzied with rage, began to still, their eyes flickering—not in fury, but in release. The battle transformed before their eyes, shifting from a fight for survival to a field of liberation—a sacred space where even the most corrupted could find their return to the light.

Not all were saved.

But many were.

And in that, there was miracle.

When the last shadow fell, the land exhaled—a deep, slow breath, filled with sacred release and profound relief. It was as though the earth itself had been held in suspension, and now, in the quiet aftermath, it was finally free.

The light-beasts remained, their eyes glowing with an eternal wisdom that transcended time. They stood as guardians of the earth, their presence a reminder of the divine forces that wove through every blade of grass, every tree, every heartbeat.

Lumeria had not only survived.

It had been transformed.

The trees, once silent in their watch, began to sing again. Their song was deep, rich, and wise, resonating with the heartbeat of the earth, a melody that echoed through the very marrow of every living being. The rivers ran clearer than ever before, their waters shimmering with the light of renewal. Flowers bloomed brighter, their petals unfurling in sacred reverence.

The laughter of children rang through the hills, pure and sweet, like the chime of sacred bells ringing through the heavens.

And far across the sea, something ancient stirred.

It had felt the light awaken.

And it was coming.

CHAPTER FIFTEEN

THE WATERS OF THE BECOMING

T ime had passed, yet it felt as if the world stood still in a quiet breath.

Lumeria, the sacred island, had settled into a golden rhythm once more. The air carried the delicate scent of flowering ethari vines, mingling with the sweet, sun-warmed fruit that hung heavy on the trees. This fragrance drifted on the soft winds, curling like sacred incense through the forest canopy, invoking the timeless pulse of life and renewal. The laughter of the people echoed through the groves, a sound so full and rich that it felt like the laughter of the earth herself. It was laughter born not just of joy, but of peace—hard-won, deeply rooted peace.

Beneath the laughter, harmony whispered through the land, felt in the rhythm of every step upon the moss-covered earth, in the flutter of wings, in the sigh of the wind. Everywhere, the pulse of life beat in steady waves—each heartbeat aligned, sacred, and true. The island, once again, breathed in seamless unity with its people—heart to heart, soul to soul.

Solei awoke gently, the first rays of dawn slipping through the canopy, casting golden beams that flickered like firelight across the woven walls of their shelter. The crystalline songs of morning birds filled the air, each note a hymn to the sacred union of light and life. The air was thick with the scent of dew-kissed blossoms, their fragrance sweet and wild, carried in by a soft, reverent breeze. She turned to Pehani, her hand still clasped in his, feeling the warmth of his presence, a constant anchor in the sacred dance of love and life. His touch was both grounding and elevating, a bridge between worlds. She gazed at him with eyes that shone with something ancient—knowing, yet new, a spark of the divine within her.

"Come with me," she whispered, her voice the soft murmur of the earth itself, pulling him into the stillness of the morning, the sacred pause between breaths.

They moved together through the waking jungle, hand in hand, each step a soft prayer. The trees, with their great and ancient wisdom, parted before them as they approached the Maer'Alasha—the Waters of Becoming. The ground hummed underfoot, and a wave of reverence passed through the air, as though the island itself had been waiting for this moment, waiting for them.

The Maer'Alasha—this place of ancient power, where the river met the tide pools, where life was woven anew from the threads of the cosmos. This sacred glade was whispered of in lullabies and chanted in the hymns of priestesses, a place where the divine energy of creation flowed freely, as though the very stones of the earth held the memories of all that had ever been. Here, where the pulse of the island was strongest, the veil between worlds was thin, and every breath felt like a call to the stars above.

As Solei and Pehani stepped into the shallow, crystal-clear waters, the surface rippled with recognition, as if the very earth knew them. A soft silence fell over the grove, and the water began to glow, not with an earthly light, but with the glow of the stars themselves, a radiance born of the island's own sacred breath. Beneath the surface, the sacred stones—smooth river gems in hues of silver, rose, and deep aquamarine—began to stir, rising from their slumber in slow, celestial spirals, orbiting Solei as if drawn by the call of her soul.

Each stone pulsed with the rhythm of her breath, aligning with the unique frequency of her divine essence. She stood in the center of the waters, her arms outstretched, feeling the cosmic energies flow through her as if she were both the conduit and the receiver of all creation. Her skin shimmered with a soft, ethereal glow, a reflection of the light that poured from the earth and the heavens, blending into one harmonious, sacred dance.

Her womb—her sacred temple of creation—glowed with golden light, a sun reborn within her, expanding with each heartbeat. She could feel it—this new life stirring inside her, not just a physical life, but a soul, a consciousness—an ancient, timeless presence, waiting to enter this world. The glyph of

Shal'Vorei, the mark of the sacred birthright, shimmered faintly across her abdomen, glowing softly as though the very soul of Lumeria was embracing the child within her.

Solei felt her heart swell with the weight of this moment, and yet, it was not the weight of burden, but of grace. It was the sacred weight of knowing that life, in all its mystery, was unfolding within her. She was becoming the doorway—the sacred passage through which a new soul would enter this world. A divine current rose from the depths of the waters, a warm, golden light spiraling up through her feet and along her spine like a serpent of light, awakening every cell of her being. It bloomed within her chest like a radiant lotus kissed by celestial fire.

Pehani stood across from her, his hand pressed to his heart, his eyes steady and filled with reverence. He was the steady flame to her dancing light, the grounding force in this sacred ceremony. His presence anchored the field, and he stepped forward with a slow, deliberate reverence, his aura a soft golden halo of warmth and love. He bowed his head slightly, then spoke in a voice that carried the weight of millennia, a voice that had been passed down through priest-kings and celestial warriors.

"Eshalama thren'ari, solan de'kai,
Let light be woven, let love not die.
By stars above and earth below,
Seed of the soul, begin to grow."

As his words unfurled into the air, the waters responded, rippling outward in waves of iridescent light, their glow shifting into colors beyond the earth's spectrum—lavender, peach, jade, and moonstone blue. These colors—these sacred frequencies—carried with them the memory of creation itself, the song of the stars, the heartbeat of Lumeria.

The stones, in perfect harmony, began to hum, sending waves of celestial sound through the air. Their glow bloomed brighter, each hue intensifying as the stones circled Solei's body, weaving sacred geometry in the air—a dance of spirals and circles, symbols of the infinite, of the divine, of the eternal. The energy they carried was one of pure remembrance, a recall of all that had ever been and all that was yet to come.

The sacred light spiraled through her—through her crown, her throat, her heart, and her womb. Each sacred energy center aligned—Ishal'ra, the crown of knowing, Thal'sari, the throat of truth, and Maralai, the womb of becoming—until the light cascaded through her like a river of living frequency, illuminating her from within. Her breath caught—not from pain, but from the overwhelming wonder of it all. She was not merely being filled—she was becoming. Becoming something beyond herself. Beyond the boundaries of time and space.

Tears filled her eyes, falling in silent devotion, a silent prayer to the universe, to the soul that had chosen her, to the island that had cradled her. She met Pehani's gaze, her eyes shimmering with the glow of the stars, and whispered, "It has begun."

The light around them swirled, the water rippling in perfect harmony, as though the very cosmos had turned its gaze upon them. The jungle—alive with the sacred pulse of creation—held its breath in reverence.

The trees, ancient sentinels of the land, bowed in quiet reverence, their leaves shimmering in sacred hues of violet and gold, as though the very foliage had been kissed by the divine. Blossoms unfurled slowly, their petals opening to reveal hearts of light, releasing fragrances that were both ancient and new—fragrances that spoke of prayers and dreams long forgotten by time. The winds, too, hushed in reverence, carrying only the soft murmur of spirit voices rising from the roots of the earth, a song that was older than the stars themselves.

Above them, the stars blinked brighter, their light intensifying as though they were watching with a gaze full of ancient wisdom. The elders of the heavens, watching with love and reverence, their luminous eyes casting their gaze upon the lovers below.

The water stilled, becoming a mirror—clear and still as a sacred pool of memory.

In that mirror, a vision formed. A luminous cradle of energy, spiraling with potential, glowing with the song of an arriving soul. The reflection was not just that of two bodies standing together, but of a soul—the soul of a child, a spirit that had heard their call. It was a soul woven from light, waiting to be born. The vision shimmered before them—a soul's reflection, radiant with the energy of creation itself.

Time softened, stretching into eternity. The very air seemed to breathe in sync with the pulse of life, as if Lumeria itself were singing, rejoicing in the divine union that had birthed this moment. And in this union—this sacred act of creation—a new soul was born into the waiting arms of the earth.

A soul had heard their call.

And it was on its way.

Chapter Sixteen

The Parting Light

Zambia and Luneia had settled into their new homes, cozy dwellings nestled near the heart of the village where flowering trees grew in arcs above the rooftops. It was a place filled with braids of light, symbols of connection, and the laughter they had sewn into the walls with their love. Their walls held the scent of their shared mornings, the warmth of tea brewed in harmony, and the softness of Luneia's touch still lingered on every surface. The air was thick with anticipation. Luneia's time had come.

As the day faded into lavender dusk, Luneia's labor began. At first, it was as expected—deep breaths, strong waves, steady pain. Zambia stayed close, her arms around Luneia, whispering encouragements, anchoring her through each contraction, brushing the damp curls from her brow. But something was wrong.

Luneia's breath turned shallow. Her skin lost color. Her light began to flicker, her body shivering between worlds.

Panic rose in Zambia's chest like a storm, consuming all clarity. Her voice cracked, her hands trembled.

"I'll find her," she whispered, her voice barely a thread of sound.

Zambia ran through the village, barefoot, wild-eyed, her hair clinging to her tear-soaked face. Panic coursed through her veins like fire, each heartbeat a thunderclap in her chest. Her cries echoed through the quiet pathways, calling for help, for hope—but the midwife was nowhere to be seen. Doors cracked open, faces peeked out in concern, but she had no time to stop, no words to explain. Her legs trembled beneath her, lungs burning, as if her soul might shatter with each step. She stumbled into the training grounds and saw him—Pehani. Relief broke through her panic for a moment before she collapsed against him, clinging to his arms like they were the only solid thing in a world that had turned to water.

"She's not well. I can't find the midwife. Pehani, please."

Without hesitation, Pehani steadied her, grounding her with the calm strength in his eyes.

"Go back to her. Don't let her be alone. I'll find the midwife. I promise."

Zambia turned and ran, her chest burning, her prayers silent and frantic.

The stars wheeled overhead. The village held its breath.

Luneia's pain deepened. Her moans turned to gasps. The room was filled with flickering candlelight and desperation. The midwife finally returned with Pehani, her healing glow a final hope.

The night was long. The cries were fierce. But the sun rose.

Solei and Pehani came with the morning, bringing warmth and hope. They had risen early, their hearts guided by love and concern, wanting to check on Luneia's progress and offer any help they could. Solei carried with her a bundle of fresh linens and a bowl of rosewater; Pehani brought a small pouch of herbs meant to ease pain. They expected to find laughter or perhaps weariness, but joy nonetheless.

The air was hushed, heavy with the scent of blooming starflowers and something unspoken, like the village itself was holding its breath. The morning sun filtered through the flowering trees, casting golden dapples on the earth, but it could not lift the quiet weight pressing on Solei's chest. She and Pehani moved slowly, steps syncing as if guided by something unseen. Solei's fingers tightened around Pehani's as they approached the house, her senses prickling with unease—like a song had ended mid-note. Something was wrong. Something had shifted in the air, a stillness too deep, a silence too sharp.

Just before she reached the door, the veil shimmered.

Luneia's spirit stood before her—soft, radiant, and otherworldly. Her form shimmered like moonlight on still water, edged in glimmers of stardust that gently floated in the air around her. Her eyes were luminous pools of amethyst, calm and knowing, and her long hair billowed as if moved by an unseen breeze. A soft white glow enveloped her, pulsing faintly with the rhythm of the cosmos. Her presence was warm and weightless, and as Solei looked upon her, she felt both comforted and deeply undone—like standing in the presence of a sacred farewell.

"Help her," she whispered, her voice like wind through chimes. "Zambia will need you more than ever."

And then she was gone.

Solei's heart pounded as she pushed open the door, her mind still spinning from what she had just seen. Luneia's spirit—so vivid, so luminous—lingered in her vision like a sunspot etched into her soul. A part of her questioned whether it had truly happened or whether it was a vision born of anxiety and intuition. Her breath caught in her throat, a strange mix of fear and awe tightening in her chest. Confusion swirled through her thoughts, but she moved forward, pulled by something deeper—an urgent knowing that whatever she was about to face, it had already begun to change everything.

Pehani followed close behind her, silent but alert, his senses sharpened by the tension hanging in the air. As he stepped into the room, his hand instinctively rested on Solei's back, steadying her. His gaze swept over the scene—midwife, child, blood, stillness—and stopped abruptly at the sight of Luneia's unmoving form. His breath hitched. His jaw clenched. And then his face dropped into still grief, his eyes locking with Solei's in stunned recognition of what had happened.

The baby's cries pierced the air—bright, raw, and filled with life. The midwife stood with the newborn wrapped in golden cloth, her face streaked with tears.

Zambia knelt beside the low bed, still as stone, her arms wrapped around Luneia's lifeless body. Her sobs came in choking gasps, the kind that hollow you from the inside out.

Solei's breath caught in her throat.

Her eyes fell upon Luneia's still form, and something inside her broke open. The air seemed to collapse around her, as if the light itself had dimmed. It wasn't just the silence that hit her—it was the absence. The void left behind by a soul so radiant, so gentle, that the room itself now felt unanchored.

Grief surged through her—not only for the sacred sister who now lay still, but for Zambia, whose wails tore at the fabric of the air, and for the newborn child, wrapped in gold and grief before she had even drawn her second breath. Solei sank to her knees.

She had lost a beloved friend. A soul she had journeyed with across lifetimes. A light that had braided hope into every sunrise. Her heart cracked wide, the loss a soundless scream within her. And yet, even in the depths of that heartbreak, she knew her role was not to fall—but to hold. To hold this grief. To hold Zambia. To hold the fragile thread of new life trembling in the air.

She bowed her head, her hand trembling as it brushed a lock of hair from Luneia's cooling brow. "I will carry her with me," she whispered silently to the stars above, "in every step I take from this day forward."

Zambia clung to her body, trembling violently, her face buried in Luneia's chest as though she could will her heart to beat again.

"Why did you leave me?" Zambia choked out, her voice raw and broken. "You were everything. You were my heart. My light. How do I breathe without you?"

Her words spilled out between sobs, each one a knife carving into the silence. "I told you I'd protect you. I was supposed to protect you. And I wasn't enough. I wasn't enough."

She rocked back and forth, her forehead pressed to Luneia's, her cries turning into guttural wails. Her whole body convulsed with grief, her soul cracking open in the echo of her loss.

"I don't know who I am without you," she whispered. "I don't know how to be in a world where your voice is gone."

Solei stepped closer, her tears falling faster, the weight of Zambia's sorrow wrapping around her like a storm. There was no healing in this moment—only witnessing, only holding space for the ache that could never be unmade.

"No..." Solei breathed, her chest tightening with shock.

Zambia looked up, her eyes bloodshot and brimming, her voice a raw whisper of devastation.

"She's gone," she said, breaking open with each syllable. "I held her. I held her, and she still left."

The baby's cries rang out again, insistent and searching.

The midwife, gently cradling the baby, looked to Solei with glistening eyes. "She needs to hold her," she whispered softly. "For the bond between mother and child to form, their hearts must touch. She needs to feel her daughter's warmth, or something vital may slip away."

Solei hesitated, her hand brushing Zambia's shoulder.

"Zambia, she needs you. Your child needs you. Please—just hold her."

Zambia's face contorted with anguish. Her shoulders heaved. "I can't," she cried, her voice sharp with grief. "I can't look at her... because I'll see Luneia. I'll see what's missing."

Then she rose with sudden motion, stumbling away from the bed. Her arms wrapped tightly around herself as she ran from the room, her sobs echoing through the doorway like thunder.

The midwife watched her go, then turned to Pehani. Her voice was low and exhausted. "I'll care for the baby until she's ready. But she must return to her soon."

Pehani nodded, his jaw tight. "You've done all you can. Please, go and rest. Send word to the wetnurse. We'll make sure the child is cared for."

The midwife nodded and stepped away, leaving behind the tiny bundle of new life—wrapped in golden cloth and glowing faintly in the soft morning light.

Solei stood by the cradle, brushing her fingers over the baby's silken brow. A tear slipped down her cheek and landed on the child's forehead, catching the light like a drop of starlight. She leaned down, whispering a gentle blessing in the old tongue, letting her voice tremble with both sorrow and hope.

Pehani came beside her and placed a hand on her back. They stood in silence, gazing at the child who had entered the world through heartbreak.

"She's light," Solei whispered, her voice cracking. "Even in this... she's light."

The baby stirred, her tiny fingers curling into a fist before opening again, reaching instinctively toward the warmth around her.

Outside, the morning sun broke fully through the trees, casting rays through the open doorway and flooding the room in golden glow. The scent of the blossoms on the wind carried into the space, mingling with quiet tears and sacred stillness.

And in that moment, with pain still heavy in their hearts, something soft unfurled—like the first sprout of a flower reaching toward the sun after the storm.

Love, aching and tender, began to rise again.

And the room, though filled with loss, pulsed gently with the sound of new life beginning

Solei's breath caught in her throat.

Her eyes fell upon Luneia's still form, and something inside her shattered. It wasn't just shock—it was heartbreak, vast and soul-deep. A grief that clawed through her chest, splintering the steady center she so often stood in. She had known Luneia across lifetimes, braided joy with her in laughter, shared silence and ceremony in equal measure. Her light had been a gentle rhythm in the symphony of Solei's world—and now, it was gone.

The absence rang louder than the newborn's cries.

Solei's knees gave way, and she sank to the floor, her body trembling as her hands pressed to the earth, seeking something solid in the hollow of loss. Her tears fell without restraint—not only for the woman she loved as a sister, but for Zambia, broken open in grief, and for the child now wrapped in golden light and longing. The ache was too large to hold alone. And yet, she held it—because she must.

Because she was the High Priestess.

Because no one else could hold this moment like she could.

She reached forward with a trembling hand and brushed a strand of damp hair from Luneia's brow. Her touch was reverent, her heart silently crying out to the stars.

"You should still be here," she whispered. "You were so much light... too much to vanish."

She bowed her head, allowing herself a breath of mourning, a breath of sacred goodbye.

CHAPTER SEVENTEEN

THE FAREWELL OF LIGHT

T he sun did not rise. It unveiled itself.

It slipped through a lavender mist like a divine hand parting the veil between worlds. The sky was not simply lit — it was painted, a living canvas of rose-gold, deep amber, and opalescent pink. The clouds glowed with iridescent light, swirling slowly above the village like ancient spirits bearing witness. The soft whisper of their passage stirred a sacred anticipation in the air, filling every corner of Lumeria with a pulse that hummed in the bones of the earth, as if the very fabric of existence held its breath.

The entire grove held its breath.

Birds did not sing. Leaves did not rustle. Even the sea beyond the trees stilled, holding its waves in reverent silence. All of Lumeria seemed to pause — listening, remembering, honoring. The morning, like the very heartbeat of the land, held space for the sacred grief that pulsed in every soul. There was no rush in the moment — only the endless expansion of time itself, a heartbeat that vibrated through the sacred soil beneath their feet.

At the heart of the sacred grove stood the ceremonial altar, carved from luminous white stone veined with threads of violet crystal. It shimmered beneath the canopy of flowering trees, their blossoms unfurling in colors rarely seen — celestial blues, soft peach-fire, radiant gold. The altar pulsed with gentle light, as though aware of the soul it cradled, reverberating in harmony with the breath of the land itself. It was as though the stone had absorbed every whisper of the earth, every tear, every prayer that had ever been spoken into its embrace.

Luneia lay atop it, serene as starlight. Her body, though still, radiated presence — an ethereal glow that seemed not of this world, but a glimpse of the divine. She was wrapped in robes of woven silk infused with crushed moon petals and stardust — hues of indigo, ivory, and pearl that glimmered as the sun kissed them, casting her in a sacred glow. Her hair had been lovingly braided with nightshade lilies, dream root blossoms, and the tiny white tears of the Lu Leya vine — flowers that bloomed only once, during a soul's final departure, symbols of her transcendence, her divine release.

The scent of sacred oils filled the air — spiced amber, sun fruit resin, and moon-milk balm — mixed with the delicate fragrance of crushed ceremonial petals scattered across the ground in intricate spirals, symbols of both life and death, their delicate beauty ephemeral, as all things in this world were. It was as if the very air itself had absorbed the grief, the love, and the sacred beauty of this moment.

Around the altar, the entire village stood in a wide circle, clothed in flowing garments dyed with earth-pigments and astral light. Each robe shimmered slightly — not from thread, but from the energy of the beings who wore them. Their faces were open, solemn, luminous. In each hand, they held orbs — crystal spheres glowing with the colors of their hearts, infused with prayers, memories, and soul-light. The light from the orbs flickered like the heartbeat of the community, pulsing with their collective devotion, radiating their presence as individuals, as one.

Zambia stood at the altar's foot, motionless — but not lifeless. Grief had turned her to stone, but there was fire beneath it, quiet and burning. Her eyes were hollow with pain, her jaw locked, but her arms cradled something sacred:

The child.

Wrapped in a ceremonial swaddle the color of sunrise, the baby rested against her chest — a flickering warmth of life amid the cold ache of goodbye. Mihati's aura glowed with gentle pulses — a soft halo of pinks, greens, and golden white, flickering like a newborn star learning to breathe. Her little hands twitched in her sleep, her breath feather-light, yet beneath the fragility of her form was an unspoken strength — the continuation of something sacred, something divine. Her presence was a bridge between worlds, holding the love and light of her mother's passing and the infinite potential of the future.

Solei stepped forward into the center of the circle, her robes trailing behind her like molten gold across the earth. The moment her bare feet touched the glowing soil, a ripple of light spread outward. The energy of the grove awakened, vibrating softly as if recognizing her presence, as if the earth itself responded to the divinity that coursed through her. The ground beneath their feet thrummed with the pulse of the sacred.

She lifted her hands to the sky and released a sound — not a cry, not a song, but an ancient call. It was the frequency of remembrance, the key to the sacred.

A deep, resonant tone vibrated from her chest — soft at first, then rising in harmonic waves. It stirred the trees, danced across the leaves, and sank into the earth. The villagers joined her, their voices layering like woven silk — some high and celestial, others low and thunderous. The sound surrounded them, lifted them, bound them. It was the song of the soul itself, of lifetimes unfolding in a single moment, of every heart beating in unison.

The orbs in their hands lit brighter.

Beams of light emerged from each — threads of soul-color that reached toward the altar like rivers flowing upstream, converging above Luneia's body in a whirl of energy. Hues of rose quartz, celestial blue, citrine gold, and emerald green spun together in a spiral of soul-light, wrapping around her like the cocoon of rebirth.

And Luneia responded.

From her heart, a single pulse of white-gold light expanded outward in a radiant wave. It wasn't simply light — it was feeling. It carried love, grief, serenity, gratitude, and infinite peace. The wave passed through every villager's chest, igniting their hearts like stars flaring to life. It was a cosmic kiss, a tender, timeless embrace from a mother's soul to her children. Some dropped to their knees, overwhelmed by the intensity of the love that flooded them. Others raised their hands to the sky, trembling with the sheer force of the sacred release.

Zambia gasped as the wave struck her. Her legs shook, but she did not fall. Instead, her arms instinctively drew the baby closer, wrapping her body around Mihati like armor and home. The baby stirred, opened her eyes — and for the briefest moment, they glowed with Luneia's light.

"I see her," Zambia whispered, voice breaking. "I see her."

Above the altar, Luneia's body began to rise.

She floated upward, held aloft by the web of soul-light spun from the villagers' hearts. Her silks flowed like water, her skin radiant with the afterglow of a soul mid-passage. Her spirit — no longer bound — shimmered in layers of translucent light, phasing gently between dimensions. She was both here and not here. Her essence stretched across the fabric of time, touching all the souls who had ever known her, and all those who would come after. Her love, infinite and all-encompassing, a bridge between this world and the next, radiated into the hearts of every being present.

The trees bowed.

The air shimmered with fine particles of golden light, like pollen mixed with stars. A low wind stirred the ground, causing the flower petals in the grove to lift and spiral around her ascending form. They, too, honored her departure. They danced in the sacred rhythm of the earth's eternal heartbeat. Every petal that floated upward seemed to whisper of eternity, of memories not yet made and stories that would never end.

Then — her voice.

A whisper on the wind. Not sound, but knowing.

"She will carry my dawn."

Zambia sobbed, collapsing to her knees, the baby cradled against her heart. She did not weep in despair, but in the sweet, heart-breaking realization that this was both an end and a beginning. The light of her love had become the light of her child. A promise. A legacy. Her soul trembled in the recognition of this sacred truth.

Solei moved to her side, one hand resting gently on Zambia's shoulder. The connection between them ignited — not as fire, but as warmth. Safe. Anchoring. A divine thread passed between them. In that sacred moment, there was no separation — only the deep, flowing current of sisterhood, of the feminine bond that transcended time, grief, and life itself. They were one in the truth of this moment, held by the earth, the sky, and the love that had created them.

Pehani stepped forward, his energy strong and grounding, and together, he and Zambia gently guided Luneia's floating body toward the sacred cliffs. As they walked, the path before them bloomed. Flowers opened mid-step, their petals unfolding as if in response to a prayer long held in silence. Light poured from the ground like breath exhaled from the core of the earth. It was as though the very land itself had answered the call, had heard the sacred longing and responded with grace.

The burial cave awaited — carved into the cliffs of crystalline stone. Its entrance glowed with soft golden mist, and the air around it shimmered with ancestral energy. Inside, the chamber was filled with softly pulsing crystals, luminous moss, and vines of remembrance. The walls themselves seemed to hum with the reverence of generations. The space was sacred beyond comprehension — a hallowed temple where time itself bent to honor the divine.

They laid her gently upon the crystal bed.

Zambia knelt beside her, one hand trembling above Luneia's chest. Her voice cracked.

"I told you to wait. I told you..."

Tears fell freely.

"...but you already knew."

She leaned forward, touching her forehead to Luneia's. A final flash of light passed between them — one last goodbye, one last blessing. The light was not bright but soft, like a twilight kiss. When she rose, her grief no longer drowned her. It walked beside her. It became part of her. She had learned to walk with her grief, to cradle it as she cradled Mihati — in reverence, in love, in the sacred knowledge that loss is never truly an end.

When they returned to the path, Zambia was quiet. But her silence was different now. It held something new. A new light, a new depth, a new strength. The weight of her grief no longer crushed her, but she carried it gently, like a treasure held close to her chest. She would not bury it. She would honor it.

She looked down at Mihati in her arms — the baby was awake, blinking slowly, her gaze steady and clear.

"She named her," Zambia said softly to Solei, voice raw with memory. "Before she crossed. I laughed at her certainty, told her to wait... but she knew."

Solei gently smiled, her voice no louder than the wind, "And the name?"

"Mihati," Zambia whispered. "It means dawn. The first light after darkness."

Solei touched the baby's cheek with her fingers, warm and glowing. "She is the light that rises when all seems lost."

The wind stirred again, gently, like the breath of the earth itself.

As they stepped beneath the ceremonial archway, the village bells rang — three notes that echoed across the valley. Not in mourning.

In recognition.

Zambia walked with strength now, Mihati held not in obligation, but in devotion. The villagers stood silently as she passed, their hands pressed over their hearts. No words were needed.

A mother had been born.

A soul had been honored.

And a new light now shone in the sacred land of Lumeria.

Chapter Eighteen

THE RETURN OF THE DEEP

The wind howled that night, a wild, primal force, as if it had swallowed the heart of a storm. It whipped through the trees, its breath carrying a fierce urgency, an untold story of the earth's ancient pulse.

Solei stood in the threshold of her dwelling, her delicate hand pressed gently against the curve of her swollen belly, her fingers trembling against the soft rise of life within her. A sharp gust of wind swept through the branches above, a flurry of petals and ash dancing through the air like sacred embers, scattering across the ground. The scent of burning sage, rich and earthy, clung to the breeze, mingling with the faint, salt-tinged kiss of the sea. The night air was cool, crisp, biting with a chill that made her skin prickle, the sensation crawling up her arms, awakening something deep within. The twins stirred beneath her palm—a double thrum of life, an ancient rhythm pulsing through her. Solei's breath became slow and measured, grounding herself against the sacred stone beneath her feet, the earth's pulse syncing with her own.

Something was coming.

She could feel it—not just in the land or the sky, but in the very marrow of her bones. It was the way the air seemed to hum, the sky whispering of change. A vibration she couldn't ignore. Her soul trembled with the knowing, a call so deep it echoed through her body.

Her gaze shifted from the warm glow of her chamber, and with a quiet breath, she turned to face the wilderness beyond. The ceremonial robe she wore fluttered around her ankles like an ethereal smoke, catching the moonlight in delicate waves. The silken fabric shimmered as she stepped onto the moss-covered earth, her bare feet moving silently through the night, each step carrying her closer to the water. Every breath she took was filled with a quiet dread that weighed heavy in her chest. The land, the night, and the stars themselves seemed to hold their breath, as if the very world was waiting for something to unfold.

Solei didn't know why she was walking toward the sea—only that her soul was being pulled there, a thread that connected her to something far beyond her understanding. The ocean had always spoken to her. Whispered her name through the waves. Pulled her spirit close when her mind wandered too far from center. As a child, she would slip away to this very cove, where the land met the sea, and sit in silence, waiting for a voice she could never name.

And once—just once—it came.

A creature so vast, so ancient, that she thought he must surely be a dream.

He had no name. But his presence, his very essence, was a warning. "The Shadowed are stirring." His voice had vibrated through her soul, leaving an imprint that would never fade. Then, like a shadow swallowed by the waves, he had disappeared, leaving her heart racing, shaken to the core. The vision had haunted her for years—his storm-dark eyes, the ancient wisdom etched into his gaze, and the echo of his voice that rippled through her dreams, waking her to something greater. That warning had forever altered her path, opening a doorway to a destiny far beyond the rituals and rhythms of her people.

Now, centuries later, her feet carried her back to the place where it had all began.

The sacred crescent of the cove. The place where the world had shifted.

The moon hung low, its silver fire spilling across the water like liquid light. The ocean mirrored its glow, each wave shimmering with a ghostly luminescence. The tide was unnaturally calm, as though the sea itself held its breath, suspended in the moment, waiting. Solei stepped closer to the edge of the tide pool, her feet sinking into the cool, damp earth, the phosphorescent glow of the water rising like gentle flames beneath her. She sank to her knees, her breath shallow, her pulse quickening in her chest as the world around her seemed to hold its breath.

"If you are there," she whispered, her voice quiet, reverent, laced with a tremor of desperation. "I need you."

For a heartbeat, there was nothing.

Her heart pounded louder, the sound deafening in her ears. Her fingers clenched at the earth, digging into the soft sand. And then—a vibration. A subtle shift, like the pulse of a forgotten heartbeat. It wasn't a sound, but a sensation, like the world beneath her feet was stirring, waking from a long slumber.

And then, from the depths of the sea, he emerged.

The water arched upward, alive, as if the sea itself was rising to meet her. A colossal figure began to take form, emerging from the depths in a majestic display of power. His scales shimmered in hues of obsidian, emerald, and blue-fire silver, each glimmering like a star in the night sky. His body was long and sinuous, a creature of both serpent and spirit, a being of the deep whose very presence seemed to command the world around him. His eyes, storm-dark and filled with ancient sorrow, locked onto hers, and time seemed to stand still.

Solei gasped, stumbling backward into the tide. The water surged around her, soaking her robes instantly, but she did not flee. She could not.

He had returned.

"You came," she whispered, her voice trembling, awe and fear swirling within her like a storm.

"You called," the creature's voice resonated deep in her mind, thunderous and ancient, as if the sound of the ocean itself had taken shape in his words.

She placed a trembling hand on her belly, her heart racing as the twins responded to the rising tide of energy in the air, their movements mirroring the storm that churned within her. "You warned me once... long ago. About the Shadowed."

His eyes dimmed with remembrance. A sorrow so deep, it rippled through her own soul. "And now you understand."

"They've found a way off the island, haven't they?"

A heavy silence fell between them, the air thick with the weight of his words. Then, slowly, with a nod that felt like the earth itself conceding to fate, he answered.

"They have torn through the final seal. The island no longer holds them. They rise now—unbound, ravenous, drawn to Lumeria like predators to the scent of light."

The world tilted, the ground beneath her feet seeming to tremble in response to the revelation. Solei's breath caught in her throat, panic rising in her chest as her vision blurred. She fell to her knees, clutching her belly as the twins kicked fiercely, as though they, too, could sense the incoming storm. "No... no, not now. Not with the veil thinning. Not with the children coming. We are not ready."

The creature's massive form lowered, his great head coming to hover just inches above her, his luminous eyes full of an ancient sorrow.

"I do not know how long it will take," his voice rumbled softly, reverberating in her very bones, "the tides no longer tell time as they once did. But I felt it... they have left the island. They are moving, inching closer, drawn to Lumeria with purpose. The sea carries their scent. The deep quakes in fear."

A cry broke free from Solei's chest, raw and full of despair. She bent forward, clutching her belly, the tears spilling freely, hot against her skin, a torrent of grief and fear. "What do I do? How do I protect them?"

The creature's great eyes softened, and though he trembled with uncertainty, his voice was filled with an ancient, painful truth. "I am the last of my kind," he said, his voice trembling, "and I fear I am not enough."

Solei's heart broke for him, for the weight of his solitude, the centuries he had carried this burden alone. With trembling steps, she waded deeper into the tide, the cool water rising around her, her hands reaching for his shimmering head. She closed her eyes, calling upon the sacred light within her palms, sending healing energy into the deep, old wounds he carried—loneliness, fatigue, the eternal burden of watching worlds rise and fall.

"You are enough," she whispered, her voice thick with emotion. "But not for this. You must survive, Tidekeeper. You are sacred. Go, now—before the storm comes. Find the deepest trench. Let the sea hold you safe."

He stared at her, his ancient gaze soft with sorrow, and then, with a slow bow of his massive head, he turned and disappeared beneath the waves, his form dissolving into the deep in a glowing spiral of bioluminescent light.

Solei stood there, trembling, her heart shattered. The weight of what she had just learned pressed down on her chest, as though the very air had become too heavy to bear. Her body, swollen with life, ached under the gravity of her responsibility. She sank to the sand, her tear-streaked face lifted to the sky, her eyes wide and unblinking as she stared out at the endless black water. Waves lapped softly at the shore, but they brought no comfort. Only questions. Only dread.

She didn't know what to do—only that time was slipping away. And soon.

"Lu Mai," she cried, her voice hoarse, cracked with desperation. "I need your guidance. I can't do this alone. Please... please show me what to do."

The clouds above her split, parting like the veil between worlds, revealing a column of celestial light that descended from the heavens. It was a river of divinity, a living, breathing current of power that flowed toward her, bathing her in warmth so profound it brought her to her knees. Solei gasped, overwhelmed, as the light wrapped around her, filling her with a deep, soul-stirring heat. Her breath caught in her chest, the pulse of Source beating in time with her own heart. Her eyes welled with tears as the energy pressed into her, an overwhelming force that made her feel both small and vast, like the universe itself was embracing her.

Her twins within her responded, their tiny movements gentle and reverent, as though they too felt the presence of the divine.

Solei placed both hands over her womb, her heart wide open, surrendered to the pulse of Source that filled the cove with its silent, sovereign grace.

A voice, soft yet powerful, rose from the light.

"In three days, the waters will rise. A great flood shall come to purge the Shadowed—whether they have reached your shores or not. But water does not choose. It will cleanse all. Unless..."

"Unless?" Solei whispered, her voice trembling with a thread of hope.

"Unless Lumeria is shielded. One among you carries the gift—the light to protect, the power to veil the land. You must find them. Before the flood arrives."

The light began to fade, the energy retreating into the heavens. The sea calmed, a stillness settling over the cove, leaving Solei to sit in stunned silence, the weight of the prophecy settling like a stone in her chest.

The creature, watching her from the depths, tilted his great head, his eyes filled with an ancient wisdom.

"I never asked your name," she whispered, the last vestiges of her tears slipping down her cheek.

He blinked slowly, his massive form glowing in the dark water. "I never had one. But if it steadies your spirit, you may call me Tidekeeper."

Solei nodded, rising unsteadily to her feet, her body trembling. "Thank you."

"Go," his voice was a low, commanding echo. "You must run. You must warn them. Time no longer waits."

Solei turned and fled.

Through the glowing woods, over stone and root, her soaked robe clinging to her body like a second skin, heavy with the weight of destiny. She reached the healer's temple breathless, her heart hammering like a war drum.

Pehani met her at the doorway, his face pale, eyes wide with alarm.

"What happened?"

"They've escaped," she gasped. "The Shadowed. They will be here in three days. Lu Mai said a flood is coming to destroy them... but it will destroy us too unless we find the one who can protect Lumeria."

He caught her before she fell, his strong arms enveloping her, anchoring her to the moment.

"And you believe this protector is among us now?"

"Yes," she breathed. "They are here. One of us carries the light. We must find them."

Her hand pressed to her belly, her voice quivering with the weight of it all. "If we fail, Pehani... everything we've built, everything we love, will be washed away. They will never know the light of this land."

He grasped her hand tightly, his voice low, unwavering. "Then we do not fail. We search. We rise. And we protect them—all of them."

The torches flickered in the stillness. The earth groaned beneath their feet.

Somewhere far beneath the sea, darkness stirred.

And in Lumeria, the countdown had begun.

CHAPTER NINETEEN

THE SEARCH FOR THE SHIELDBEARER

The skies over Lumeria had darkened by morning.

A low, dense fog had crept over the island like a shroud, clinging to trees, rooftops, and skin with damp fingers. The air was heavy with silence, the kind that pulsed with foreboding — like the world itself was waiting.

Solei stood in the center of the Temple of Gathering, surrounded by flickering lanterns and the scent of smoldering cedar. Her damp robe had been replaced with a fresh wrap of garnet and ivory, her hair still half-wet, coiled and pinned behind her ears. But her heart pounded with the same urgency that had driven her through the forest just hours before.

Pehani knelt beside her, chanting softly into a shallow bowl of sacred water. The ripples moved not from his breath but from the vibration of the words — an old divination song used to call forth the presence of hidden truths. Around them, the

Elders had gathered in a crescent circle, their eyes wide, faces tense.

Solei gripped the edges of the bowl. "We don't have time to wait for visions," she said through clenched teeth. "We need to search. House to house. Aura to aura."

"We will," Pehani replied calmly, never breaking rhythm. "But if the one we seek carries such power, their soul will leave traces in the field. We must try to feel for it."

The bowl shimmered.

Suddenly, the water surface flared gold.

A single image flashed within it — a hand, outstretched. Young. Bare. Surrounded by light.

Then it vanished.

Gasps rose from the Elders. Solei blinked, chest heaving.

"A child?" one whispered.

"Or someone cloaked in innocence," Pehani replied.

Solei stood abruptly. "It doesn't matter. We search. Now."

They moved through the village like wildfire.

Solei and Pehani walked door to door, followed by seers and acolytes trained in energy sensitivity. At each stop, the villagers were asked to open their doors, their homes, their hearts. Some responded with reverence, others with confusion — but all obeyed.

Every man, woman, elder, and child was seen. Read. Felt.

Solei's own hands trembled with exhaustion, her senses worn raw from reaching into field after field, searching for a pulse that matched the divine code.

By nightfall, the last house on the southern rise had been checked. Nothing.

They returned to the central square, where the sacred flame burned low and blue.

Solei collapsed to her knees beside it, cradling her belly.

"What if we're too late?" she murmured. "What if they've been hidden too long — even from themselves?"

Pehani knelt beside her. "Then we draw them out."

He turned to the Elders. "Prepare the circle of awakening."

At midnight, the villagers gathered in the amphitheater carved into the hillside.

Torches lined the steps. Incense swirled through the air in fragrant spirals. Children sat on laps, elders stood leaning on staffs, the rest murmured prayers under their breath. All eyes turned to the center — where Solei stood, belly round, palms raised.

She spoke not from her throat but from her heart, her voice projected with energy.

"If you carry the light... if you were born with the code of protection... you may not even know it. But now is the time. We ask you to step forward. Not for power. Not for glory. But for the soul of Lumeria."

Silence.

The earth held its breath.

But no one else stepped forward.

Solei looked around the amphitheater, her voice trembling as she called again, "Please... if you feel anything—if something inside you stirs—step forward. We don't have time."

But only silence answered.

A cold wind swept through the torches, and the flames dimmed.

Pehani's face tightened. "We have to prepare. If we can't find them, we must shield what we can."

They worked through the night, every soul in the village pouring heart and sweat into the effort to protect what they had built. Seers drew vast runes of protection across the cliffside, while elders traced energy glyphs into the ground with trembling fingers. Children carried stones soaked in sun energy, and warriors stood guard with staffs imbued with old spells. Lanterns of white flame burned along the borders of the temple, flickering with fragile hope. Crystals were laid in sacred patterns, and prayers echoed through the stone halls like incantations.

But even with all their efforts, the light wavered. The pressure in the air deepened.

And still, no one came forward.

With mounting dread, Solei and Pehani continued channeling what light they could into the temple walls. Solei's strength waned. Her body ached. Her breath grew shallow. The twins stirred constantly within her, as if sensing the rising tide.

Then, the skies opened.

It began with a whisper—raindrops as soft as breath. But they carried a chill unlike anything Lumeria had felt in generations. A rumble rolled through the mountains, deep and ominous, like the voice of the earth groaning beneath the weight of what was coming. Then came the roar.

A curtain of rain dropped from the heavens with violent suddenness. It struck the ground with such force the very soil seemed to recoil. The sky blackened until it was indistinguishable from the sea. Lightning crackled from cloud to cloud, revealing brief flashes of the village below—torn banners, panicked birds, trees bending in unnatural shapes.

The great flood descended like a beast unleashed. Waves of water surged from the horizon, merging with torrents from the sky. The storm enveloped the entire island in a relentless spiral, like a living entity closing its grip around Lumeria. Rain pounded the rooftops until clay cracked and caved. Sacred shrines were ripped from their moorings, tossed like toys into the rising tide.

Mountains groaned. The sacred river that once flowed gently around the village now swelled into a savage force, dragging away anything in its path—stones, statues, even trees. Thunder cracked so violently the skies seemed to split open. Lightning shattered the tops of towers. The wind screamed, howling through the village with a voice like a thousand ghosts.

Villagers locked their doors and shuttered their windows. Homes that had stood for lifetimes trembled on their foundations. Inside, the people clung to one another — some wrapped in blankets, others gripping whatever sacred tokens they had left. The scent of burning oil, wet stone, and fear filled every room. Elders mumbled protective chants through clenched teeth, while children whimpered into their mothers' arms. Fathers paced like caged animals, powerless to protect the land they'd sworn to defend. Some whispered ancient prayers, others wept without sound, their tears indistinguishable from the storm outside.

And still, the rain came. Sheets of it, tearing across the land like blades. Water ran in rivers through the streets, turning paths into torrents. Crops were pulled from the ground. Statues of old gods and guardians crumbled beneath the weight of the downpour.

The temple floors began to flood. The flames sputtered and died. Mud and debris surged through the paths.

Solei and Pehani stood at the edge of the central hall, water rising past their ankles.

"We failed," Solei whispered, her voice broken. "Lu Mai warned us, and we couldn't find them."

Pehani reached for her, holding her trembling form. "We did everything we could. The one may still awaken. But for now... we survive."

Outside, the island of Lumeria trembled under the weight of the storm.

And the light they had protected for centuries threatened to be swallowed by the sea.

That night, Solei and Pehani lay curled in the corner of their home's highest room, the stone walls moaning with every gust of wind. The rain pounded like fists upon the roof. Each crack of thunder shook the bones of the modest structure, and the twins stirred uneasily in Solei's womb. Neither she nor Pehani spoke. There were no words left — only a silent current of fear and defeat flowing between them.

They eventually drifted into a restless sleep, lulled not by peace, but by sheer exhaustion. The storm roared on through the night, snarling against the walls of their home like a wild beast trying to break in.

And then — stillness.

Solei blinked awake to the sound of birds.

She sat up sharply, heart pounding, unsure if it was a dream. Pehani stirred beside her, eyes fluttering open.

"Do you hear that?" she whispered.

Pehani sat up, listening.

Birdsong.

Not distant. Not imagined. Real.

They scrambled to their feet and pushed open the heavy wooden doors, the hinges groaning. A golden-pink light flooded the room — the sky painted in soft pastels. Steam rose from the earth where the sun kissed soaked stone. The storm had passed.

Outside, the village was a ruin of mud and debris. Statues lay toppled. Walls had collapsed. Trees were half-uprooted, their limbs hanging like broken arms. But in the center of it all, something shimmered.

Solei and Pehani rushed barefoot into the muddy streets, the chill of the wet earth biting at their skin as they sprinted through the wreckage. The mud clung to their feet, thick and slippery, splattering their legs as they stumbled forward, driven by instinct and disbelief. Their lungs burned with the morning air, damp and thick with the scent of rain-soaked ash and trampled blossoms. All around them, the remnants of Lumeria groaned beneath the weight of what had passed.

From broken doorways and leaning walls, the villagers emerged — dazed, shivering, and barefoot. They blinked against the gentle sunlight filtering through the dissipating storm clouds, their expressions caught between disbelief and hope. Faces were streaked with dried tears and soot, their eyes wide as if unsure whether to weep again or fall to their knees in prayer.

At the center of the village — in the heart of what had once been their ceremonial grounds — sat a figure.

Cross-legged, unmoving, his body still as a stone, Lehari sat at the center of the devastation. He was surrounded by a radiant sphere of soft, golden energy that shimmered like sunlight filtered through morning mist. The shield pulsed with a quiet heartbeat, a living barrier between what remained and what could have been lost. The energy around him rose and fell like breath, humming faintly with ancient power, grounding itself in the earth as though drawn from the roots of the island itself.

It was Lehari.

Gasps rippled through the crowd. A few villagers covered their mouths. Some exchanged wide-eyed glances, as if unable to reconcile the man they had once overlooked with the miracle before them.

Solei stopped cold. Her mouth parted in disbelief.

Pehani whispered, "It's him... He's holding the shield."

Lehari was a plant healer. A quiet man who kept to the outer edges of the village, tending herbs and roots in the shaded groves where few ventured. He was not beautiful like the others — his features were asymmetrical, his hair always unruly, his robes stained with soil. He rarely spoke unless spoken to. He had never attended council. Never offered his opinion.

And yet... he was kind.

He healed without expectation, without ever asking for thanks. With quiet hands and dirt under his fingernails, he tended to the sick and the weary. He brewed teas from rare flowers that only bloomed in moonlight and ground salves from moss that grew in the silence between the stones. To those with aching bellies, he offered fragrant leaves wrapped in silk. For broken skin, he mixed oils that smelled of mint and sun. Once, in a quiet grove beneath a dying moon, he brought a withering tree back to life with nothing but his breath, his tears, and the steady hum of an ancient chant known only to those who listened to the roots. He did not seek attention — he simply served, in his quiet, sacred way.

But no one had ever considered he might carry such power.

Not until now.

Lehari's eyes were closed. The shield pulsed gently around him — a living sphere of light that extended upward like a dome, protecting what remained of Lumeria.

Tears streamed down Solei's cheeks as she whispered, "He saved us. When we'd given up... he woke."

And all around them, as the villagers gathered in reverent silence, the first rays of morning broke through the clouds.

Lumeria still stood.

And in that moment, Solei understood — the shield was never about power. It was about devotion, rooted in silence. And that kind of light... could never be hidden for long.

Because of the one they least expected.

Solei stood in the rising light, a hand over her womb, eyes locked on the quiet miracle before her. Gratitude swelled in her chest, but it was braided with something deeper — humility. She had searched the entire island, looking outward, demanding signs, missing the truth that sometimes the sacred hides in plain sight, within the overlooked and unseen.

She thought of the long nights, the prayers unanswered, the fear that had choked her breath. All along, the light they needed had been gently growing in silence, like a seed beneath the soil — waiting not for recognition, but for the right time.

Her heart ached with reverence. Lehari had not been chosen for his strength or stature, but for his quiet consistency, his devotion to life. And now she understood: the shield of Lumeria could only be held by a soul who had mastered stillness, patience, and care.

And as the dawn painted golden lines across the sky, Solei whispered a silent vow to honor the unexpected, to listen more deeply — not just with her gifts, but with her whole being.

Chapter Twenty

THE SHIELD

T he storm had not passed.

Beyond the shimmering shield, the world was still raging — a cataclysm of nature and ancient force. Wind howled like a wounded beast, lashing the sea into mountainous waves that crashed against the barrier in relentless fury. Rain fell in sheets so dense they blurred the horizon, slicing through the air like icy daggers. Thunder cracked in violent succession, echoing across the heavens like celestial drums of war. Lightning split the sky, illuminating the chaos in strobe-light flashes of terror and beauty.

But within Lumeria, inside the golden dome, there was a fragile stillness — a quiet heartbeat beneath the roar.

The dome shimmered like woven sunlight, stretching high above the village in a perfect curve. Its surface rippled gently, as if breathing. Each flicker of its glow held back destruction, and with every breath Lehari drew, the shield pulsed in kind.

The air beneath it was heavy with tension. The villagers moved slowly, speaking only in whispers, as though afraid even their voices might disrupt the delicate miracle. Water pooled around their ankles, brought in by the floodwaters licking at the edge of the shield. Yet they stood in hushed circles, not fleeing, but watching — as if in the presence of something holy.

And at the center of it all, Lehari remained — a lone figure bathed in divine light, unmoving, unyielding, and becoming something more than he had ever been. Still, steadfast, surrounded by his golden dome.

The villagers moved like threads drawn to a center, gathering around him not out of curiosity, but out of reverence. They brought offerings of water, cloth, healing balm. Children placed feathers and stones at his feet. Warriors stood quietly along the edges, guarding the space with unsheathed blades held like staffs of honor.

Lehari, though held in quiet glory, bore the weight of the shield with growing fatigue. His muscles trembled from the strain of stillness. Sweat slicked his brow. His fingers, extended outward in constant offering, ached as if carved from stone. His breath grew shallow at times, chest rising in slow, controlled effort.

And yet he held it.

Eyes closed, he searched inward — feeling for the rhythm, the balance, the way to draw not only from himself, but from the land, the people, the sky. He whispered ancient words beneath his breath, words not spoken aloud since the oldest roots had touched the ocean floor.

He wasn't just shielding Lumeria.

He was becoming part of it.

The villagers noticed. And they acted.

The builders — once focused on homes and temples — turned their skill to Lehari's aid. They crafted an intricate support structure out of sacred cypress and wind-polished stone. With soft leather loops and moss-lined rests, they created an armature that held his limbs gently in place, letting him extend his arms in offering without exhaustion. A rounded seat was woven from thick reeds, shaped to contour his body like an embrace.

A canopy followed — suspended from tall sun-carved beams, it sheltered him from wind and rain while casting dappled light upon the dome. Beneath it, vines were strung with crystal beads and white shells that tinkled softly in the breeze.

The women — mothers, sisters, and grandmothers — came in shifts with food and drink. They brought thick root stews, sun-baked fruit, and jars of herbal tonics. They wiped sweat from his brow. Massaged his hands. Whispered songs while feeding him sips of honeyed tea. Their tenderness became a rhythm, a devotional dance that sustained him.

And slowly, something extraordinary unfolded — not with the flash of miracles, but with the quiet glow of reverence.

But even miracles can tremble.

It happened in a blink.

A sound — sharp, foreign — cracked through the stillness. The dome around Lumeria pulsed erratically. Lehari's body jolted as if struck from within, and for a breathless moment, the shield flickered.

Just beyond its curve, the storm surged, sensing weakness. A fissure opened in the barrier — only a breath wide — but it was enough. Wind screamed through the gap. Rain crashed into the village with brutal force, toppling baskets, slamming doors, soaking villagers in an instant. A bolt of lightning cracked a tree in the central square, sending splinters flying.

Gasps rang out. Children cried. Some villagers fell to the ground in shock, shielding their heads as the sky seemed to reach inside their sanctuary. Others screamed names of loved ones, scattering to protect elders or children. Fear surged like a second wave — raw, human, immediate. Solei grabbed her belly, shielding her unborn twins as Pehani moved instinctively to her side, his arm wrapping protectively around her. Their eyes locked with a single thought: not now, not after everything. Not after they had come so far.

And then — Lehari roared.

Not in anger, but in focus. His hands, still trembling, flared with light. The dome surged back into place, sealing the break. The storm slammed against it once more, but this time, it held firm.

Silence fell inside the village — save for the patter of rain upon the barrier.

Lehari panted, chest heaving, eyes blazing. And then... he laughed.

Softly at first. Then louder, almost joyfully.

"I felt it," he whispered to no one and everyone. "Where the strength comes from. It isn't just here." He touched his chest. "It's everywhere."

From that moment on, the shield no longer wavered.

And something in the villagers shifted.

Where awe had once been quiet and uncertain, it now blossomed into fierce devotion. They had witnessed the fragility of their protection, had felt the cold kiss of chaos slip through. And they had seen Lehari rise — not in perfection, but in perseverance.

Mothers who had once doubted now wept openly when they passed him. Children, who had cowered in fear, now approached with offerings of song and laughter. The men who had once cast sidelong glances now spoke his name with pride.

They didn't revere him as a god.

They trusted him as one of their own — a brother, a son, a guardian who had stumbled and stood stronger.

Lehari, too, felt the shift. In the hands that passed him bowls of food, in the shoulders that leaned against his platform in quiet solidarity, in the laughter that returned to the air like birdsong after storm.

He no longer bore the shield alone.

He bore it with Lumeria.

Lehari didn't just hold it — he *became* it.

And though the storm raged on beyond the dome, something in the air had changed. The pressure began to ease. The wind, while still wild, felt less wrathful — like a tantrum nearly spent. Even the thunder seemed to echo from farther away. Solei, watching from the canopy, could feel it: the storm was beginning to lose its grip. The balance had shifted. The shield had turned the tide.

The more Lehari held the shield, the more the villagers began to see him differently.

His face, once regarded as unremarkable, now seemed carved with a sacred symmetry. His skin, once hidden under shadow and soil, now gleamed with a soft golden hue. Even his posture changed — no longer hunched or awkward, but tall, rooted, noble.

The energy flowing through him was transforming not only Lumeria — but himself.

And the people noticed.

They began to speak his name with reverence. Some traveled from distant parts of the island just to glimpse the man who held the shield. Others lingered for hours, hoping for a smile or a nod. The village children made flower crowns for him. Young women blushed when their hands brushed his. Old men came to offer ancient blessings, bowing before him with tears in their eyes.

Lehari, to his quiet credit, received all this with humility. He remained grounded, his presence serene, almost monastic. He offered smiles like blessings, soft and knowing, and when he chuckled, it was with the lightness of someone who had never imagined himself worthy of praise — and now chose to meet it with grace.

When he spoke, his voice felt like roots unfurling beneath the soil — deep, steady, and alive with ancient memory. It was not loud, but it made the listeners lean in, wanting more.

"I do not hold the shield alone," he told one small boy who sat beside him. "The roots help me. The wind helps me. The people help me. I only opened my palms."

And it was true. While Lehari remained the center, it was the village — their effort, their faith, their care — that kept the light alive.

Solei watched from the periphery, a soft hand on her belly, heart swelling with awe and quiet emotion. The twins within her stirred gently, as if responding to the golden current pulsing through the air. Tears blurred her vision, not from sorrow, but from the profound recognition that something sacred had shifted — not just in the village, but in the very heart of their people.

This was not just the rise of a protector. It was the blooming of a people. A transformation seeded in crisis, watered with unity, and now flowering beneath divine light.

Lumeria had been saved — not by force, but by communion. Not by command, but by calling. Not by glory, but by grace.

And as the golden shield shimmered on, still whole, still glowing — the people of Lumeria began to rebuild, one sacred step at a time.

From her place beneath the crystal-laced canopy, Solei sat in silent contemplation. Though peace pulsed just beyond the curve of her hand, her heart ached with questions she could no longer ignore.

A soft voice, laced with fierce wit and feminine power, stirred Solei from her contemplation. "Is that... *Lehari*? Our Lehari? Root-muddler, cloak-tripper, never-makes-eye-contact Lehari?"

Solei turned, lips already curving with amusement. Zambia stood there, one hand perched on her hip, the other clutching a damp shawl like a warrior brandishing her banner. Her hair, wild from the mist, framed her face like a crown of dark flames.

"Mm-hmm," Solei said, raising a knowing brow. "The same Lehari who once asked if dreambark was edible because it 'smelled like pudding.'"

Zambia gave a mock gasp. "The same Lehari who accidentally planted sacred herbs in a funeral mound and swore it was a 'blessed coincidence'?"

They both dissolved into laughter — not small, polite laughter, but full-bodied, divine feminine howling. It echoed between the sacred stones, drawing a few curious glances.

"I mean..." Zambia finally said, exhaling like she'd danced the storm from her chest, "I always thought there was something about him. Not obvious. Not polished. But ancient. Like he remembered something the rest of us forgot."

Solei nodded, her hand resting protectively over her belly. "He listened when no one asked him to. Watched without needing praise. That's a rare kind of strength."

Zambia sank down beside her with a grace that belied her power. "It's divine. It's... Lumerian. We've been trained to look for light in thunder and fire, but maybe the truest glow is the one growing slowly in the dark."

Solei smiled, eyes misting. "And now look at him — the shield-bearer, the heart-rooted guardian of an entire civilization."

Zambia arched a brow, glancing toward the dome. "Do you think he knows? That he's become the dream we all carried?"

Solei paused, gaze soft. "I think he's not thinking about himself at all. And that's the most beautiful part."

Zambia reached over and took her hand. "We're going to be alright, High Priestess. Not because we're protected — but because we remembered how to protect each other. And when this storm ends, I'll help rebuild. Brick by brick. Blade by blade. For Mihati. For all of them."

"We are," Solei whispered. "And this is just the beginning."

The trembling during Lehari's falter had reminded her: everything sacred is still vulnerable. And her children, still forming inside her, would be born into this new world — one forever changed.

She looked to the dome, to the man now rooted at its heart, and felt something shift within her.

Not fear.

Readiness.

The time was coming.

She could feel it in the aching swell of her belly, in the energy gathering low in her spine like an ancient tide. Soon, she would give birth — not just to children, but to a new era.

And when the shield eventually fell, as all shields must, she would be ready to rise.

CHAPTER TWENTY-ONE

BETWEEN THE VEIL AND THE LIGHT

It began in the softest hours of night, when the world itself seemed to hold its breath. The air was thick, saturated with the heavy scent of jasmine and damp moss, the very essence of the earth breathing in the stillness. Every inhalation carried with it the weight of ancient memory, the pulse of life thriving in the soil. Above, the canopy stretched endlessly, bathed in silver mist that hung between the trees like a veil separating worlds. The stars barely glimmered through the haze, their lights absorbed by the eternal shroud, as though the heavens themselves were holding their breath in reverence. Inside their small sanctuary, Solei stirred.

At first, it was nothing more than a pull—a faint, almost imperceptible tug in the deepest part of her belly, like the smallest ripple on an otherwise calm sea. But then, it deepened. It sharpens. It struck.

A cramp, sudden and violent, tore through her body, radiating from her womb like a shockwave, each pulse reverberating through her, shaking the very core of her being. It felt as if the Earth itself had roared and now shook beneath her. Her breath caught, momentarily stolen by the force. Her body felt as though it was being torn apart by the pull of gravity itself, every fiber of her being drawn toward some sacred, inevitable truth. She gasped, clutching the edge of the woven mat beneath her, its texture rough against her palm, as if grounding her in a world that was slipping away. Her body arched in response, instinctively trying to escape the fire racing through her veins, but it was futile.

Another wave came. Stronger. Deeper. More insistent. This was no ordinary pain—no simple ache of the flesh. It was an ancient ache, one that stretched back to the beginning of time, to the very birth of the cosmos. It was the ache of becoming. Of creation. Her glyphs, ancient symbols etched into her skin like sacred markings, shimmered to life—slow, molten gold tracing across her skin like rivers of light, filling the room with a soft, radiant glow.

The cry that escaped her lips was not human. It was primal. Raw. Elemental. A sound that echoed through the very fabric of reality itself. It was a sacred resonance, a vibration of the soul that could not be contained.

Pehani was already waking. His energy flared into the room before his body even moved, like a flame igniting the very air between them. He was at her side in an instant, crouched beside her, his hands trembling as they sought her shoulders, as though trying to steady the very storm that raged within her.

"Solei?" His voice was thick with concern, but there was something deeper there—something ancient, a knowing that ran as deep as the roots of the Earth itself. He was with her, always.

Her eyes met his—wide, luminous, filled with a mixture of terror, awe, and something more. "It's time," she whispered, her voice barely audible, tremulous with fear. "But... I don't know if I can do this."

His hand cupped her face, his touch warm and steady. He was the calm in her storm, the rock against which she could lean. "You already are," he said softly, his voice a promise. "You're not alone."

But even as he spoke, her body tensed again, each muscle clenching in agony as the next wave of energy gripped her. Her hands curled into the woven mat beneath her, its fibers digging into her skin. She cried out again, a sound so raw it shook the walls of their sanctuary, reverberating like the toll of an ancient bell, signaling a momentous, sacred occasion.

Outside, the village shield pulsed—a deep, resonant thrum that could be felt in the very marrow of the bones. Far across the compound, Zambia jerked awake. Her body responded as if guided by some unseen force, the change in the air electric, tangible. The air itself seemed to thicken, carrying with it a deep, reverberating hum, the heartbeat of the Earth, a song of life that reverberated through every living thing. She felt it in her bones.

It was not fear, but a knowing—a knowing that something ancient, something monumental, was unfolding.

Without hesitation, she rose.

Barefoot, her cloak flowing behind her like a dark flame, she sprinted through the mist-filled paths, her breath sharp in the cool night air, her heart pounding like a drum. Her glyphs, painted in violet and indigo, flared to life with each step, glowing like the night sky, lighting her way through the heavy mist. She moved with a sense of purpose, drawn to Solei as if the very earth was pulling her toward the source of the shift.

She burst into Solei's room, her energy colliding with the thick tension inside. "I felt it," she said, her voice breathless, her chest heaving as though the air itself had become too heavy to breathe. "The shield flickered. I knew something had changed."

Solei groaned again through another wave, sweat slicking her brow, her skin flushed with heat. She trembled with the force of the pain, her body wracked with each surge of energy. Zambia knelt beside her, her hand finding Solei's with a fierce tenderness, her fingers grounding her, offering comfort in the midst of the storm.

"You are not allowed to leave me," Zambia said, her voice thick with emotion, a strength forged from the deepest parts of her soul. "I swear it on every sacred breath I've ever taken—I will tear through the veil, drag you back, and curse every realm in between if I must."

Tears welled in her eyes, but they did not fall—no, they pooled in her gaze, the strength of her love shining through, steady and unyielding. "I can't lose you too."

Before Solei could respond, the door opened again, silently, like the turning of time itself. Amara, the elder midwife, entered, her presence filling the room with a reverence that softened the tension, turning it sacred. Her robes were the color of the deepest twilight, as though the very night sky had been draped over her. A silver braid, woven with wisdom, rested upon her head like a crown. In her hands, she carried bowls of sacred herbs, oils, and firestones—tools of an ancient craft, each one steeped in centuries of wisdom.

Her eyes swept over Solei with a reverence that was both gentle and knowing. "She carries light," Amara murmured softly, her voice low and full of awe. "And light never comes quietly."

Pehani stepped back, his energy weaving with Solei's as Amara knelt beside her. Her hands were warm as they sought Solei's pulse, and she placed warm cloths beneath her hips. Her chant filled the room—soft, rhythmic, like the beating of a distant drum. The air shifted, calming, softening, wrapping around Solei in a blanket of sacred rhythm, as though the entire universe had joined in her labor.

"Open," Amara whispered, her voice like a breeze through the trees. "Let the stars speak through you."

The labor began in earnest. And it was fire.

Solei's body became a vessel, a conduit for the cosmic forces of creation. Her hips split with pressure, her thighs trembling, her spine arching as if pulled toward the heavens. Every inch of her body felt as if it were being torn open by the power of creation itself, the pain so intense it blurred the lines between life and death. It was not her pain. It was the universe's. She was both the creator and the creation, the pain and the light.

She screamed—a sound that shattered the air, a primal cry that resonated with the deepest forces of the universe. Her soul called out, a desperate plea to the stars above, to the spirits who had woven her into being.

She wept—her tears mingling with the sweat of her brow, each one an offering to the unseen, to the journey of life and death. Her breath was ragged, her chest rising and falling like the tides of an ocean caught in a storm.

She called out to Lu Mai, her voice shaking with every breath, "Help me... please..."

Amara laid glowing stones across her abdomen and forehead, their warmth a contrast to the fire raging inside her. "Breathe," she said softly, her voice the balm to Solei's soul. "You are not alone."

But Solei was no longer sure she was here. The world around her dimmed, the edges of her vision blurring as she slipped beyond the realm of the physical. Everything faded, except for the rhythmic beat of her heart, the fire that burned in her bones, and the two souls flickering within her.

She reached for Pehani's hand, trembling as their fingers intertwined, a sacred vow shared between them. He held her hand like the promise of all eternity.

Zambia knelt behind her, her presence a constant, steady force that anchored Solei to this world. "You are strong," she whispered, her voice thick with reverence, with love. "You are sacred. You are needed."

And then—silence.

Her head fell to the side, her breath stilling, her heart faltering.

"Solei?" Pehani's voice cracked, torn by fear, his hand desperate against her chest.

"No," Zambia whispered, her throat thick with panic, her voice breaking. "No."

Amara pressed her fingers to Solei's neck, her touch careful, deliberate, searching. Her eyes softened as she felt the faintest pulse. "She's not gone," she said firmly, her voice carrying the weight of truth. "She's between."

And she was.

No longer in her body. No longer in the pain. No longer bound by breath.

Solei stood barefoot on luminous sand—the radiant shores of Sirius A, her soul's celestial origin. The twin suns bathed her in their soft, golden glow, casting no shadow, only light, filling her with warmth and peace. Above, the sky was a deep, endless indigo velvet, dotted with floating crystals that shimmered like the stars themselves, hanging suspended in the air. The air hummed with an eternal, silent song—an ancient melody that spoke of everything that had ever been and everything that would ever be.

Solei took a breath—not with her lungs, but with her soul, drawing in light, the very essence of creation itself. There was no ache here. No fire. No blood. No pain. Only peace. Only peace.

"Solei."

The voice called her name, soft and reverent, like stardust on still water. She turned and saw Lu Mai—the High Mother of their lineage—walking toward her, her presence radiating wisdom, compassion, and love. Her robes flowed like liquid moonlight, shimmering with opalescent veils that danced like the night sky itself. Her skin glowed with the light of the stars, not of the sun, but of the soul—the eternal light that never fades. Glyphs of living light shimmered across her arms, chest, and forehead, each one a testament to the ancient wisdom she held. Her hair floated around her like mist, braided with the stars, a part of the very fabric of the cosmos.

And her eyes—her eyes held galaxies, swirling with the knowledge of time itself.

Lu Mai stepped forward, and Solei, trembling, stepped into her embrace. It was like sinking into the heart of the universe itself. All pain, all fear, all doubt, all confusion dissolved in the light of her love. There was only peace.

"You have come far," Lu Mai whispered, her voice soft, resonating with love that was older than time itself.

"I couldn't hold on," Solei replied, her voice breaking under the weight of her fear. "It was too much. I thought I lost myself."

Lu Mai pulled back just enough to meet her gaze, her eyes filled with a love so pure it seemed to burn like a star. "You were never lost. You simply reached the edge of remembrance."

Tears welled in Solei's eyes. "I want to stay here. It's so beautiful. So... easy."

Lu Mai smiled—a smile that held the sorrow of the ages, and yet a knowing, a truth. "But the children," she said gently. "They still burn within you."

Solei looked down.

And there they were.

Two radiant flames—one golden-orange, wild and fierce like the heart of the sun; the other soft blue-violet, calm and deep, like the pulse of the ocean's heart. They flickered within her, synchronized with her heartbeat, alive and waiting.

"They are starborn," Lu Mai said softly, her voice filled with the depth of ancient wisdom. "They chose this world because of you."

Solei's voice trembled as she spoke, her heart breaking with love and fear. "I'm not ready. I don't know how to be a mother to... that."

Lu Mai's eyes softened, filled with compassion. "You are not here to be perfect. You are here to remember love in the face of pain. To show them how to rise after the breaking. That is motherhood."

Solei dropped to her knees, overwhelmed by fear and love. "I'm afraid."

Lu Mai knelt with her, her presence grounding, steady, a reminder that she was not alone. "Then carry your fear as you would carry them—close, but not in control."

For a long moment, they knelt together, beyond time, beyond space, two souls entwined in the sacred dance of remembrance.

Then Lu Mai reached forward, her hand soft as she touched Solei's forehead. With a single word, she breathed into Solei's soul.

"Return."

And light surged through Solei—not gentle, not quiet, but fierce. It was the light of creation itself, the light of a soul reborn. It was the roar of life, the scream of love, a cosmic embrace.

Solei returned.

Her body arched, struck by the force of a thousand stars. Her eyes flared open, wide and bright, her breath coming in ragged gasps. Her glyphs exploded in golden light, filling the room with divine energy.

"She's back!" Zambia cried, her voice breaking as her hands pressed to Solei's chest, grounding her, holding her close.

Pehani collapsed beside her, relief flooding through him as tears streamed down his face. He held two golden-swaddled infants in his arms, the miracle of life resting between them.

"You came back," he whispered, his voice trembling with emotion. "You came back to us."

Solei reached out, and as her fingertips brushed her children, the room transformed.

Light bloomed.

Not from fire or flame.

But from memory.

From soul.

A radiant pulse surged from Solei's chest, golden and warm, spiraling outward like sunlight through crystal. Pehani's aura responded instantly, expanding like a tidal wave of honeyed light. And from the twins—silver-blue and rose-gold threads unfurled, reaching outward, searching for their roots.

The air grew thick with vibration, a pulse of life that resonated through every being in the room. The midwife gasped, stepping back, her hand pressed to her heart. "The soul-bond," she whispered in awe. "It's awakening."

Solei felt it first in her skin—a tingling warmth, like starlight tracing every nerve. Then deeper, into her bones, into her womb, into the very thread of her being.

From the twins, two distinct energies rippled outward:

One—bright, pulsing, fierce. The energy of fire wrapped in laughter.

The other—deep, rhythmic, oceanic. The calm strength of water remembering the stars.

They reached not just for her body, but for her spirit.

She met them there.

And Pehani—holding them both—felt it too. His glyph of the Protector glowed across his chest as the energies of their children wove into his own, braiding them together like a living tapestry of light.

Mother.

Father.

Child.

Child.

A constellation of light. A soul-net of frequency.

The weavings didn't just link their hearts. They wrapped around their entire beings—spiraling through time, across past lives and future dreams. Glyphs shimmered into the air, ancient symbols of lineage, purpose, and love. They hovered, danced, and then gently dissolved into their skin, leaving behind a soft, sacred glow.

The twins' eyes opened—wide, ancient, filled with the wisdom of the stars.

They saw her.

Not as a stranger.

But as the one who had answered their call.

Tears streamed down Solei's cheeks. She gathered them into her arms, her body weak but held upright by something larger than flesh. Pehani knelt beside her, wrapping his arms around them. Their foreheads touched. Their breath synchronized.

And in that moment, they became one.

A soul weaving complete.

Zambia dropped to her knees beside them, her face flushed with tears, her hands pressed to Solei's knee in reverence. She didn't speak at first—only pressed her forehead to the earth.

Then, her voice cracked, but strong: "You brought back the light. You left the veil and returned holding stardust."

Solei smiled weakly, her heart full. "They called to me. I came for them."

Zambia looked up, her voice steady, unwavering. "Then I'll protect them with everything I am. I swear it on Luneia's name."

Solei reached for her hand, and they sat together—two women, two flames, softened by grief, glowing with love.

Outside, the village stirred. The shield surrounding Lumeria pulsed once—soft, shimmering, as if acknowledging what had just been born. The air shifted. Trees bent toward the house. Crystals in the walkways chimed like wind-bells, their tones light and jubilant.

In the distance, birdsong broke the morning silence—notes that hadn't been heard in eons. Flowers bloomed, petals unfurling as if drawn by the breath of new life.

And overhead, the twin moons gleamed brighter, glowing for a moment before fading into the rising dawn.

The Earth had felt it.

Lumeria had received them.

And in the heart of the village, something ancient had been reborn.

CHAPTER TWENTY-TWO

THE INTEGRATION OF THE TWIN FLAMES

When Solei awoke the next morning, what remained was a stillness unlike any she had ever felt. The air outside shimmered with gentle mist, dew-kissed leaves glistening beneath the pale sunlight, as if nature itself was breathing in the newness of life. Birds sang softly from the forest's edge, tentative notes fluttering into the silence, as if they were testing the calm that had settled over the land. Inside the birthing hut, time itself felt suspended—each passing second hanging in reverence for the sacredness that had transpired.

Solei lay propped against a mound of soft pillows, her body sore and trembling, each breath a fragile testament to the strength that had carried her through the night. Yet, her eyes—those deep, radiant eyes—were clear and luminous, glowing with wonder and disbelief, as if she were seeing the world through a veil of holy remembrance. Her heart swelled with an emotion too vast for words, a rush of relief, awe, and something ancient, as if her very soul had unlocked a long-forgotten truth. It was as if she had touched something eternal, something her soul had always known but had not yet remembered.

The twins lay beside her, nestled in the warmth of her skin, their breath light and rhythmic, a divine lullaby. Solei studied them as though memorizing the very stars that had shaped their essence. One child had skin like sunlit pearl, soft and radiant, glowing faintly in the morning's light. Their skin, a blend of bluish-greenish-grey, held the ethereal quality of the Lumerian lineage, almost translucent—like the light itself was woven into their flesh. Tiny strands of dark silver-blue hair curled delicately against their forehead, and their eyes, barely opened, shimmered with the flicker of a forest fire—wild, untamed, alive.

The other child, slightly smaller, shared the same luminous hue, but their skin carried the cool tones of moonstone, with lavender undertones that seemed to shift with the light. Their eyes, calm and open, mirrored the depths of ancient oceans, infinite and knowing, holding memories of a time before time. Unlike the others of their kind, the twins bore delicate, glowing symbols etched only on their hands and feet—intricate spirals and lines, sacred markings, as if the stars had kissed them before they ever took form on Earth.

Both children radiated the unmistakable Lumerian glow—a soft, shimmering light beneath their skin, as if galaxies themselves coursed through their veins. Their presence was magnetic, drawing the sacred energy of the island itself, filling the space with an almost tangible reverence. Sacred.

Zambia knelt nearby, her face caught between awe and devotion, her breath barely escaping her lips. "They don't look like babies," she whispered, her voice trembling with the weight of her reverence. "They look like love made visible. Like light wrapped in skin and born from the stars themselves."

Pehani chuckled softly from where he sat behind Solei, his hand resting gently on her shoulder, but his eyes were brimming with unspoken emotion. "They are what Lumeria has been waiting for," he said, his voice low, reverent. His gaze never left the twins—there was no awe alone in his eyes, but a deeper recognition. He saw not just his children, but the beginning of a new era. The dawn of something sacred and powerful, a turning of the age that trembled through his very soul.

Solei blinked slowly, her lips parting, as tears pooled once again in her eyes—silent and steady. "I saw them before they came," she whispered, her voice thick with emotion. "I saw their souls in Sirius. I didn't know their names then... but I do now."

She turned to the child on her left, the warmth of their tiny hand cradled in her palm. "This one is named Kael. Flame of the forest. Spark of transformation."

Then she looked to the smaller child, cradling their hand with the same reverence. "And this one... Amari. Stillness of water. Heart of the divine."

Zambia pressed a hand over her mouth, tears streaming silently down her cheeks, her whole being trembling with emotion. The sight of Solei—radiant, alive, and holding the children they had once feared might not come—broke something open in her. Her heart surged with pride, reverence, and an unexpected, fierce protective love. It was a love so primal, so deep, it felt like it had always been there, buried beneath the surface, waiting for this moment to unfold.

Pehani leaned in, his lips pressing softly against Solei's temple. "Kael and Amari," he echoed, his voice filled with tenderness. "The future of Lumeria."

Outside, the first rays of full sunlight broke through the clouds, casting golden beams across the village, as if the heavens themselves were offering a blessing. Birds soared above, and the trees seemed to lean closer, their leaves whispering in the soft morning breeze.

And the people—sensing the shift, feeling the divine pulse—began to gather at the edge of the birthing hut. They were not drawn by curiosity, but by something much deeper. A knowing. The twins had arrived—the children of the High Priestess of Lumeria, born of starlight and prophecy, carrying the legacy of a divine bloodline written in the very codes of the cosmos. And nothing—nothing—would ever be the same again.

Three days later, under a sky cleansed by storm and brushed with golden mist, the villagers gathered once again for the Integration Ceremony—an ancient rite, reserved for the arrival of prophesied souls.

At the center of the ceremonial grove, a vast circle of moon-stone had been prepared, etched with ancient glyphs that shimmered softly beneath the morning light. The trees surrounding the clearing bowed gently inward, their limbs adorned with silken ribbons, feathers, and bells that chimed with the slightest breeze, a sacred melody carried by the wind.

Solei stood at the edge of the circle, robed in flowing white and lavender, her body healed, strong, and serene. There was a quiet power in her, a grace that radiated from within. Beside her, Pehani stood, cradling Amari, the sacred child, against his chest. Zambia, wrapped in ceremonial copper and turquoise, held Kael close, her posture proud, protective, her heart swelling with the love she had for both children.

The entire village had come—elders leaning on staffs, their eyes glistening with emotion; children holding bundles of herbs, their small hands steady with the weight of responsibility; warriors and healers wrapped in radiant cloth, their faces open with reverence, their hearts full of silent prayer. The air was thick with the fragrance of sacred herbs, rich with the energy of collective anticipation. There was no need for words—only the silent communion of souls bound together in reverence.

The High Seer stepped forward, her hands graceful as she anointed the twins' foreheads with shimmering stardust oil. The liquid shimmered with the light of distant galaxies, a balm of divine blessing. She placed a sunstone crystal at each child's feet, and golden threads of energy unwound from the stones, spiraling around the twins like strands of living light. The glyphs etched into the moonstone beneath them pulsed with soft hues of aqua and rose, casting radiant patterns into the air—sacred breath, sacred light.

The energy in the air thickened, and invisible threads of light spiraled above the children's heads, a swirling lattice of protection, wisdom, and ancient lineage. These were not just lights, but living, breathing symbols of divine purpose.

"These are not just children," the High Seer intoned, her voice rich with reverence. "They are keys. Bridges. Portals between worlds. They carry memories not written, and light not yet seen. And we—the people of Lumeria—are the stewards of that light."

A soft hush fell, and then, like a prayer released into the air, the chorus of crystal bowls rang out, their tones cascading in waves of pure resonance. Each note shimmered with color—violet, gold, teal—sending ripples of energy through the grove. The vibrations moved through the bodies of the villagers, cleansing old grief, aligning their hearts with the ancient frequencies of the Lumerian bloodline. The light above the twins danced, swirling and spiraling, as if in response to the sound—a sacred exchange of energy and memory.

Kael stirred, his soft cry rising in harmony with the breeze, and a nearby flame leapt higher, responding to the energy in the air.

Amari blinked slowly, and the wind itself seemed to pause, holding its breath.

Gasps rippled through the crowd.

Zambia laughed through her tears, her voice full of wonder. "I told you they weren't normal."

Solei stepped into the circle, the hem of her robe trailing behind her, leaving a trail of soft silver sparks in her wake. As she lifted both children into the light, beams of golden energy from above seemed to converge around them, forming a halo of radiant tendrils that danced like gentle flames. The energy was palpable—ancient, intelligent, and full of grace. It shimmered in hues unseen by the human eye, infusing the breath of every villager present, and filling the space with an overwhelming sense of sacred recognition.

"They are not meant to be hidden," Solei's voice rang out, clear and steady. "They are meant to be known. Witnessed. Integrated."

And in that moment, the people bowed—not in worship, but in awe, recognizing the divine truth that stood before them.

The Integration Ceremony had begun.

As the final note of the crystal bowls faded into the air, a pulse of light surged upward from the moonstone circle. The ground beneath the twins glowed with brilliant white-gold light, and from it emerged two small stones—smooth and perfect—each etched with intricate spiraling glyphs that shimmered with blue and silver fire. They hovered for a moment before gently lowering into Solei's open palms, the crowd watching in stunned silence.

The High Seer stepped forward again, her voice a soft whisper, reverent and full of awe. "A gift from the Source," she said.

"Two stones of living protection. One for each child. Carved not by hand, but by energy—encoded with the language of the stars."

The stones pulsed with quiet power.

Solei cradled them close to her heart, tears falling freely down her face. "They will be shielded," she whispered. "By light. By memory. By love."

As she held them, the stones hummed with ancient promise—alive, warm, and radiant.

The High Seer nodded solemnly. "These stones are to be placed within their home," she said, turning to the village. "One at each entrance, where the energies of the world cross the threshold. They will guard not just the children, but the sanctity of their soul paths—the sacred contracts they were born to fulfill. Nothing misaligned shall enter."

A murmur of awe rippled through the gathered villagers as Solei cradled the stones to her chest, understanding their sacred purpose.

Lumeria would never again be only what it was. It was becoming what it was always meant to be.

Chapter Twenty-Three

SACRED RHYTHMS OF LOVE AND GROWTH

In the days that followed the Integration Ceremony, a gentle rhythm returned to Lumeria — not marked by urgency, but by reverence, like the Earth itself exhaled. Mist clung softly to the trees at dawn, catching the early light like strands of silver silk. The stone paths shimmered with dew, and laughter spilled like warm honey through the winding village corridors. The storm was a memory now, its scars softened by sunlight and the sounds of laughter drifting through the village paths.

Yet beyond the soft rhythms of renewal, one force remained unbroken — Lehari. Still seated at the edge of the village, beneath the ancient arch of flowering stone, he held the great shield steady. Day and night, the dome of light shimmered above them, powered by his breath, his will, and the rising current of love from every soul he protected. His presence was both beacon and boundary — the unseen sentinel guarding their rebirth. Though the rains had slowed, the floodwaters still raged beyond, and the energy required to keep the barrier strong flowed constantly from his core like an unending prayer.

At the heart of Solei and Pehani's home, where Kael and Amari now lay nestled in soft woven cradles, a sacred presence had begun to form — not of celestial light or ancient magic, but of something even more enduring: the circle of elder women.

From the moment the twins arrived, the elder women of the village took it upon themselves to surround the young family with loving, purposeful support. They were a mix of warmth and fire — loving but sassy, bossy yet full of timeless wisdom. They moved like a silent symphony — shawls fluttering like wings as they drifted from room to room, arms laden with baskets of sun-ripened fruit, bundles of luminous healing herbs, and cloths still warm from stone-washed rivers. Their voices wove through the air in lilting song, harmonizing with the gentle coos of the twins like lullabies of the ancestors. A few of them, especially the sharp-tongued Auntie Kelaya, had no qualms about teasing Pehani whenever he fumbled a diaper wrap or held a baby like a ceremonial staff.

"Oh, child," she'd chortle, hands on hips, "that's a baby, not a scroll of prophecy. Support the neck, not the stars!"

The others would laugh softly, shaking their heads as Pehani blushed and adjusted his hold with a sheepish grin. It became part of the morning rhythm — the babies cooing, the elders bustling, and Pehani being lovingly corrected as only village aunties could.

It was not just a tradition — it was their purpose. Their joy.

In Lumeria, it was well understood that the first years of a child's life were sacred — a time meant for deep bonding, for quiet presence, for the kind of connection that would echo through generations. And so the village made space for that bond to grow without interruption.

No mother or father was left to shoulder the weight of care alone. The elder women had done their part in seasons past, and now, they offered their wisdom and their hands freely — not out of duty, but out of devotion.

"This," one of them whispered to Solei as she braided a garland of glowing blossoms, "is the current that keeps the river of love flowing in our village."

Their presence brought more than help — it brought sacred balance. It was as though the very walls of the home softened under their touch, the air becoming thicker with warmth, a fragrant blend of crushed jasmine, simmering root stew, and rose oil. Their laughter bounced off the stone like wind chimes stirred by memory. By relieving the family of everyday tasks, they allowed Solei and Pehani to remain fully present — to nourish their children with undivided hearts, to sleep when they could, to rise with joy instead of exhaustion.

And perhaps most importantly, their gentle care rippled outward like waves of golden light moving through the village. Gardens seemed greener, the air sweeter. Children played with more ease. Even the birds flew lower, singing lullabies over rooftops as if blessing every soul beneath them. The entire village felt the ease. There was more laughter. More softness. More space to breathe.

Love was the lifeblood of Lumeria. And in those early days, it flowed strongest through the arms of the elders who had carried it the longest.

Yet beneath the softness, Solei and Pehani were learning to navigate a new rhythm — not just as parents, but as partners. They were adjusting, day by day, to the delicate balance of holding space for their children while still tending to the sacred flame between them.

Solei, the High Priestess, was filled with wisdom and deep intuitive knowing. When she became a mother, her gifts amplified — expanding her already powerful awareness with heightened instincts, gentle sensitivity, and a new layer of fierce, nurturing presence. She could sense the subtlest shifts in her children's energy and knew how to calm them with just a breath, a touch, a hum of her voice. Pehani, with his Lumerian warrior energy, found his own gifts transforming as well. The moment he held their newborns, his protectiveness deepened into something primal and sacred. His senses sharpened, and his movements became more attuned — not only to danger, but to tenderness. His strength bent toward service. His courage took the shape of fatherhood. Together, they were powerful. But power did not make things easy.

They butted heads from time to time — a clash of sacred roles, a dance of fire and water. One evening, as the moon cast soft light over their home, Solei sat cradling Amari while Kael fussed restlessly in the cradle nearby.

"I think they need to be fed again," Solei said gently.

"They just ate an hour ago," Pehani replied, already reaching for the calming stones.

Solei watched him for a moment, her brow furrowing slightly. "Their energy feels unsettled. Kael especially."

Pehani sighed. "They're babies, Solei. Of course they're unsettled."

Solei's voice softened. "Sometimes they cry because of what *we're* holding, not just what *they're* feeling."

Pehani turned, eyes narrowing just slightly. "Are you saying this is my fault?"

"I'm saying..." Solei paused, choosing her words with care. "I can feel something in you. Tension. Anger. You haven't said anything, but it's there. And Kael, especially, seems to be responding to it."

Pehani clenched his jaw, looking away. "I didn't want to burden you."

"You're not burdening me," she said, placing a gentle hand over his. "You're my partner. Whatever you carry, I carry too. But you have to let me in."

A long silence followed. Then Pehani whispered, "I just feel like I'm failing. I'm supposed to be strong, but half the time I don't know what I'm doing."

Solei leaned in, pressing her forehead gently to his. "You're not failing. You're learning. Just like I am."

She pulled back just enough to look into his eyes, her voice soft and steady, but laced with a sly smile. "And it's okay not to get everything right the first time. That's what being human is — especially when we're stepping into something new like this. Parenting doesn't come with a scroll of instructions."

She leaned in, eyes glinting playfully. "Because let's be honest, if there *was* a scroll of instructions, you'd skip straight to the part titled 'Warrior's Guide to Baby Swaddling and Not Freaking Out — With Diagrams.'"

Pehani let out a reluctant laugh, and Solei continued, her tone warm. "We make mistakes. We stumble. But that's how we grow. That's how we learn. And every time we choose to try again — with more patience, more presence — we empower ourselves."

They stayed like that for a moment — until Kael let out an impressively loud spit-up that landed directly on Pehani's chest.

Solei burst into laughter. Pehani groaned. And even Amari gave a hiccup that sounded suspiciously like a giggle.

And just like that, the tension would break — not with words, but with laughter, with grace, with a reminder that divine love often hides in the smallest, messiest moments.

Solei would laugh. Pehani would groan and reach for a cloth. And somewhere in the space between, there'd be a whisper —

not always heard, but deeply felt. A reminder from Lu Mai, as if woven into the moment itself:

This is not a battle. This is a dance. You are not here to win — you are here to rise together.

And so they did. With laughter, with humility, with sacred imperfection, they rose again and again — a priestess and a warrior learning to parent the future of Lumeria, one sacred mess at a time.

Through each misunderstanding and every minor clash, something sacred began to root between them — a deeper knowing of each other's rhythms, an unspoken language carved in quiet moments and softened edges. They learned that their differences were not obstacles, but mirrors — ways to see each other more clearly. And with each moment of frustration that transformed into laughter, with each disagreement that became a doorway to deeper understanding, their love grew stronger.

Once they remembered what was truly important — their connection, their family, their sacred purpose — they stopped trying to be right and started learning how to move as one. Side by side. Heart to heart. Solving each challenge not as opponents, but as co-creators of a life woven in light.

One morning, golden light spilled through the vine-covered windows, casting dancing shadows across the stone floor. The soft murmur of morning songbirds echoed from the garden, and the scent of sweet lotus root tea lingered in the air. Pehani gently rocked Kael in his arms, his warrior frame swaying with surprising grace, while Solei rested nearby on a woven floor cushion, the glow of early light kissing her skin.

Auntie Kelaya sat peeling fruit at the table, humming a tune older than memory, her hands moving with the ease of a hundred lifetimes. Her skin shimmered in hues of greenish-greyish-blue, aged but radiant — like the last light of dusk resting on sacred waters. Her hair, wild and lighter than sky-soaked midnight, was tangled with feathers from exotic birds — so many, in fact, that when she walked away, she seemed more creature of the air than elder of the earth. She wore flowing, boldly colored garments that caught the light with every movement, and her arms jingled with an outrageous number of bracelets, each one a story from another time.

She was fabulous, fierce, wise, and beloved.

Without looking up, she said, "You know, child, all the best fathers and husbands I've ever known made every mistake under the stars. Burnt the stew. Forgot the herbs. Wrapped babies like scrolls. But they kept showing up. They kept trying. That's the trait your little ones will look for in their own partners someday. Not perfection — but presence. And you know what else? It'll make you a better father," she added, her tone both firm and kind. "When they grow up and face their own storms, you'll know how to guide them — not by fixing everything, but by standing beside them. Holding them with love, but giving them room to fall, to learn, to rise. That kind of quiet wisdom from the divine masculine? That's what stays with a child. That's what shapes who they choose to walk with in life.""

Pehani paused, his arms tightening slightly around the baby, but his brows furrowed. His voice was low, uncertain. "I hear what you're saying, but... it's hard to feel like that's enough. When I'm in it — when I feel like I'm getting everything wrong — I can't see the lesson. I just feel like I'm failing, again."

Auntie Kelaya looked up at him then, her eyes sharp with clarity and kind with age. "That's because you're still seeing through the lens of your fear, not your truth. Let that soften. Let it pass. Because fear will always tell you you're not enough — but love will remind you that your presence is what plants the roots."

She set down the fruit and reached across the table, tapping his hand lightly. "And let me offer you one more thing, child. You and Solei? You need time. Not just as parents, but as lovers. As individuals. There's no balance when you forget who you are beyond the crying and the cradles. Make space for yourselves, for each other. That's how the roots grow deeper. That's how you keep your bond sacred. And remember — you are not just new parents, you are also Solei the High Priestess and Pehani the Lead Warrior. You carry sacred roles beyond your home. You must learn to balance the call of your people with the call of your hearts. That balance, child — that's the true art of union."

Pehani looked toward Solei then, his eyes softening with a kind of awe, as though seeing her for the first time — not only as the High Priestess or the mother of his children, but as the radiant soul whose light had always guided his path. The golden sunlight pooled around her like a halo, casting soft shadows across her cheeks, her expression both tender and ancient. Her smile was small but knowing, and when their eyes met, something sacred stirred in the air between them — a stillness, a hum, a pulse of recognition. It was a moment of quiet revelation — not loud or ceremonial, but soul-deep, as if time itself had paused to witness their love become something even more enduring. The air shimmered, the walls of their home seeming to breathe with them, letting love in a little deeper than before.

It was a reminder he didn't know he needed — and it landed like a blessing in his soul, spreading warmth through his chest like the morning sun rising after a long, starless night. Outside, the light stretched softly across the village, touching every leaf, every stone, as if honoring the quiet miracle unfolding inside their home.

Chapter Twenty-Four
THE HEART OF LIGHT

Y ears had passed.

Though the great flood no longer roared with the same fury, Lehari still remained at the edge of the village — seated beneath the ancient flowering arch — holding the protective shield over Lumeria with unwavering strength. His body was older now, but his spirit burned with quiet devotion. And he was not alone.

Every morning, just as the sky blushed with the first breath of sunrise, the villagers emerged from their homes, cloaked in the glow of early light. The air shimmered with dew and the sweet scent of crushed hibiscus and sandalwood. They walked in reverent silence, the soles of their feet brushing against the sacred earth, leaving trails of warmth with each step. Birds circled above, their cries like songs of remembrance. As the villagers arrived at the sacred grounds, a quiet current of anticipation rippled through them. They moved like a river of souls flowing toward purpose, forming a great circle around Lehari — the heart of their protection, their enduring sentinel of light.

Together, they joined hands — fingers woven not just in gesture, but in spirit. A pulse moved through the circle the moment skin met skin — a soft jolt of connection, a breath shared by many. In perfect silence, their hearts opened like flowers in bloom, and golden filaments of energy began to rise from their bodies — ribbons of light that swirled through the air, weaving a tapestry of collective devotion above them.

This was the Elaran'Shae Ritual of Universal Gratitude — a ceremony of cosmic remembering. As they gave thanks for all that existed — within themselves, within one another, in this world and all others — the energy around them thickened with light. Gratitude pulsed through the circle like a golden heartbeat, stretching across timelines and dimensions. The earth beneath their feet hummed. The sky shimmered in response. It was more than a ritual. It was their lifeline — a sacred pulse that tethered them to the divine.

As they channeled unconditional love and reverence, currents of iridescent energy rose from their bodies, spiraling into the dome above. The shield shimmered with renewed brilliance — luminous layers of blues, violets, and silver dancing like flames of protection. It flickered with cosmic patterns — ancient glyphs and swirling runes that only appeared in moments of highest resonance, forming and dissolving like breath on glass. Lehari, seated at the center, felt the surge move through him like lightning wrapped in silk. His fingertips tingled, his spine alight with the pulse of divine presence. The flood of energy entered his chest and unfurled like a great lotus — wide, radiant, eternal. His eyes, closed in devotion, shimmered with moisture as the energy moved deeper. His aging bones were kissed with light, his spirit buoyed by the breath of the collective. The weariness that clung to his muscles melted like morning mist, and in its place rose a sense of quiet bliss — a sacred fusion of strength and surrender. It not only sustained him — it healed the village. Wounds in the hearts of warriors dissolved into peace. Old aches in the elders' joints softened into song. Children ran freer. The land pulsed with restored vitality.

At the center of the circle, Solei sat in deep meditation. Her robes shimmered with threads of crystal and shadow, reflecting both light and remembrance. Her presence was an anchor — serene, divine, utterly present.

She served as the sacred conduit — the anchor of celestial alchemy.

She drew in the villagers' gratitude like a chalice being filled with light, her hands open on her knees, fingers glowing with translucent gold. Her breath moved in perfect harmony with theirs — inhaling the vibrational field of their unified devotion. From the depths of their offering, she called forth unspoken burdens — tension in the bellies of mothers, doubt resting in the shoulders of young warriors, grief curled inside the chests of widows. These emotions rose like shadows, spiraling around her in mist-like tendrils. They passed through her body, alchemized by her love, and descended into the earth beneath.

The stones glowed faintly, pulsing in time with her heartbeat. She whispered ancient phrases, words passed down from Sirius A, and sent the energies back to the Great Mother — who wrapped them in her earthen embrace and returned only light. It was a sacred alchemy. A transmutation of sorrow into sacred fuel. A recycling of pain into peace — nourishment for all beings, seen and unseen.

This act, repeated each morning, was more than spiritual maintenance. It was evolution. It was what allowed them to thrive — not just as individuals, but as a collective family. The Ritual reminded them that they were one — not despite their differences, but because of them.

And so each day began not with worry, but with wonder.

Not with fear, but with unity — a pulsing remembrance that they were not broken, not separate, but pieces of the same divine song, rising together in harmony.

It was the rhythm of Lumeria.

The rhythm of remembrance.

The rhythm of love.

Life in Lumeria blossomed with radiance. The golden years flowed like a river of honey, and the presence of the twins, Kael and Amari, brought a kind of magic that softened the edges of time. It wasn't just that they were children of prophecy — it was the way they *lived*. They laughed with the purity of stars, argued like ancient spirits learning to be human, and carried the subtle light of something far beyond what words could hold.

They were growing quickly, with curious hearts and vibrant minds. Each day they danced barefoot through sacred lessons — practicing the ancient movements that once summoned rain, reciting chants that could realign a soul, and sitting cross-legged beside elders who told stories woven with constellations and the breath of the sea. Their learning was not structured — it was sung, touched, danced, lived. They were being shaped by love itself, and joy was their most devoted teacher.

One warm afternoon, Solei walked barefoot through the village, her long silk robe trailing behind her like a veil of twilight stitched with starlight. She had always loved the feeling of bare feet on the sacred earth — the way the blue moss seemed to pulse gently beneath her soles, whispering ancient songs to her spirit. It grounded her, made her feel more alive, more whole. The soft contact between skin and soil reminded her she was both stardust and seed.

The moss beneath her feet glowed with her steps, as if greeting her soul's radiance. The air shimmered with warmth, touched by the fragrance of wild plum, goldenroot, and something soft and sweet — perhaps from the flowering skies that hung low over the trees. Her fingers trailed along ivy-covered walls, her heart attuned to the pulse of the land.

Ahead, she heard it before she saw it — the sound of childhood bursting open. Laughter — high, wild, and free — rang through the village like sacred music. And then she saw them.

Zambia sat in the middle of the play circle, arms overflowing with giggling children, including her spirited daughter Mihati, whose laughter rose like bells on the wind. The warriors — some of the most stoic and scarred protectors of Lumeria — knelt nearby with the grace of boulders being asked to pirouette. They had been conscripted into an elaborate game involving painted stones, glittery cloth, and the official title of "Royal Rainbow Dragons." One warrior, infamous for his stone-faced silence and stormy gaze, now sat with his legs tucked beneath him, a lopsided flower crown perched precariously on his head. A tiny girl, perhaps three, was patting his cheek gently with her palm and nodding with solemn approval, as if to reassure him, "You'll do just fine." The sight of it — the warrior's wide-eyed bewilderment, the child's fearless tenderness — was enough to make the stars themselves giggle.

The elders lounged in nearby hammocks like guardian spirits at rest — their silver-toned skin catching flecks of sunlight like stardust on still waters. Some knitted with threads that shimmered under the sun, weaving not just garments but blessings into every stitch. Others hummed lullabies that carried old magic — notes that vibrated through the trees and seemed to calm even the wind. Their eyes glistened — not just with amusement, but with the kind of tears that come from witnessing the very thing they had prayed for: generations healing, lineage restoring. Each child was a prayer returned, each laugh an answered call — echoing into the soul like the gentle bell of prophecy fulfilled.

Solei paused, her heart swelling so fully it ached — in that good, ancient way. Her eyes welled with tears she didn't bother to wipe away. The sight before her was breathtaking — not because it was grand, but because it was sacred. This was what they had bled for, fought for, waited lifetimes to remember. A village in bloom. Children as bridges. Warriors kneeling in play. Elders humming blessings through time. A sacred orchestra of souls in harmony, wrapped in light and held by love.

She saw Pehani watching the children too, a half-smile softening his usually guarded expression as Kael darted toward him, shrieking with joy, curls bouncing, arms flung wide like wings. Pehani bent to scoop him up, and in that moment, he looked less like a warrior and more like a starstruck father caught in the gravity of love. Nearby, Amari was cradled in the lap of an elder healer, her greenish-blue eyes unblinking, soaking in every shimmer, every sound, every breath of magic around her like a tiny oracle reading the heartbeat of the world. She held the elder's thumb with one hand and a petal in the other, still and powerful in her watching — as if memorizing the soul of the day.

Solei pressed a hand to her heart, overcome by the swell of love that rose like a wave within her chest. Her fingers trembled slightly against her breastbone, not from weakness, but from the sheer beauty of witnessing her people living in such radiant harmony. The laughter of children danced through the air like sacred song, and the sight of warriors adorned with flower crowns and elders cradling joy in their arms made her spirit shimmer. A single tear traced down her cheek, kissed by sunlight. She whispered softly to herself, voice thick with reverence,

"They are the light we've been preparing for — the dream we planted long ago now blooming before our eyes."

And in that moment, Lumeria glowed — not from the shield above, but from the love that pulsed through its people, bright as the stars they had once descended from.

Yet even wrapped in such beauty, Solei felt a quiet tension beneath her joy. It was difficult to even think of the Shadowed in the midst of such radiant living — to imagine that anything so dark could find its way into something so luminous. But she knew better. She had seen too much, carried too much. She could not let herself be lulled into forgetting.

She whispered a silent promise into the breeze: to remain focused, strong, and balanced — for her children, for Pehani, for the village.

Even Lu Mai and the sacred flood, as powerful as they were, may not be enough to keep out the evil of the Shadowed. The dreamweavers had warned her in visions woven from starlight and shadow — the Shadowed were driven by a hunger that did not tire. A lust for light so deep it warped their very essence.

And no flood could stop what would come if they found their way.

Solei turned her face to the sky, her eyes reflecting both the joy of now and the storm of what might be.

The joy in her chest, as warm and radiant as it was, lived alongside an ancient knowing — that love this powerful always attracted shadows that longed to consume it. As the golden air whispered around her, Solei felt the pull of something stirring far beyond the horizon, like thunder drumming beneath the sea. She didn't know when the Shadowed would come — only that they would. The dreamweavers' visions haunted the edges of her sleep. They showed flickers of clawed hands reaching through veils of light, voices twisted with hunger for what they could never create — only steal.

Her hand returned to her heart.

She closed her eyes and breathed in the scent of jasmine and plum, grounding herself in the beauty of now, anchoring her spirit to the present.

She would protect it.

Even if the stars themselves trembled.

CHAPTER TWENTY-FIVE

THREE FLAMES, ONE HEART

One night Solei and Zambia went on their night walk, one they had done for many years, they loved to soak in the moon at its fullest.

The forest glowed around them — a living sanctuary of light and breath, cradled in an ancient lullaby sung by the land itself. Emerald leaves quivered with crystalline dew, reflecting scattered rainbows with every subtle shift of wind, as if the trees were painting the air with color. Violet blossoms unfurled in slow, sacred spirals, releasing soft waves of fragrance that smelled of honey, cedar, and starlight — a scent that lingered like a memory at the edge of dreams, tugging gently on the heart. Luminous vines draped overhead like glowing rivers of spirit, weaving in and out of the ancient trees, each one pulsing faintly with iridescent energy that mirrored the quiet rhythm of the heart. The canopy above shimmered with hues of turquoise and rose gold, as though the sky itself had come closer to witness their sacred walk. Tiny orbs of bioluminescent light floated lazily through the air, trailing sparkles behind them like echoes of magic, some resting briefly on petals, others dissolving into dust the moment they touched skin. The very ground beneath their feet seemed to hum, the moss warm and yielding, rising slightly with each step as if the Earth herself breathed beneath their soles — aware, loving, alive. It was a realm between worlds, where every root held memory, every breeze carried prayer, and time bowed in reverence to love.

This garden, nestled deep within the ancient forest, was a place of otherworldly magic — the kind that held time in a soft pause, that wrapped around sorrow like a shawl, and healed wounds too old for memory. Every leaf shimmered with intention. Every breeze carried whispers of ancestral prayers.

Solei and Zambia walked side by side, their robes whispering against the forest floor, trailing behind them like stardust threads, catching on the tips of the moss like threads of a greater tapestry being woven by the Earth itself. Hints of opal and moonstone shimmered from the woven fabric, catching the flickering sunlight that streamed through the canopy in soft waves, casting living patterns of light and shadow across their skin like blessings from the sky. The colors shifted as they moved — blush golds, aquamarines, hints of pale amethyst — an ethereal dance of harmony between fabric, form, and forest. Their silence was not emptiness — it was a communion, a wordless prayer shared between two hearts tethered by lifetimes of devotion, forged through tears, triumphs, and soul-bound trust.

With every step, they moved like a single breath, echoing the rhythm of a sacred bond that needed no voice to be understood.

They said nothing at first — they didn't have to. The trees bore witness. The wind listened. The air pulsed gently with their love and trust.

"I don't say this enough," Zambia finally whispered, brushing a vine aside as they passed beneath an arch of flowering moon-vine that shimmered like woven starlight, her voice trembling with the weight of the truth it carried, "but I am so grateful for you. Truly. You carry so much, Solei — more than any one soul should ever have to. And still, you move through it all with such grace, like moonlight dancing across the ocean, never breaking even when the waves rise. I see you. We all do. And I thank the stars every day that I get to walk beside someone like you — not just as our High Priestess, but as my sister."

Her breath hitched, emotion flooding her chest. "And after Luneia... after I held her hand and felt her leave this world... I don't know how I would have survived. You were there when I collapsed. You stayed through every silence, every scream, every hour when I felt like my bones might shatter from the weight of grief. You helped me care for Mihati when I didn't even know how to rise in the morning. You reminded me I was still a mother. You reminded me I was still a soul worthy of healing. Your healing, your presence... your love — it didn't just help me. It saved me, Solei. In every way that mattered. You were my light when I couldn't see."

Solei's lips curved in a soft, tender smile, her eyes glimmering with unshed tears that caught the forest light like morning dew on crystal petals. A tremor moved through her chest, the kind of ache that came when love was so full it had nowhere to go but out through tears. The emotions rising within her were ancient and profound — the kind that lived deep in the soul, passed through lifetimes. She reached out, her fingers trailing gently along Zambia's arm before placing her head on her shoulder, exhaling softly as if that simple act allowed the weight of her heart to be shared. The warmth radiating from Zambia wrapped around her like a sacred cloak, pulling her into the safety of remembrance, of sisterhood, of a love so unconditional it left the soul bare and whole all at once.

For a moment, the world vanished. There was no war, no prophecy, no pressure to be anything other than this: a woman in the arms of someone who had chosen her a thousand times. Her breath caught — not from sadness, but from the overwhelming rush of love, of gratitude, of awe at the depth of this bond. "And I'm grateful for you, my sister," she whispered, voice soft as prayer, breaking only slightly with emotion. "I never walk alone. Not really. Because you're always right there — holding the parts of me I sometimes forget to carry. Loving the parts I sometimes struggle to see."

Zambia stilled, her eyes glistening as she turned toward Solei. She placed a firm, reverent hand over her friend's. "You are the anchor that keeps this world upright. I will protect you with everything I am, Solei. Everything. Lumeria breathes because of your breath. The stars sing because your heart remembers how to listen. The village, our children, Pehani — they need your light. They follow your rhythm. And your children — they carry the light, but *you* are the source."

A silence followed — heavy, sacred.

And then, the moment cracked — a sharp snap of a branch echoed through the hush like thunder shattering glass. Both women turned, startled, their sacred stillness interrupted by the presence now standing at the edge of their sanctuary.

Pehani stepped into the clearing, his shadow stretching long before him like a specter of unease. The golden glow of the forest clung to him like armor, but it did little to hide the storm brewing within. His posture was taut, a coiled current of tension that threatened to snap, and the rise and fall of his chest betrayed the battle between instinct and reason. His brow furrowed, eyes scanning the scene before him — Solei nestled against Zambia, their hands gently intertwined, their forms bathed in the ethereal light of the garden.

They looked radiant, otherworldly, almost mythic — like two priestesses lost in a sacred vow. The sight struck him like a blow to the chest, knocking the air from his lungs. His jaw tensed, a pulse ticking visibly at his temple. There was no malice in his gaze, only a raw confusion, an ache that spiraled into his chest — a mix of love, longing, and a fear he couldn't quite name. The emotion burned at the back of his throat, thick and hot, a wildfire of vulnerability ignited by a moment he didn't understand — and yet couldn't ignore.

"What's going on here?" he asked, his voice low, laced not with accusation, but with the wounded rumble of a heart unsure of its place. There was no threat in his tone — only the sharp edge of a sacred protector who had momentarily lost his center, a guardian spirit caught between instinct and insight.

Zambia straightened. "What does it *look* like? I'm loving your wife the way any fierce soul should be loved."

Pehani's eyes flared. "With her head on your shoulder? That's—"

"Easy," Solei said, her voice soft but commanding, raising a hand between them like a veil of moonlight between two flames. "This is not a duel, my love. It is a sacred moment between hearts that know how to honor each other. Friendship can be a form of devotion, too."

Zambia raised a brow and smirked with the grace of a wild rose in full bloom, sunlight catching the shimmer in her eyes. "Oh, he's jealous," she said with a teasing lilt, her voice curling like warm incense. "Look at that warrior pride puffing up like a moonbird trying to guard the stars — all feathers and fire, forgetting we all shine from the same sky." Her words danced in the space between them, light but edged with the wisdom of someone who knew exactly when to wield softness and when to stand tall.

Pehani blinked, a flicker of self-awareness rising behind his eyes. Then he sighed, his breath carrying away the last of his resistance like smoke caught in sunlight. Finally, he chuckled — low, warm, almost sheepish. "Maybe I am," he admitted, glancing between the two women with softened eyes. "Maybe I forget sometimes that love comes in many forms — and that all of them are sacred in their own way."

Solei stepped forward, her presence serene and luminous, like the moon gliding over still waters — radiant, calm, yet deeply commanding. The soft glow of the garden danced across her skin, casting halos of gold along her arms as she reached for Pehani's hand. Her fingers, warm and sure, pressed his palm to her heart, where her heartbeat pulsed like a sacred drum. "You're not wrong to feel, beloved," she whispered, her voice a blend of honeyed compassion and crystalline knowing. "Sacred masculinity is not the absence of emotion — it is its graceful mastery. It is the courage to feel deeply, to hold the fire without being consumed by it. Feel, but let it guide you back to truth, not away from it." She leaned in just enough that her breath brushed his cheek, her eyes searching his. "You know what we are — light and root, breath and fire. We are creation and keeper, storm and stillness. And you are never alone in that."

Pehani's shoulders dropped, the tension melting from his frame like storm clouds dissolving into dusk. He stepped closer, his eyes softening as he looked between them. A flicker of shame passed through his gaze, followed by understanding. "You're right," he said, voice quieter now, reverent. "I was blinded for a moment — by fear, by pride, by love I didn't know how to place. Forgive me, both of you. I see it now — the beauty of this bond, the wholeness it brings."

Zambia clapped him on the back with mock drama, her hand landing with a playful thump that echoed slightly in the stillness of the garden. "Forgiven," she said, her voice light but laced with love. "But only because you're pretty when you're flustered — like a storm cloud that forgot how to thunder." She winked, the glint in her eyes reflecting both her teasing nature and the unshakable loyalty beneath it.

The three of them laughed, the sound blooming through the garden like crystal bells carried on moonlight — a melody of healing and release that shimmered through the sacred air. It fluttered like golden silk through the canopy, wrapping around each blossom, each stone, as if the land itself leaned in to listen. Petals quivered in response, and a flock of tiny, radiant winged creatures flitted overhead, stirred by the vibration. Their laughter faded into the hush of something holy. The laughter echoed in the branches above like an offering of joy to the spirits of the forest, blending into the wind as if becoming part of the eternal hum of the land.

It was the kind of laughter that softened ancient wounds, that mended the invisible threads of kinship, that reminded them they were still human, still divine, still alive — breathing proof that love, in all its forms, could hold the world together.

And the forest held them — glowing, breathing, remembering.

Pehani lowered himself beside them, his movements slower now, thoughtful, like a warrior laying down not just his weapon but his armor — willingly, reverently. The golden light caught in the strands of his hair as he exhaled deeply, the breath leaving him with the weight of things he hadn't realized he was carrying. He placed one hand on the mossy ground, grounding himself in the heartbeat of the earth below, and let the other rest gently on his knee. The forest's glow wrapped around him like a benediction, as if the land itself was welcoming his surrender. The tension he'd carried unraveled, thread by thread, dissolving into the sacred earth beneath them like rain finally falling after a long drought.

"I needed this," he said softly, his voice carrying a rare vulnerability, a crack in the steady cadence of his usual strength. "Sometimes I forget to just stop... to breathe it all in — what we've created here. This sanctuary. This life. This sacred tapestry between us." His gaze drifted from the glimmering canopy above to the sacred faces before him. "You two... you are the roots and rhythm of Lumeria. The way you hold space, the way you love and lead — it humbles me. You make this place feel eternal, like it has always existed because of your presence within it."

He paused, emotion tightening his throat. "There are days I feel like I'm still learning what it means to hold this world with balance. I know I'm fire... but even fire needs direction. And the two of you — you are my compass. I don't say it enough, but I see you. I feel it. And I cherish it more than I know how to put into words."

Solei leaned into him gently, her hand resting over his. "We feel you too, Pehani. You are the fire that protects it all."

Zambia smirked, brushing an invisible speck from his shoulder. "Even if that fire occasionally flares up with a touch of jealousy."

Pehani chuckled. "What can I say? Sacred protector, remember?"

Solei's laughter joined his, light as breeze. "Sacred and slightly dramatic."

"But earnest," he added with a grin, looking between them. "I couldn't have asked for stronger souls to walk this world beside me. And I'll spend every breath making sure this Lumeria we've built — this sanctuary — stays sacred."

Zambia nodded solemnly. "Then we'll do it together. All of us. Light, root, fire... and feathers."

They laughed again, softer this time, and leaned into each other in a triangle of trust and love, the bond between them deepened not only by purpose, but by presence.

Above them, the garden shimmered as if in blessing — a living witness to the devotion that held Lumeria strong.

The sacred quiet returned, and for a few long breaths, they sat in stillness, their bodies relaxed, but their spirits radiant with the golden hum of soul-deep connection. Their hearts beat like synchronized drums beneath a shimmering canopy of living light, each breath a sacred offering to the earth and stars alike. The air was thick with reverence, shimmering faintly as if laced with invisible threads of memory and magic. It felt as though the ancestors were watching, their presence woven into the breeze that kissed their skin.

The luminous glow of the garden wrapped them in an embrace beyond time — a place where the sacred feminine and divine masculine didn't just coexist, they danced. Not as opposites, but as sacred complements: moon and sun, water and flame, grace and power, weaving into one fluid force of creation. Their stillness wasn't emptiness — it was recognition. Their silence was not quiet — it was communion. This was a moment suspended in the breath of the cosmos, where time dared not interrupt the soul song rising between them — a harmonic alignment of purpose, love, and ancient remembering vibrating through the earth beneath them and the heavens above.

Pehani looked at them again, his voice low and steady, reverent as the roots beneath them. "You've both taught me how to feel deeper and love wider than I ever believed I could. This isn't just a village we've created — it's a sacred weave of soul threads. It's our legacy."

Solei brushed her fingers over his cheek with a smile soft as starlight. "And it's only just beginning."

Zambia reached for both their hands, squeezing them with warrior strength and sisterly devotion. "Let's promise each other now — that no matter what comes, we'll keep choosing each other. Again and again."

They nodded in unison.

Three flames. One heart.

And above them, the sky shimmered in quiet agreement, as if the stars themselves had borne witness and sealed the vow with light.

CHAPTER TWENTY-SIX

WHEN SHADOWS FELL (WOMB OF THE STORM)

S olei gently rose, offering a parting smile to Pehani and Zambia, her heart still radiant from the sacred communion they had shared. As she turned and walked back through the winding paths of the glowing forest, her spirit floated somewhere between awe and stillness. Each step was a prayer, each breath a benediction. Her robes flowed like rivers of starlight, catching glimmers of the bioluminescent orbs that still lingered in the air. The scent of blossoms swirled around her, soft and familiar, and the distant laughter of children seemed to echo like a blessing across the trees.

Her heart swelled with a tender ache — the kind that comes only when one realizes how utterly beautiful life truly is. She felt it in the warmth of the earth beneath her bare feet, in the soft caress of wind against her cheek. She felt it in the memory of her children's laughter, in the way Zambia had held her through grief, in the steadiness of Pehani's eyes. The sacredness of being human — of being part of something ancient, divine, and alive — wrapped around her like a promise she never wanted to let go of.

Life in Lumeria was breathtaking. She was surrounded by love — from her family, from her friends, from the village that had bloomed like a living soul around her. There was beauty in the simplicity: meals shared under the moon, elders singing old stories into the fire, children laughing through gardens. And in that moment, Solei felt as though she had never been more alive.

But then — something shifted.

The light faltered.

She stopped mid-step, every fiber of her being alert. The vibrant glow of the forest dimmed around her, as though the trees themselves had inhaled and forgotten how to exhale. The air thickened, no longer sweet with blossoms but tinged with the metallic scent of dread. A low hum began in the distance — no melody, no rhythm, just an eerie vibration that settled beneath her skin.

The warmth on her cheeks from the sun faded into a chill that licked the back of her neck. Her senses narrowed to a single thread of awareness. The birds had stopped singing. The orbs of light that danced among the trees had vanished. Even the wind — the ever-whispering breath of Lumeria — had stilled.

Her breath caught in her chest, held captive by the sudden, terrible stillness. It was as if time had bent around her, coiling tight in warning.

Then she saw it — a flash. A flicker of something dark cutting across the path, too fast for her eyes to catch fully, yet unmistakable in its wrongness.

Not light. Not love. Not Lumerian.

A shadow.

Her chest tightened. Her skin buzzed. And deep in her womb, a knowing rose. Something was terribly wrong.

She crept forward, following the trace of whatever had passed. The village was silent now. Too silent.

Her bare feet padded over warm moss and stone as she wound her way through Lumeria's sleeping paths. Her eyes scanned every movement, her heart pounding harder with each step. And then —

She saw it.

Her soul shattered.

Lehari — radiant, kind Lehari — was no longer standing.

He was strewn across the stone, a tangle of broken limbs and spilled light, his lifeblood painting the ancient ground in sacred red. It glistened in the low twilight, pooling like liquid rubies against the moss-covered earth. The once-living glow of his Lumerian skin had faded to an otherworldly pallor—sea-glass green now streaked with arterial crimson, dulled like a memory erased in shadow.

A deep gash split his side, torn ragged as though something feral had ripped through the soft divinity of his flesh. His robes—once pristine and white, embroidered with celestial glyphs of protection—were soaked through, clinging to his body like heavy silk drowned in grief. The golden threads that once sang with light were frayed, torn, their music silenced.

His chest rose no longer.

The shimmering shield he had always carried—a protective frequency that hummed through the air like a soft chant—lingered faintly for a heartbeat, then shattered into flecks of light that evaporated like dew beneath a burning sun.

His eyes.

Those starlit eyes, so often filled with laughter, mischief, and radiant calm, now stared upward—wide, glassy, vacant. They reflected the sky above not with wonder, but with a hollow stillness, as if they had seen too much beauty to survive the brutality of this end.

And still, something sacred clung to him.

A whisper in the wind. A hum in the stones beneath him.

Time knelt with him.

And the land mourned.

A strangled cry ripped from her throat before she even knew it had come. It sounded feral—like something ancient and wounded had awoken in her soul and clawed its way out through her mouth.

Solei's body seized, muscles locking in shock, her breath shattering into fragments as the truth struck like lightning down her spine.

"No... no, no, Lehari... please..."

She pressed her palms to his chest, trembling as she poured her essence into the fading glow of his body, willing — begging — the light of healing to return. Golden sparks flickered weakly beneath her hands, but they sputtered and died, unable to take root. Her breath broke in ragged sobs as she whispered incantations through her tears, her voice cracking with desperation. "Please... please, come back..." But the light would not rise. The soul she had known — the friend who had guarded Lumeria with unwavering devotion — was gone. Her hands, slick with blood and lightless power, trembled over his chest, unable to feel the pulse that once sang with ancient rhythm. It was too late. The stars had claimed him.

His spirit had flown.

The garden no longer shimmered. It wept.

And standing in the shadows, watching — a being of twisted sorrow and desecrated purpose — a creature cloaked in writhing darkness, its form folding in and out of itself like smoke mourning its source. Its face, a grotesque mask of forgotten creation, held black, depthless eyes — voids that devoured all they gazed upon, as if love itself had never touched them. From its jagged mouth, black ichor dripped in slow, deliberate trails, sizzling against the sacred moss like venom falling on prayer. Obsidian-like teeth, uneven and cracked, jutted from its trembling jaw, twitching with primal hunger. The stench that followed it was not just decay — it was despair itself, thick and bitter, coiling through the air like a warning.

It radiated not simply cold, but the aching hollowness of something that once knew light — and had turned away from it.

The Shadowed.

Her scream caught in her throat, raw and silent — a cry not just of fear, but of heartbreak. It rose from the womb of her soul, ancient and full of knowing, as if every woman who had ever held love and lost it cried with her in that moment.

The Shadowed.

The shield was broken.

As the creature turned and vanished into the shadows, Solei rushed to Lehari, dropping to her knees beside him. She placed trembling hands over his wounds, trying to summon healing light — but it was too late. His soul had returned to the stars.

The earth beneath her rumbled.

A sound like roaring waves split the night. The shield was gone. And the sea had remembered.

The great flood surged forward, pouring over the shores of Lumeria, as if the ocean herself wept with Solei — a sacred mother mourning the unraveling of her radiant child.

Solei's breath was ragged, tears streaking down her cheeks like threads of sacred water, drawn from the ocean of her womb — from the grief of every mother, healer, and goddess who had ever loved and lost. But her body moved on instinct. She turned and ran, the wind catching her hair like wings of starlight, her heartbeat pounding with the rhythm of generations before her — the ancient call to protect, to rise, to love even in the face of darkness. She sprinted through the village, guided by the primal knowing that her children were the light of what still could be saved.

The alarms rose — crystal chimes and horn bells echoing into the night.

"Pehani!" she cried, her voice a tremor of both terror and hope as she ran, feet pounding the sacred earth, her breath tearing through the silence like a prayer breaking against stone. Her hair streamed behind her like a flame in the wind, eyes wide and wild with the vision of what she'd just seen — the death of innocence, the breach of their sanctuary. Her soul called for him, not just in name but in essence, as though his spirit alone could steady the unraveling she felt rising all around her.

Villagers were pouring into the streets, panic beginning to bloom in their eyes. Zambia met her halfway, eyes wide with terror.

"The Shadowed," Solei gasped, "They're here. The shield is broken. Lehari is gone."

Zambia grabbed her hand without hesitation, her grip firm, grounded, and full of silent strength. Her eyes scanned the village with the keen awareness of a warrior, but her heart pulsed with the fierce tenderness of a mother, a sister, a soul protector. "We need to protect the children," she said, her voice low and steady — not with fear, but with sacred purpose. Her presence was a balm and a blade, and in that moment, Solei felt the immense, unbreakable force of the divine feminine beside her — steady, unwavering, and ready to do whatever it took to keep the light alive.

Pehani rushed toward them, sword drawn — a weapon forged of sacred crystal and blacksteel, etched with ancestral glyphs that shimmered faintly with protective light. Its blade, curved like a crescent moon, seemed to hum with ancient memory, a living extension of his vow to defend Lumeria. His face was pale, but burning with a quiet, searing fury. His eyes met Solei's, and in that instant, a thousand soul-threads tied between them — fear, love, protection, and the unspoken promise that if it came to it, he would offer his final breath to keep them safe. The sacred masculine rose in him like a storm guided by purpose, unwavering and fierce.

"Zambia, go with Solei. Take the villagers to the Protection Temple. Guard the children. I'll lead the warriors to the shoreline. We can't let them breach the heart of the village."

"But you'll be outnumbered," Solei cried.

"I won't let them take our home," he said, eyes glowing with sacred fire. He kissed her forehead quickly, pressed his hand to her stomach, and turned to his warriors.

Solei turned with Zambia and ran. The sky was already darkening with unnatural clouds. The storm had begun.

And with it, the war for Lumeria had returned.

Solei and Zambia reached the edge of the village center, breath heaving, hearts pounding, as the ground trembled again beneath their feet — the pulse of a sacred land in distress. Without speaking, they understood their mission. Zambia raised her voice with commanding clarity, calling villagers to gather, her tone steady and firm despite the chaos rising around them.

"To the Protection Temple! Move quickly! Take nothing but your children and your breath."

Solei moved through the growing crowd, gathering mothers, elders, and trembling little ones, her hands radiating a calming presence even as her soul trembled. She placed one hand over each child she passed, whispering blessings of light and protection. The cries of fear were rising, but so was the strength of unity.

Thunder cracked above them, and still they moved — through mud, through smoke, through the memories of peace that now crumbled behind them.

The Temple stood like a beacon in the distance, aglow with the faint flicker of sacred runes. In Solei's satchel, wrapped in soft woven cloth, she carried the two ancient protection stones — perfectly etched with intricate designs of power and light. Gifted during the twins' integration ceremony, the stones pulsed faintly, sensing the urgency. She clutched them as they ran, trusting their ancient energy to shield the children and the light of the village from what was already at the gates. Zambia led the way, sword in hand, shielding the rear, while Solei kept the children close in the center of their formation. The village they loved was disappearing behind them, but the future they still believed in had to be protected.

And with every step, every whispered prayer, every tear shed in silence, they carried Lumeria's light toward safety — even as the shadow closed in.

But even as they reached the threshold of sanctuary, the wind whispered: the storm had only just begun.

CHAPTER TWENTY-SEVEN

THE LAST BREATH OF LIGHT

The Protection Temple pulsed with a calm, steady glow, like the heartbeat of the earth herself — ancient, steady, maternal. Sacred runes danced faintly along the curved stone walls, casting halos of warm gold and violet light across tear-streaked cheeks and wide, searching eyes. The air was thick with incense — lavender, myrrh, and sacred resin — meant to soothe the mind, but unable to mask the rising current of fear.

Children huddled against mothers, their little hands clutching woven charms of protection. Elders rocked gently, whispering prayers into their palms as if speaking to the ancestors. The entire temple felt like a womb — sacred and sheltering — yet filled with the tension of labor, of something being born through pain and upheaval.

Zambia stood at the main entrance like a living shield, eyes unblinking, her breath even but ready. Solei moved like flowing moonlight through the chamber, her hands glowing with soft pulses of warmth as she placed them over trembling hearts, her voice a lullaby of sacred invocations meant to calm, to anchor, to hold.

But her own heart was not still.

The ache in her chest tightened with each moment that passed. Her breath caught every time she felt the distant echoes of chaos — the clashing of energy, the dull boom of elemental rings colliding with darkness. She felt Pehani.

And she knew he was giving everything.

When she could no longer sit in the sacred stillness, she slipped toward the back chamber of the temple where an ancient tunnel, long hidden from common use, led through the underground roots of the land — toward the shoreline.

But before she could lift the stone threshold, Zambia's hand landed firmly on her shoulder.

"You're not leaving me behind again," she said, her voice low, soft, but fierce. "What are you doing?"

Solei turned slowly, her eyes shimmering with determination. "I have to go. I can feel them weakening. The warriors... Pehani. They need more light. I can help them."

Zambia shook her head. "You are the High Priestess. You are needed here."

"I am the High Priestess," Solei said, stepping closer, her voice steady with the weight of lifetimes. "And that means I go where the light is most threatened. Right now, it's at the edge of the sea. I feel the thread fraying — the tether between what we love and what they would steal from us. I will not let our warriors fall if there's even a single breath of light left in me to give. My place is not behind stone walls. It is at the mouth of the storm."

Zambia stared at her a long moment, then nodded. "Then I'm coming with you."

Together, they descended into the earth, the stone passageway greeting them like an old memory. Their footsteps echoed like heartbeats in the silent corridors — steady, reverent, and full of knowing. The walls pulsed faintly with the memory of ancient rites, their surface etched with symbols that flickered softly as Solei passed by, recognizing her essence.

The air grew cooler, but it was not cold — it was charged with sacred awareness, as though the land itself was awake, watching, praying with them. Each breath they took tasted of salt and stone, of roots and legacy. The deeper they went, the more Solei could feel the pull — not of fear, but of destiny.

As they neared the exit, the roar of battle rose like a storm in their bones — a deep, guttural sound that shook the stones and stirred the soul, vibrating up through the soles of their feet as if the land itself cried out. A heavy wind met them at the tunnel's mouth, thick with salt and smoke and the scent of burning energy. When they reached the narrow outcrop overlooking the shoreline, the vision below seized their breath and held it hostage. Solei's heart clenched as her spirit trembled, overwhelmed by the magnitude of what she saw. A deep knowing surged within her — a fusion of awe, sorrow, and divine urgency. She could feel every pulse of light, every scream of defiance, every ounce of her warriors' fatigue like it was etched across her own skin. The ground beneath her feet vibrated with ancestral cries, and the weight of prophecy coiled in her chest like a flame begging to be released. Her breath caught, and tears sprang to her eyes — not from fear, but from the sacred ache of knowing that she was watching the story of their people being written in light and shadow before her very eyes. It was not just a battlefield — it was a sacred reckoning. The sea glittered like molten obsidian beneath the moonlight, while bursts of light carved through the night like the breath of gods. The clash of forces echoed like a war drum for the stars themselves.

The scene was breathtaking and terrible — like a celestial war carved into earth's skin and set ablaze by the heartbeat of the gods. Below them, the beach pulsed with bursts of radiant power, wild arcs of energy flickering like lightning caught in sacred ritual. Bolts of golden light lashed across the field as shadows erupted in snarling counterforce. Warriors moved like divine silhouettes caught in a trance of death and devotion, their limbs slashing through the dark with the elegance of sacred dance. Pehani was a vision of sacred fire — his armor a gleaming vessel of moonlit steel and etched runes, his energy ring whirling with blinding light as he drove back shadow after shadow. The air cracked with tension and power, and every strike sent waves of light shivering up to the heavens. It was not just battle. It was the embodiment of prophecy — love and rage and legacy forged into motion.

Pehani and the warriors were luminous in the fray — their forms glowing like sacred flames moving through a sea of darkness. Circles of spinning energy rings whirled around them like galaxies in motion, each one etched with ancient glyphs that glowed like stardust, pulsing with sentient rhythm and radiant color. Their edges shimmered with the razor brilliance of sacred flame, alive with purpose. Each ring cast sparks of sapphire and gold, carving sigils into the night sky. Their movements were fluid and divine, as if choreographed by the stars themselves. Shields of translucent light bloomed like sacred petals of crystalized moonlight, forming sigils in the air as they unfurled. They shimmered with hues of violet, azure, and gold, absorbing dark impacts with rippling pulses of protective energy before releasing them in radiant shockwaves. The monstrous creatures lunged with claws and teeth, shadows twisting and snarling, but the warriors held the line, golden-blue beams slicing through the dark with the precision of cosmic judgment. It was not just a battle — it was a ballet of survival, of light refusing to die.

But it was what lay beyond the brilliance that stole the breath from her lungs.

Silence.

The jungle behind her, once alive with rustling wings and the soft padding of paws, was still—unnaturally still. There were no bird calls, no insect hums, no rustling leaves stirred by animal life.

The wild had gone quiet. Not from peace... but from absence.

Her gaze drifted to the shoreline, where the sea met stone and sand. The waves rolled in slowly, mournfully, carrying more than foam.

Bodies.

Feathers soaked in salt. Antlers tangled in seaweed. Small paws curled and lifeless, half-buried in glimmering wet sand. The ocean, once their sanctuary, now returned them like broken offerings to the land.

Not a single creature moved.

Not one remained.

A sickly shimmer clung to the air—residue from the corrupted. Those who hadn't fled in time had been taken, twisted into something monstrous. The ones who had not turned... had perished.

Solei's heart clenched. Her throat tightened.

The battlefield rippled with primal rhythm — the sound of power against power, light meeting void, like thunder crashing within the bones of the world. Screams of effort and cries of pain sliced through the storm, raw and unfiltered, the voices of warriors giving every breath they had, their souls etched into each strike. The Shadowed shrieked like broken wind and poisoned flame, their rage a howl of forgotten light twisted into hunger. Their movements were desperate, chaotic — tendrils of shadow writhing through air thick with charged magic.

Energy clashed and collided, ringing out like ancient bells torn between realms, a sound that echoed deep into the heart's memory. Some Lumerians stumbled — shields cracked, knees struck ground, sacred garments torn and bloodied — yet they rose again, eyes aflame, bodies trembling but unbroken. Their wounds glowed faintly with lingering light, as though even their pain refused to surrender.

For every burst of brilliance, a shadow lunged darker and louder, the space between breath and scream filled with tension and sacred violence. The clash was not just terrifying — it was transcendent. It was a sacred storm of spirit and shadow, visceral and raw, as if the very soul of Lumeria was being rewritten — not in silence, but in screams of devotion, in blood and brilliance, in the pulse of every warrior who dared to still rise.

Above them, the heavens split open with lightning. The sea — that ancient witness — rose in great spiraling tides around the shore, mirroring the chaos below with its own divine unrest. Salt spray kissed Solei's cheeks, mixing with her sweat and tears.

But the Shadowed were unending. Their growls rippled across the shore like a curse torn from the underworld, and for every one that fell in a blaze of light, two more rose from the mist — clawing, slithering, moaning as they surged forward with eyes void of mercy. Their twisted forms pulsed with a hunger that could not be reasoned with, only resisted. And worse — with every touch, every claw that tore through armor or skin, something darker unfolded. The infection of shadow passed like wildfire; warriors struck by the Shadowed began to shake, their auras dimming, their light draining as the darkness took root within them. It was a transformation swift and brutal.

Screams turned to snarls. Allies became threats. Lightbearers, corrupted.

It was terrifying.

The warriors began to slow, weariness weighing down their limbs like stone. Some fought beside friends who moments later turned into enemies, cloaked in blackened fire and hissing void. And in that moment, despair flirted with the edge of the light.

For every one that fell to the Lumerians' might, another rose from the mist. The tide was shifting.

Solei stepped forward, her robes whipping in the wind like prayer flags in a sacred storm, her eyes no longer filled with fear — but with sacred resolve, drawn from the deepest well of her divine feminine knowing. She felt the call of her foremothers echoing through her spine, the sacred hum of the womb from which creation is born, rising in waves through her bones. Every part of her being — her breath, her pulse, her spirit — harmonized with the rhythm of the land, the moon, and the cries of those she loved. Her fingertips sparked with rising power, tingling with ancestral fire, as she raised her arms to the sky, not with force but with reverence — opening herself as a vessel, not to control the light, but to become it. In that moment, she was not just a woman, not just a priestess — she was the memory of every healer, mother, protector, and lightbearer who had ever walked this earth.

Every breath she took was a lullaby and a roar — a sacred harmony of comfort and power. Her lungs filled with the scent of sea and storm, her breath a rhythm that pulsed in time with the rising waves and the cries of her people. Every heartbeat was a drumbeat of remembrance, echoing with the footsteps of her ancestors and the tears of every mother who had ever prayed over their children in the dark. She summoned not only the brilliance of the stars, but the primal, radiant grace of the Earth herself — a force ancient and feminine, as fluid as blood, as fierce as flame. The light didn't just answer her — it surged through her in ribbons of memory, in flashes of soul-song. The ancient voice of the Lumerian soul rose with her, trembling the ground beneath her feet and lighting the sky with the love of all who came before her.

She called down the light — not as a weapon, but as a remembering, a returning. The divine mother flame poured through her. And the earth, the sea, and the sky rose in chorus, answering her like daughters coming home.

Beside her, the warrior in Zambia could no longer stay still. The battle song in her blood surged with the cries of her people, each heartbeat echoing like a drumbeat in her chest. Her breath deepened, and her stance shifted — the ancient rhythm of war rising in her veins like a call from the ancestors. Her fingers curled into fists at her sides as her muscles tensed with sacred readiness. She dropped down the slope with divine precision, her boots skimming the loose rock like wings of purpose. Her silhouette blazed like a comet descending from the sky, the fire of her purpose burning brighter with each step. Her golden energy shimmered around her, responding to the invocation of her lineage, cloaking her in the strength of those who had come before her. With every breath, Zambia became not just a warrior — but the storm itself.

With a sharp exhale, she summoned her energy ring — a brilliant arc of golden fire that surged around her wrist with a hiss of light. She leapt into the fray without hesitation, her body a living invocation. Her strikes were fierce and fluid, swirling like fire caught in a sacred current — a dance of protection, vengeance, and ancestral grace. Each movement became a luminous sigil traced in air, a prayer written in the language of motion to shield her people and pierce the very heart of darkness. Golden pulses ripped through shadow with sacred fury, illuminating her path like a halo of war.

She fought like fire wrapped in love — the embodied soul of a protector answering destiny's call. In her every step, every swing, the spirit of Lumeria blazed alive — wild, wise, and unyielding.

Solei watched, pride swelling in her chest even as her own power climbed toward its peak. The light she summoned rippled outward in luminous waves, washing over the warriors like warm starlight. Where it touched them, their strength reignited — wounds sealed, breath returned, and their energy rings flared brighter. For a moment, it looked as if they were winning. Hope surged through her veins.

But then, from the corner of her eye, she saw it.

A Shadowed — larger, darker, vibrating with concentrated malice — lunged toward Pehani, its form moving with unnatural speed and purpose, as if it had chosen him specifically. Pehani turned to meet it, energy ring raised, his stance braced with sacred instinct — but he was a breath too late. The creature's claw, elongated and glistening with oily darkness, raked across his chest in a violent arc, and a ripple of shadow followed in its wake. A hiss of energy split the air as the impact made contact — and in that moment, something dark slithered beneath Pehani's skin. It was more than a wound; it was an invasion. The shadow didn't just cut him — it claimed him.

Solei's scream tore through the air, breaking her focus.

Zambia turned, eyes wide as she watched Pehani stagger. His aura flickered, then dimmed. Darkness spread through him like ink in water.

"No!" Zambia cried, leaping toward him. She slammed her energy ring into the creature, tearing it off him with a burst of golden fire, but the damage had been done.

Pehani fell to his knees.

Solei was already running, tears blinding her. But before she could reach him, he rose slowly. Something in his eyes had changed — the light she knew so well was gone. In its place was shadow.

He turned toward her.

And then — with a snarl that did not belong to him — he lunged.

"Pehani!" Solei cried, her voice a mixture of terror and heartbreak.

Zambia stepped between them, screaming his name.

But he didn't stop.

He crashed into Solei with terrifying force, knocking the breath from her lungs. She staggered backward, gasping, her hands instinctively glowing with light as she tried to push the darkness out of him. "Come back to me," she whispered through tears, her palms pressed to his chest, willing the infection to retreat.

But it was too late.

"Please..." Solei whispered, her voice trembling as tears streamed down her cheeks. "Please, Pehani... fight it. Come back to me." Her hands gripped his tunic as she tried to steady herself, not just from the pain, but from the crumbling world inside her. "I love you," she cried. "We need you. The children need you. I need you. Don't let this darkness take you. Please, let me save you..."

Her plea was not just a cry of survival, but a sacred invocation of their bond — a call to love, to memory, to the man who had once promised to protect her. Her voice cracked with desperation, with the raw ache of knowing she was not only losing her life, but the soul tethered to hers.

His face twisted into a grimace of dark delight, a grotesque mask of triumph where love once lived. His eyes flickered with inhuman satisfaction, and his lips curled as if he were savoring every moment of her horror. With a low growl that sounded more beast than man, he raised his blade — the sacred sword that once stood for protection, for love, for loyalty — and with chilling precision, he drove it straight through her womb. The impact was a thunderclap inside her body, a violation of every promise ever whispered between them. It was betrayal incarnate — and it shattered her.

Solei cried out, the sound primal and soul-deep, echoing through the battlefield like the wail of the Earth itself. Pain erupted in her like wildfire tearing through sacred ground, scorching every nerve and memory of love. Her vision blurred as her womb pulsed with searing agony, the betrayal cutting deeper than the blade. Her hands, trembling and blood-slicked, pressed against his chest — not in resistance, but in a last desperate attempt to find the man she once knew. And in that moment, as darkness surged into her, she felt it — the infection taking root, crawling beneath her skin like ink in sacred water. A coldness crept into her bones, threatening to smother her from within. But deep within her core, her light resisted. It pulsed in defiance, a fragile but fierce flame that refused to surrender. Her divine essence clung to every memory, every prayer, every sacred breath she had ever offered in love. It pushed back against the invasion, not with rage, but with remembering — of who she was, and what she carried. Her light sputtered, not just from her palms but from the essence of her being, flickering like a candle in the wind of a sacred storm.

And he smiled — a smile twisted with triumph, its edges sharp and cruel, as though carved from the darkest corner of a broken soul. It curled across his face like a shadow mimicking joy, hollow and haunting. There was no trace of the man she had loved — only the presence of something ancient and vile, wearing his skin with wicked pride. It was the smile of a creature that relished betrayal, that savored the unraveling of love. And it pierced her deeper than the blade ever could.

As she gasped for air, trying to hold on to her fading light, he leaned in, pressing a hand over her heart. His touch was cold and consuming, a void cloaked in flesh. From his palm came a force that gripped her very soul—like icy tendrils slithering into the depths of her being, coiling around her essence with merciless intent. She felt herself unraveling at the core, not just her light being taken, but her very memories, her sacred dreams, her divine knowing — pulled toward him in a spiraling theft of everything that made her whole.

He began to siphon her light.

Golden threads of radiance rose from her skin, swirling around him like stolen breath—glowing strands of everything sacred she had ever been. Her knees buckled, unable to hold the weight of pain and betrayal. Her eyes widened with disbelief, flooded with the agony of recognition that the love she once knew was now the vessel of her undoing. Each thread pulled from her felt like a memory unraveling—her children's laughter, the village songs, the heartbeat of her people. And still he stood tall, unflinching, devouring her light with silent pride. The brilliance of her soul dimmed, strand by strand, until only the echo of her glow remained.

Then he stepped back — and let the Shadowed close in.

They descended upon her like vultures to sacred flame, their claws dripping with malice as they tore into her arms, her legs, her back, each strike searing her flesh with the venom of the void. Her nerves ignited like shattered crystal, white-hot agony crashing through her body in waves too vast to contain. Light exploded from her wounds in desperate flickers, as if her soul was trying to escape before it could be devoured.

But the Shadowed didn't just tear — they feasted. They consumed her light hungrily, their monstrous mouths opening to drink the luminous essence pouring from her broken body. As if intoxicated by it, they grew bolder, more ravenous, clawing deeper as beams of golden-white energy were siphoned into their blackened forms. Her sacred energy — divine, maternal, ancient — was ripped from her like sacred silk shredded by monsters who craved only destruction.

Her scream tore from her like thunder torn from the heavens — raw, sacred, and excruciating — echoing across the battlefield with such ferocity that time itself seemed to freeze, caught in the echo of her pain.

Zambia fought with wild, feral strength, her body driven by a storm of grief, fury, and unwavering love, trying to tear through the encroaching Shadowed to reach her sister of the soul. Her golden energy ring blazed like a comet streaking through the darkness, casting sharp, radiant light with every arc of her arm. Shadows hissed and recoiled as she carved a path through the chaos, each movement executed with the precision of instinct and the desperation of heartbreak. Her breath came in gasps, raw and ragged, as she screamed against the roar of the battlefield. Each swing was fueled by memory — of laughter, of shared pain, of sacred sisterhood. Her strikes became a hymn of rage, a chorus of devotion to the light she refused to let slip away.

Her feet pounded the earth like thunder, kicking up blood-soaked soil, her limbs trembling with exhaustion but refusing to yield. Hair wild and matted with sweat and ash, she was a vision of holy war, of raw love turned into flame. Her voice cracked the air like lightning.

And then something in her heart shifted. A knowing. A scream from within the soul.

She paused for only a moment — just long enough to see Solei's body fall, to hear her last breath in the air, to feel the shattering pulse of the High Priestess's light collapse into the earth.

Zambia looked toward the temple in the distance, her breath catching. The children. The villagers. The stones of protection.

Tears mixed with fury on her face.

With a final, trembling glance toward Solei's crumpled form, Zambia turned and sprinted from the battlefield, her boots kicking up mud and ash. Her body screamed in protest, her spirit torn, but her purpose clear.

She would protect what remained.

She would carry the light back to the ones who still lived. "SOLEI!" It was not just a name—it was a battle cry, a plea to the stars, and a promise stitched into every cell of her being: she would not let the light die without a fight.

But Solei was already falling. Her body collapsed under the weight of suffering, and everything around her blurred.

Then — silence.

She rose above herself, watching from beyond her body, floating in some sacred space between.

She saw her own limp form being ravaged, torn between agony and the flickering remnants of her light. Pehani... or what was left of him... stood amidst the chaos, laughing. Not the laughter of the man she loved, but the hollow, venomous laugh of something monstrous, his eyes glowing with shadowed pride and cruelty. She looked into those eyes one last time, desperate to find even the smallest flicker of the love they once shared. But there was nothing. No warmth. No recognition. No remembering. Only a consuming hunger — ancient, merciless, and void of all that was once human.

Solei, heartbroken and mortified, reached out from beyond — her arms trembling with urgency, her fingers reaching for the fabric of life she no longer belonged to. But her hands passed through everything, like wind through smoke. There was no weight, no hold, only the aching realization that she could no longer touch the world she had given everything to protect. Grief welled in her chest, heavy even in spirit form, as the sounds of Zambia's cries and the thunder of battle became distant echoes, fading like the last notes of a sacred song.

The light was leaving her.

And the world she loved was slipping away.

Her soul, wrapped in the remnants of sacred memory and divine love, drifted higher into the realm between worlds. The stars above dimmed as her lifeforce flickered. A final tear traced across her cheek in the physical, even as her spirit ascended.

Solei — the High Priestess, the healer, the light of Lumeria — exhaled one last breath.

But in the final breath that left her lips, the veil between pain and peace parted. And within that hush — that sacred stillness — Solei's spirit was wrapped in a cascade of memory.

She saw flashes of love: her twins swaddled in her arms, their tiny fingers wrapping around hers as their eyes blinked up at her with eternal trust. Pehani laughing under the golden sun before the war, his face soft and radiant, whispering dreams of their future together. Zambia holding her through nights of sorrow and mornings of hope, her arms a sanctuary of sisterhood and soul-bond.

She felt the warmth of the village — the elders singing beside firelight, their voices cracked with wisdom and joy, the children weaving blessings into her hair with giggles that echoed through the dusk. She felt the ocean breeze that once carried her prayers into the sky, salt and starlight brushing her cheeks like kisses from the Divine. The scent of blooming crystal-fruit trees, the rhythm of dancing feet during moonlit rituals, the laughter that rippled like healing wind through every home.

Each heartbeat of her life danced before her, a mosaic of tenderness, triumph, and the kind of love that only blossoms when souls live in truth and light.

And in those sacred echoes, she remembered who she truly was: not just the High Priestess of Lumeria, but a vessel of love, of hope, of light. Her essence shimmered, not with sorrow, but with quiet radiance.

Then, with one final smile — soft, knowing, and whole — her soul released into the stars.

And far above, the stars wept — not in grief, but in reverence.

CHAPTER TWENTY-EIGHT

THE SACRED RETURN

S olei's spirit drifted, weightless and free, beyond the veil that separates the living from the eternal. Her body, broken and bloodied by the Shadowed, lay abandoned on the battlefield, but her soul rose, lifted by an unseen force — ancient, tender, and infinitely familiar. She ascended through the heavens like a leaf caught on a gentle breeze, floating upward into a vast, infinite expanse. The darkness that had once sought to smother her light faded into nothingness, replaced by a soft, radiant glow that enveloped her, drawing her ever higher into the boundless soul world.

Her journey was a slow, graceful dance of light and sound — ethereal and flowing, as if every star, every breath of wind, and every pulse of energy moved in perfect harmony with her. The air shimmered with a fragrance that felt like home — the heady scent of lavender, jasmine, and fresh earth. It was a fragrance that carried with it a sense of remembrance, a connection to all she had been and all she was becoming. The colors of this place surpassed anything she had ever known in the material world — rich lavender melding into deep sapphire, glowing emeralds swirling in a cosmic symphony, their hues alive with compassion and wisdom. Each color shimmered like water bathed in moonlight, rippling with an energy so pure it felt as though the very fabric of existence itself was embracing her. Solei moved through this living landscape, merging with its beauty, its vitality, the essence of the universe humming softly within her.

Her skin tingled with the energy of all that surrounded her, each pulse like the heartbeat of the cosmos. She felt untethered yet completely whole — no longer confined by the earthly wounds that had once burdened her. She was at once infinite and grounded, embraced by a love so vast, so deep, it transcended time, space, and matter. Solei's soul floated in an eternal embrace — the softest, most peaceful sensation she could ever know.

And then, she felt it. A presence. Warm, familiar, and utterly undeniable. Her heart fluttered in recognition before her mind could fully grasp it. She knew, before even seeing her, who it was.

"Luneia?" Solei whispered, her voice soft with awe, each syllable trembling with the depth of their shared history, their sacred bond.

A warm laugh echoed through the space, sweet and familiar, like the sound of a gentle river winding through a quiet forest, soothing and eternal. And then, Luneia appeared, radiant and shimmering with purity, her form aglow like a golden sun at dawn. Her presence was both tender and powerful, a light so warm it seemed to envelope the entire universe in its embrace. Her eyes — the same deep, knowing eyes that Solei had loved across lifetimes — met hers with a gaze of unconditional love and understanding.

"You have come home, my dear sister," Luneia said, her voice a melodic fusion of compassion and love, carrying the weight of ages. "You did so much on Earth. Your light shone brighter than you know."

Solei's heart ached with the weight of the love and gratitude that surged through her. Her hands, trembling, reached toward Luneia, her voice barely a whisper. "I couldn't save him. I couldn't save Pehani," she confessed, her words quivering with the grief she had carried through her mortal journey. "I failed him."

Luneia's eyes softened, and the light surrounding her grew even warmer, more radiant, wrapping Solei in a cocoon of loving energy. It was as if the entire cosmos had reached out to cradle her in a mother's embrace, tender yet powerful, infinite yet deeply personal. "You did not fail, beloved," she replied, her voice soothing like the sound of the wind in the tallest trees. "You gave your light freely, and that was all that was ever asked of you. His soul chose its path, as did yours. Now, it is time for you to rest."

Luneia extended her hand, and as it touched Solei's heart, a wave of healing light flowed through her. It poured into every corner of her being, soothing every ache, every lingering sorrow. The warmth of it was profound, as though the universe itself had reached down to cradle her, to heal her, to hold her. It was the kind of love that felt like the embrace of the Earth itself — vast, all-encompassing, and tender beyond measure. As the healing light enveloped her, the weight of grief melted away, leaving only peace, a soft, radiant surrender.

"Rest now, dear one," Luneia whispered, her voice a lullaby woven from the stars. "You have earned it."

Solei closed her eyes, surrendering to the love that enveloped her. The peace she felt was eternal, a peace unlike any she had ever known. It was a deep, sacred rest, cradled in the divine embrace of the universe. She felt no need to hurry, no need to rush. All around her was still, calm, and perfect — a space filled only with the purity of being, with the joy of simply existing in the loving embrace of the cosmos.

For what felt like an eternity, she rested in that space. Time ceased to exist. There were no worries, no fears. There was only the peace of sacred existence. It was a restful stillness that wrapped her soul like the softest of blankets, a peace that sang through every fiber of her being.

But then, as though she were being gently woken from a dream, a voice — soft yet insistent — called her name.

"Solei, my dear one," came the voice of Lu Mai, vast and soothing as the wind that whispers through the tallest trees. "The world needs you once more. The Shadowed have taken over, and humanity is in peril. Will you return to Earth and help them? Will you return to your people, to your children, and help them find their way?"

Solei's heart fluttered, and a great wave of love surged through her, as though her very soul had awakened. She thought of her children — their small, trusting hands reaching toward her, their innocent love an anchor in her heart. But even more, she thought of the world, the lives she had touched, and the love she had shared. The world was in turmoil, and her soul knew that her work was far from finished.

"I am ready," Solei whispered, her voice steady, clear, and filled with divine purpose. "I will go back."

The energy around them flared, bright and radiant, a warm, golden glow that filled the entire space with love. The universe seemed to shift, opening before them like a vast, sacred portal. Before them stood a library — ancient, boundless, and sacred. Shelves stretched infinitely, their books glowing softly with the wisdom of countless souls. The air around them was thick with the scent of parchment and stardust, as though the knowledge of the ages had been woven into the very fabric of these sacred books.

"Choose your next life, Solei," Lu Mai's voice carried the weight of both gentleness and power. "This library holds many possibilities. Each one is filled with lessons, growth, and trans-formation. Choose wisely."

Solei's eyes widened with awe as she approached the shelves, the books gently glowing, their energy pulling her forward. She stopped before one golden book, its cover shimmering with a light that seemed to invite her in. The energy of the book was warm, like the embrace of a long-lost friend. As her fingers brushed against its cover, the book opened on its own, the pages turning, each one offering glimpses of the many lives she could live.

Each life was a possibility, a path filled with lessons — some of peace, some of struggle. She saw herself in different bodies, in different places, walking different paths. She saw the faces of her children, her family, and the lives they would lead, the lessons they would learn together. Every life was rich with love, sacrifice, joy, and pain — each one an invitation to become something more.

Lu Mai's voice, soft yet guiding, whispered through the silence. "You have chosen this life, Solei. Your light is meant to guide others. The wisdom you carry is vast. Now, it is time for you to return, with all that you have learned."

Solei nodded, the weight of her choice settling deep within her heart. She was ready. Her purpose had not been fulfilled. The world needed her.

With one final embrace from Lu Mai, Solei felt herself being drawn back to Earth. The warmth of the sun, the scent of the flowers, the joyful laughter of children filled her senses once again. The world she had once loved — the world she had fought for — was waiting.

Her journey was not yet finished. She had chosen her path.

As Solei began her journey back to the world she had once known, the future awaited her — filled with lessons, love, and challenges. A future where her light would not only guide her, but the entire world, toward a new beginning.

And just as she began to step through the veil, a sudden, sharp feeling of dread swept over her — a coldness, fleeting but powerful, like a shadow passing over her heart.

The air shifted, the starlight flickered, and for a brief moment, the very fabric of the universe seemed to tear.

A voice — not Lu Mai's, not Luneia's — whispered through her mind. It was dark, hollow, and relentless.

"The light you bring will not save them all. The Shadowed are not finished. They will return... stronger."

Solei froze, her heart sinking. The weight of the words crushed her chest, and in that moment, she understood — the battle was only just beginning.

To be continued...

Reflections for the Priestess Within

A *Sacred Journal of Remembrance, Awakening & Devotion*

You are not merely reading a story. You are tracing the contours of your own soul.

Before You Begin: A Soft Unveiling

Place one hand on your heart, the other upon your womb or solar center. Close your eyes. Breathe in the light of the stars and the song of the Earth. Speak softly within: "I open the temple of my being.

I allow the ancient to rise.

I remember myself through sacred story,

and walk the path of the priestess with devotion and grace."

Take your time. You are not rushing toward answers. You are softening into truth.

◻ Chapter One: The Descent of Light

Theme: Soul Landing, Divine Purpose, Sacred Remembering
Whispered Invocation: "I came not to forget—but to reawaken.
I descend not in punishment—but in promise."

Reflections to Receive:

- When have you felt the quiet ache of being far from home... even while standing on Earth?

- What if the very place you resisted arriving in... was the altar you came to bless?

- If your arrival on Earth was a sacred choice, what prayer did your soul whisper as you crossed the veil?

Closing Devotion: "I have not fallen. I have returned. I remember why I came."

▢ **Chapter Six: Sacred Union**

Theme: Inner Marriage, Embodiment, Love as Temple

Whispered Invocation: "Within me lives the beloved. In my touch, I remember wholeness."

Reflections to Receive:

- How does divine love feel in your body—when it is not seeking, but simply being?

- Where have you fragmented the feminine and the masculine within you—and where do they long to entwine again?

- What becomes possible when your body is no longer a battleground—but a sanctuary?

Closing Devotion: "In loving myself fully, I remember what has always been holy."

▢ **Chapter Nine: The Sea Guardian's Warning**

Theme: Intuition, Oceanic Wisdom, Deep Listening

Whispered Invocation:

Reflections to Receive:

- What ancient voice stirs beneath your skin when silence surrounds you?

- Have you ever sensed a shift before it arrived? What did you do with that knowing?

- How do the waters within you speak—through dreams, through emotion, through sacred ache?

Closing Devotion:

◻ Chapter Fourteen: The Mother's Flame

Theme: Rebirth, Sacred Grief, Creation through Surrender
Whispered Invocation: "Even in the ashes, I bloom.
My womb is fire, and I am unafraid."

Reflections to Receive:

- What grief has shaped you, not as a wound, but as a

womb for something new?

- When have you held both life and death in the same breath?

- What sacred expression is ready to rise from what has been released?

Closing Devotion: "From sorrow, I shape starlight. From endings, I call in beginnings."

☐ Chapter Seventeen: The Waters of Becoming

Theme: Creation, Soul Birth, Legacy of Light
Whispered Invocation: "I am the sacred chalice. Through me, light takes form."

Reflections to Receive:
- What soul-gift lives within you, stirring, swelling, aching to be born?

- How do you nourish the creative flame that flickers inside your womb—physical or energetic?

- What would it mean to live as legacy—not through deeds, but through frequency?

Closing Devotion: "I create not just with hands, but with heart, with vision, with soul. I am the vessel of the divine."

After the Final Page: Integration and Becoming

Theme: Embodiment, Awakening, Priestess Reclamation
Whispered Invocation: "I do not close this book.
I open the temple of my life."

Reflections to Receive:

- What sacred threads of remembrance now live inside you?

- What part of you is no longer dormant, no longer denied?

- If this story was a mirror... what did you see that you had forgotten was yours?

Closing Devotion: "I am the continuation of the ancient ones. I walk the Earth not in forgetting, but in flame."

Sealing the Temple

Light a candle. Lay a flower at your altar. Offer your breath in reverence. Whisper: "It is done.
What I have remembered will never be lost again.
I walk forward not as seeker,
but as one who remembers the way."

Lumerian Glossary of Sacred Remembrance

A *Guide to the Language, Light, and Legacy of Lumeria*

Ehl'Vara *(el-VAH-rah)*

The Rite of Sacred Light

A ceremonial invocation used to activate divine remembrance. Performed in sacred thresholds, it calls light through the body into the Earth to restore unity and soul alignment.

Sol'Shara *(SOHL-shah-rah)*

The Ritual of Recalling

A sunlit ceremony of soul embodiment. Through breath, light, and intention, this rite awakens the cellular memory of one's divine origin and purpose.

Eluq'ara *(el-LOO-kah-rah)*

She Who Walks Between Worlds

A title carried by high initiates who bridge realms. Eluq'ara serves as a channel of healing and remembrance across dimensions.

Zha'turim or The Shadowed

Those Who Have Forgotten the Light

Beings who exist in distortion, consuming energy rather than creating it. Their presence reflects the need for protection, clarity, and compassionate boundary.

Lu'Shael *(LOO-shay-ell)*

Stones of Sacred Protection

Crystalline guardians placed at the four corners of Lumerian dwellings. These vibrational anchors protect against distortion and amplify harmony.

Orin'thal *(OR-in-thall)*

The Order of Rememberers

An ancient council of wisdom keepers. These elders carry harmonic knowledge across timelines and hold the spiritual architecture of Lumeria.

Lu Qai *(loo-KAI)*

The Mother of Memory
A divine feminine intelligence. She whispers through wind and light, summoning priestesses and starborn souls to anchor healing on Earth.

Lu Mai *(loo-MY)*

The Voice of the Ancients
A celestial teacher and ancestral guide. Lu Mai speaks across the veil, guiding souls through cycles of initiation, death, and rebirth.

Thal'Vahir *(THAHL-vah-heer)*

Lineage of Sacred Protectors
Carried by Pehani and other soul-guardians, this glyph represents strength in stillness and the protection of light through frequency, not force.

Sael'Vahara *(SAYL-vah-HAH-rah)*

Lineage of Warrior Priestesses

Bearers of ancient fire. These women protect not through violence but through sacred embodiment, energetic defense, and unwavering presence.

Virelia *(vir-ELL-ee-uh)*

The Silent Invasion

An ancient word for energetic corruption and shadow interference. Virelia marks the moment distortion begins its descent.

Dreamweavers

Soul Seers of the In-Between

Visionaries who receive guidance in dreams and meditative states. They carry prophecies, timelines, and the subtle maps of soul evolution.

Lattice of Light

The Ancient Energy Grid of Lumeria

A crystalline structure woven beneath the land. Activated by intention and frequency, it protects, uplifts, and harmonizes the energy of the island.

Sorei'Na *(so-RAY-nah)*

Radiant Embodied One

A divine feminine leader who walks as living remembrance. She embodies truth, harmony, and devotion to sacred service.

Children of Sirius

Starborn Healers and Builders

Beings seeded from Sirius who incarnate with missions of awakening, healing, and anchoring light into density.

Womb of the Storm

The Threshold Between Death and Birth

A sacred space where transformation lives. It is both the dissolving and the becoming—a portal of radical soul rebirth.

Remembrance Scroll

The Soul's Sacred Prayer

A channeled vow written in the heart of every priestess. It is remembered at key moments of awakening and spoken when one fully returns to truth.

Golden Spiral

Path of Divine Evolution

A sacred symbol of soul return and spiritual unfolding. It appears in ceremonies, dreams, and descents into incarnation.

Sacred Grove

The Heart of the Island

A living temple deep within Lumeria. Here, elemental, ancestral, and divine frequencies converge to awaken memory and restore soul alignment.

Starfire

Essence of Soul-Light

The inner fire of priestesses, warriors, and healers. It pulses in rituals, battle, and sacred love, burning away illusion and anchoring divine truth.

The Veil

The Curtain of Forgetting

The energetic separation between form and divine memory. Lifting the veil is the path of awakening—the sacred act of remembering who you are.

Sacred Figures of Lumeria

The Living Embodiments of Light, Remembrance, and Divine Purpose

Solei *(so-LAY)*

The High Priestess of Lumeria

A radiant soul born of starlight, Solei carries the codes of divine feminine awakening. She is Elu'Vara —the one who walks between worlds—and a living transmission of remembrance. Through her journey of love, loss, union, and leadership, she anchors ancient wisdom and cosmic harmony into Earth. Her presence is a mirror to every soul who came to awaken the light within.

Pehani *(pay-HAH-nee)*

Sacred Guardian and Divine Union Partner

Pehani is a protector of light and frequency. His soul resonates with the Thal'Vahir lineage—grounded, present, and fierce in his devotion. As Solei's beloved, he anchors sacred masculine energy and meets her with deep reverence. Through his love and strength, he helps birth new timelines of balance, protection, and sacred partnership.

Zambia *(ZAM-bee-uh)*

Warrior Priestess of the Sael'Vahara Lineage

Zambia walks the path of the sacred flame—elegant, fierce, and loyal. She carries the glyphs of the warrior priestess across her body like living armor of remembrance. Her presence is both moonlight and lightning: a shield for her people and a fire in the dark. As sister, protector, and truth-seer, she stands at Solei's side through joy, loss, and legacy.

Lu Mai *(LOO-my)*

Celestial Guide and Voice of the Ancients

Lu Mai is the cosmic mother who whispers through stars and wind. She appears not in form, but in frequency—carrying guidance, memory, and grace. Her presence ripples through dream, breath, and ceremony. She is both witness and weaver, the ancestral voice that midwives the return of light to Earth.

Haelion *(HAY-lee-on)*

Sacred Builder of the Elar'Miran Lineage

Haelion crafts with soul. His hands shape sanctuaries that breathe, and his heart tunes structures to frequency. As a member of the Elar'Miran, his work echoes the soul's geometry. In silence, in stone, and in structure, he remembers the sacred architecture of harmony.

Luneia *(loo-NAY-uh)*

The Braider of Memory and Keeper of Tenderness

A gentle soul with stardust in her voice, Luneia weaves remembrance into form. As a dreamweaver and sacred braider, she anchors comfort, ritual, and divine softness into the village. Through her quiet presence, the people feel home, held, and whole. Her essence is moonlight upon water—nourishing, reflective, and eternal.

T his book would not exist without the love and support of the souls who held space for me while I journeyed deep into the sacred unknown.

To my beloved husband, Nathan—thank you for being my rock, my anchor, and my greatest support. Your unwavering belief in me gave me the strength to write when the words felt too heavy to carry alone.

To my beautiful children, Scott, Siena, Adeline, and Aiden—you are my light, my inspiration, and my greatest blessings. Your laughter, love, and wild, radiant hearts remind me every day why this work matters.

To the teachers and soul sisters who have walked beside me:

Lisa Campion, thank you for your wisdom and mentorship.

Christi Powell, thank you for your love and empowering presence.

Lisa Powers, thank you for the space you've held and the light you share.

To Hawai'i—

You transformed me.

Thank you for four unforgettable, life-changing years of healing, awakening, and returning home to myself.

To the sacred 'ohana, the crystalline ocean waters, the streams that flowed from the mountains, the forests alive with ancient mana, and the spirit of Aloha that cradled me—I am endlessly grateful.

To the *music* that moved my spirit while I wrote—thank you.

"*Seasons*" by Amistat, "*Moving On*" by Arizona, "*Elastic Heart*" by Sia, "*Everything*" by Lauren Daigle "*Om Mani Padme Hum*", and "*The Saint*" by Lincoln Jesser and "*Never Give Up*" by J Boog—each note was a frequency that lifted me, anchored me, and reminded me of the truth I came to tell. You infused this novel with soul.

To Claudia Deen, The Savannah Striders, and Sara Pelletier Norwood—

I will never forget your life-changing support and encouragement during a time in my life when I didn't think I could cross the finish line.

You believed in me at times when I forgot how to believe in myself.

You reminded me of who I am, and for that, I am forever grateful.

And to everyone who has inspired me to do the hard, scary things—the things that stretch and shape us—thank you.

You helped me in ways you may never even know.

To the Ones who dared to awaken again—thank you. You are the reason this light returns.

Dominique **Wright** is a master clairvoyant, quantum energy healer, soul progression coach, and sacred storyteller devoted to helping others awaken the remembrance of who they truly are. Her work weaves together ancient wisdom, energetic healing, and divine feminine embodiment to support healers, empaths, and visionaries on their soul journeys.

A lifelong intuitive, Dominique channels multidimensional teachings and vibrational codes into everything she creates—whether through her transformational coaching or her spiritually evocative fiction. She is the author of the award-winning *Her Side of the Story: A Psychically Channeled Untold Novel of Catherine de Medici.*

The High Priestess of Lumeria is her soul offering in novel form—a mystical remembrance of light, lineage, and the divine feminine rising. Through her words, she invites readers to reclaim their inner knowing, walk with intention, and remember the sacred power that lives within us all.

Dominique lives and breathes her work with grace, humor, and cosmic devotion. When she's not guiding clients or writing beneath moonlight, you can find her speaking to the stars, blessing the Earth, or laughing with the soul family she's called home.

To connect with Dominique's offerings, visit www.dominiquewright.com.

Solei's Closing Prayer

Great Mother, Divine Light that dances through all creation,
Sacred Source of all that flows, and all that is still,
I come to you as a daughter of this Earth,
With a heart open wide, a soul lifted in gratitude.

Through your embrace, I have passed through the fire,
Through your love, I have felt the pulse of rebirth.
I stand now, in this moment, whole and new,
A reflection of the stars, a keeper of light.

May your grace flow through me like the rivers of the heavens,
Soft, but fierce, gentle yet unwavering.
May my hands be steady in the nurturing of all,
May my heart remain open, a vessel for love,
A mirror of the divine wisdom within.

Grant me the strength to love through all,
The courage to rise when the winds of change blow wild,
And the wisdom to trust the sacred rhythm of life,
Even in the darkness, when the path is unseen.

I offer my prayers to the Earth, my Mother,
To the air, my breath, my connection,
To the waters, the sacred flow of emotions,
To the fire, the spark of creation, the light that awakens.

May all beings remember the divine within,
May we walk together, as one heartbeat, one soul,

THE HIGH PRIESTESS OF LUMERIA

Guided by the stars, united by love,
Held in the peace that is the womb of all things.
 Blessed be this moment, sacred and pure,
Blessed be this life, an unfolding flower,
And blessed be the divine feminine in all,
As it rises, always and forever.
 So it is. So it shall be.
 Aho